THE FIRST WIVES

S.E. REED

Storm
PUBLISHING

Ebook ISBN: 978-1-83700-183-5
Paperback ISBN: 978-1-83700-185-9

Cover design: Lisa Horton
Cover images: Shutterstock

Published by Storm Publishing.
For further information, visit:
www.stormpublishing.co

ALSO BY S.E. REED

The First Widows

To the ones I love and obsess over

PROLOGUE

I grip the curved wooden handle of my umbrella, waiting for the heavy rain that is sure to come, and try not to look at her. Her dress is nearly identical to mine. Black, sleek, gold zipper up the back. Mine comes down to my knees, because this is a funeral after all. While hers is mid-thigh.

The body. The smile. The laugh. She has it all.

I'm here today, thanks to her.

I reach up to wipe the tear that's trickling down my cheek from under my oversized black sunglasses. It feels foreign, the tear falling over a perfectly contoured cheekbone. Someone stands up to speak, and I'm only half-listening.

I can't help myself... I look over at *her* again, the other woman. I wonder how she's holding up. I shouldn't care, but I do. Is she crying too? I remember the screaming and tears last time I saw her in person, and a shiver radiates up my spine.

"Ma'am, the service is over, would you like to head back to the limo?" My driver taps me on the shoulder. I take a final look at the grave, shaking my head in disbelief.

"Yes, thank you." I turn slowly and take the driver's arm, letting him guide me toward the limo in the distance. The ground is uneven, and my designer heels sink into the soft, wet grass as we walk. I'm thankful to have someone to keep me standing, because honestly, it feels like there hasn't been anyone in my life holding me upright the last few months.

As we approach the limo, a clap of thunder signals the heavier rain, and the driver opens the door in a hurry. But before I can get in—a dark unmarked car pulls up and a man in a cheap suit steps out, his hair slicked back. I recognize him from the station.

"Quickly." I hand the umbrella to the driver and slide in. My flight to New York leaves in an hour, and I don't have time for this. There's so much to do now that this is all over.

"Wait, please, I just have a few questions." The man trots over to the door and flashes his badge, just as the driver closes it. I click the button to lock it, and take a deep breath. My trembling fingers move to the other button and I push it once, to open the window a sliver.

The man leans forward and I can see him plain as day through the single-sided tinted glass. He has a gun in a holster at his breast. "Ma'am, do you mind coming down to the police station, we'd like to ask you a few more questions about—"

"My flight leaves in an hour. Am I under arrest?" I interrupt him. I have an attorney on speed dial if those words cross the detective's lips.

"Well, no, you're not under arrest—technically the case is closed—but there are things we need to—"

A smile spreads over my face. I roll the window back up because there's no need to hear anything else. My driver is buckled in his seat and adjusts the mirror, looking me square in the eyes, and I nod. He pulls away, slowly at first, gaining more speed as he reaches the main road and turns out of the cemetery. I imagine the detective standing there in the rain with his hands up in disgust or scratching his head with confusion.

I let out a long sigh and lean back against my seat, the soft black leather cradling me. I open my phone and download my plane ticket to my wallet. One way, first class. My new life is waiting for me, far away from here.

Then I make one quick call.

"Hello?"

"Get out of the rain."

PART ONE

Nine Months Earlier

ONE
HANNAH

"Ruby, Rowen, look over here, smile for Mommy." I dash around the backyard, capturing pictures of the twins playing tag in between colorful birds of paradise and hot pink bougainvillea. The gardeners did a great job on short notice. Court wasn't pleased when he saw the landscaping crew knocking out part of the fence to fit in a truck full of plants. Turning our sleek, million-dollar South Florida ocean view into an over-the-top tropical oasis. But truthfully, it was something I'd wanted to do for a while. I grew up in the country surrounded by plants, and I guess I was feeling nostalgic. Plus, how could I pass up doing a series of flower pictures on my social media, when that random snap I took of the twins at Busch Gardens a few weeks ago had over a million views?

"Ruby, like I taught you. Pause and smile." She obeys, striking a pose with a huge toothy grin. God, she looks just like *him*, right down to the hazel eyes, button nose, and sandy blonde hair. Rowen runs up, grabs her hand, and they go tearing off, laughing, into the newly planted jungle.

I smile and take a few more pictures.

Court's work schedule has been daunting, meaning one business trip after another. We were lucky to get that little weekend getaway to Busch Gardens in Tampa. So I figured, why not turn our backyard into someplace beautiful that the kids and I can enjoy, since we aren't taking as many family trips these days?

Buzz.

I look at my screen. A text from SugarFairy, an adorable local bakery, letting me know the cookies I ordered are ready for pickup. Tomorrow I'm throwing the kids and their stuffed animals a tea party in our new backyard, complete with swirly unicorn frosted cookies. The owner won't stop thanking me for all the attention they're getting since I've been posting their sugary treats for my five million followers. But really, I'm the one who needs to thank them. They suggested the tea party idea in the first place.

Anything that entertains the twins is a blessing. Because at four years old, they are terrors. Well, not really, but they certainly don't want to sit in a stroller anymore. So taking them on local adventures like I used to has become completely overwhelming by myself. You know, one running this way, the other running that way. Inevitably, someone breaks down in tears (and sometimes it's me). So, I've been trying to do more at home to occupy them, hence the backyard makeover and tea party.

Don't get me wrong, we can easily afford a nanny, but Court is very private about his job working in crypto finance. I don't really understand what exactly he does, but he seems to enjoy it, and he's very good at it. He would never just leave his work lying around, where a "tech-spy pretending to be a nanny" might steal it. Yes, he actually used that phrase, but I've learned over the years not to argue. His work was his entire life before I came along, and he's—how to put this gently—very precious about it.

I suppose I could reach out to some of the other moms from the private preschool Ruby and Rowen attend three days a week to come over for a playdate. But most of them are in the same boat as me, with slightly paranoid, workaholic, wealthy older husbands. We're not housebound by any means. It's more of a pick-your-battles kind of situation.

One more year, I keep telling myself.

That's when the twins start full-time kindergarten at Beach

Ridge Prep. I'm so excited to have a steady stream of new material for my social channels. Tips for keeping uniforms clean, how to pack the perfect lunchbox, and making class goody bags. The list is virtually endless. And best of all, I can join the parent association. That's where I'll finally make some mom friends and feel less cooped up.

"No, not like that." A woman's sharp voice carries over our newly replaced fence. I look around, to make sure the twins are still in sight. They are squatting down and looking at something on the ground, giggling.

"I said *not like that*. You're holding a priceless Joan Miró for Christ's sake." The name of the artist rolls off her tongue... She's clearly not American.

My eyebrows instinctively raise. I'm not an art person, but the word "priceless" does mean *priceless* in this neighborhood. I'm actually surprised to hear a voice coming from the house next door. I've always assumed it was intentionally empty, either purchased by my husband because of his need for privacy, or the real owner keeping it strictly for their real estate portfolio.

Hmmm... I wonder if this means we'll finally have neighbors after four years? I creep over to the fence and stand on my tippy-toes. A warm coastal breeze ruffles my long blonde hair. I'd love to get a sneak peek at their furniture, you know, to get a feel for what kind of people they might be. It's kind of exciting to have European neighbors. But just as my eyes spot a woman in sunglasses marching up the steps, I hear something behind me.

"Ready, set, go!" Ruby shouts.

I spin around in time to see Ruby, Rowen, and their very muddy hands running at full speed for the house. Shit. I ditch my spying attempt and sprint to reach the back door before the kids and their handprints.

"Mommy, who was yelling?" Rowen asks. My nose wrinkles. He's covered in mud, and the smell is reminiscent of my days on the farm.

"Hey, buddy, do Mommy a favor and don't touch anything.

Straight to the bathroom for you," I say, taking a final glance over my shoulder at the house next door.

It doesn't really matter if I don't get a good look at the woman. She's probably not the owner anyway. Maybe the interior designer. Or an art dealer hired to install that priceless piece of art she was fussing over. I glance at one of our paintings in the hallway as I trail after my muddy children. It was installed by an interior designer, and he was probably rude and loud like the woman next door. I wouldn't know—we never met. I was six months pregnant with the twins when we moved in and not in the mood... *Thank god for Court.* I sigh. He handled everything, including all the contractors.

"No!" I shout as I enter the bathroom.

Ruby and Rowen squeal with laughter, and I can't help but smile.

"Oh, you two are gonna get it." I rush forward to tickle them, pausing first to take a picture. They've crawled into the free-standing tub and smeared muddy handprints all over the white porcelain. That one will be a million views, easy. And they might all be from me. I'm not sure a mom ever loved their children as much as I love these two kiddos.

After bathing the twins, feeding them some string cheese, and putting them down for a nap, I log online. It's a heap of work managing my social accounts and programming posts after I design them on Adobe. Then I verify the analytics, making sure I'm still trending. Keeping up with the algorithms is practically a full-time job.

My watch buzzes. Has it been an hour already? I stretch my arms and yawn. Wow, I guess I could use a nap too. I close my laptop, check my phone for any messages from Court, and head upstairs toward my room. Maybe I can rest my eyes for a few minutes before the twins wake up. As I ascend the staircase, I can't help but look out the giant windows that overlook our neighbors' house. A view that for the last four years has meant nothing to me

—since the chic steel and glass house was more like an art installation, than a place my brain registered as could-be occupied.

I pause.

Our own steel and glass house is coated with some kind of reflective treatment, so I know they can't see in. But still, if someone is moving in next door, it's really going to feel like we're living in a fishbowl. I know Court is going to hate it. He despises any invasion of our privacy. Which is funny, considering my internet fame as a trad wife lifestyle influencer. But my online life —it's not our real life. It is very carefully and selectively curated.

"Mommy!" Ruby shouts.

Without another glance at the house next door, I take the rest of the steps two at a time, my bare feet sinking into the plush luxury carpet on the top floor. Carpet in the bedrooms was a must for me. It makes playing, snuggles, and reading with my kids extra cozy. Something I'm obsessed with. Giving them what I never had growing up.

"I'm here," I say.

I gently push open the door to the twins' shared room. Ruby is sitting up and rubbing her eyes. Rowen is still curled in a ball on his bed, covered by his favorite blankie and clutching his plushie cow.

I grab the remote off the shelf, where little hands can't reach it, and crawl on the bed with Ruby. "How about we watch *Bluey* until Rowen wakes up?" I ask and cuddle up on the bed.

"Okay, Mommy." Ruby pats my head, then tucks her blankie over me before rolling over to her tummy so she can watch. Maybe I'll just close my eyes for a few minutes...

I wake up with a start when a toy spoon gets shoved in my mouth. "Mommy, do you want to try my soup?"

"Mmmm, yummy," I mumble and remove the spoon. I check my watch. Wow, thirty minutes—better than I expected. I climb off Ruby's bed. "Looks like you're having fun playing."

"We aren't playing, Mommy," Rowen says, very matter-of-fact. "We started a restaurant. See." He points to their setup. They've laid a perfect place setting for four around their child- sized table, and Ruby is dressing up stuffed animals in their finery. Rowen heads back to the toy kitchen stirring his fake soup with a rainbow ladle.

"Five stars." I put my hands up to my lips and make a chef's kiss at them. They both giggle as I slip out of their room to head back downstairs to check on my posts and see what I can heat up for dinner.

I'm the first to admit—I'm not a cook. Which I realize doesn't look great on my trad wife résumé. But in a world of gourmet home delivery meals that I can easily plate on our nice dishes, does it really matter? I wouldn't say that I lie to my fans. I never claim that I personally cook the food. Instead, I say things like, *Wow, chicken Kiev, yummy*. Or, *My husband's favorite, beef Wellington*. Sometimes less is more when creating authentic-sounding marketing materials. Something my favorite professor taught me at Iowa State.

I stare into my ultra-organized, color-coded fridge with its bins, glassware, and other eye-catching containers. But the thing that's really catching my eye is the view out the kitchen window. That woman from earlier, the interior designer or maybe art dealer, is sneaking a cigarette on the back deck of the house.

It's been a long time since I've been around a smoker. It's a gross habit for sure, but something about it is oddly comforting to me. So I tiptoe to the sliding glass panels that line the back of the house, chuckling at my unnecessary sneaking around, and push a button on the wall. The first panel slides open. I don't step all the way outside, but, rather, I linger in the door frame—sucking in the air, catching a whiff of Marlboro.

Just like Matt used to smoke.

TWO

For the next week, nothing changes about our daily routine. Court comes and goes. I take the children to their three days of preschool, stopping at yoga and to get my nails done. And of course, at home I spend hours planning out a series of social posts, specifically for the summer. However, I continually find myself lingering on the staircase, gazing upon the house next door.

Every day I see that woman orchestrating what appears to be some interior work. Painting, wallpaper, new fixtures. I'm starting to think that she might have purchased the home herself, but I'm not ready to walk over and introduce myself.

Court hasn't mentioned anything about the commotion, so I don't bring it up.

"I know it's only February, but I really want to start planning our summer schedule," I say to Court over dinner. The children are in bed for the night after a rambunctious day in the yard, and we are having a late Friday night meal, just the two of us. He thoughtfully chews his food, then sets down his fork, as if I'm about to get a lecture.

I hold my breath.

"Hannah," he says with a twinkle in his eye. "Is this about Disney again?"

I smile. "Oh, babe, please say yes." Disney is a huge trad wife influencer milestone. I desperately wanted to do it last year, but Ruby and Rowen weren't independent enough for those insanely adorable run-up-and-hug-a-character photos.

He double taps his watch, then reaches a hand out and clasps my fingers. My phone pings from whatever he AirDropped me. "You know I'd do anything to make you happy... and who knows, it might be fun." He pauses and smiles. "I already booked the trip—I just sent you the itinerary."

"Eeeek!" I leap from my chair and run around the table to hug and kiss him. "Oh, Court, you big softy!" I'm practically in tears. Court was such a huge help when the twins were babies. Seriously, he was the most doting father you could imagine. But the last few years have been... hard. He'd never say it, but I can tell by the amount of business trips he takes that the kids kinda get under his skin.

This is a big deal for him.

"Thank you," I exclaim between kisses and run my hands through his short, sandy hair. I keep kissing, moving them down the back of his neck and grip his shoulders. He's surprisingly strong and muscled for being, well, a nerdy tech guy. I guess he does like to work out.

"Mmmm." He kisses me deeper and his hand slides up my thigh and squeezes. Oh, okay, I see where this is going. He wants a reward for surprising me.

"Let's go up to the bedroom," I whisper. I take his hands and tug. But he isn't budging.

"No, here." He pulls me back and kisses my lips, then my neck.

"Court, you're so naughty," I tease.

He puts his hand between my legs and I gasp. I really don't want to have sex in the dining room. The twins could easily walk down the stairs and catch Daddy on top of Mommy—every parent's nightmare—but his body language is insistent.

"Just sit on me like this." He spins me by the waist, then lifts up my skirt and positions me on his lap.

We're both facing the dining room windows that look across at the house next door. He sweeps my hair over and kisses the back of my neck, then rests his chin on my shoulder—as if he's staring out the windows. His hands caress my body and I moan. A light comes on, illuminating the glass, and unlike our view-proof home, we can see the outline of a person walking around next door.

"Someone is there." His voice is husky.

Oh crap. If he gets distracted and doesn't finish, he will be a serious grouch. So I move my body up and down, gyrating my hips, hoping to recapture his undivided attention. "Oh god, yes," he growls. I turn my head and lean back so we can kiss. That does the trick and for the next ten minutes, neither of us looks out the windows. We are completely entranced by our impromptu dining room sexcapade.

I breathe a sigh of relief as I walk up the stairs when we're finished. I don't pause or look next door. Something about it feels wrong, dirty even. Maybe I'll go over and introduce myself to the woman tomorrow. Would it be rude to lead with, *Hi, I'm your neighbor, Hannah. My husband and I were having sex in our dining room last night, and we could see your shadow walking around. You should get blinds.*

The steam shower soothes my nerves, and by the time I crawl into bed, I've practically forgotten about the neighbor. Court won't come up to bed for hours—he's a night owl and often works late into the night in his home office downstairs. I open my phone, checking out the surprise itinerary for our Disney trip, and make a happy noise. Then I post a throwback of me and Court in Paris when we got married, with the phrase:

Happy wife, happy life.

The next day, I'm still on cloud nine from Court's big summer vacation announcement. I've got on my straw sun hat and I'm spraying the kids with some SPF 50 and daydreaming about the cute matching shirts I'll have custom made for our trip. There's a great breeze blowing in off the coast, keeping the humidity down, but, boy, is it making this spray get everywhere. I start coughing, and the kids screech and flail around.

"Hold still, you little wiggle worms, you don't want a sunburn," I exclaim. But the combination of squirming and slippery spray makes holding on to Ruby and Rowen like holding on to greased pigs. And no. That is definitely not something I did growing up in the country.

"Better listen to your mommy," a woman says behind me.

My back stiffens.

"All done, go play." I scoot the kids into the yard before I turn around. I flash my best smile, reach up and pull my sunglasses down, and say, "I wondered when we'd meet." I quickly assess my neighbor. Her sunglasses are on top of her head like a headband, exposing her steely gray eyes. She's swapped out the designer clothes for a plunging black swimsuit, with a sheer black sarong wrapped around her waist. Her skin is tight and glowing. Pilates, for sure.

"I was heading down to the water, but I heard you out here and thought I'd better come introduce myself," she says as she looks around my yard, taking it all in. "I'm Sophia Carter, your new neighbor." Her hand extends. But mine are greasy and I'm still holding the can of sunscreen.

"I figured you were just the interior designer." I don't mean for it to come out as rude as it does. She's not an enemy just because I saw her shadow in the window last night while Court and I were in the dining room having sex. "I'm Hannah McMillian." I set down the bottle, wipe my hands quickly, and shake her hand. "Sorry— where are my manners? Do you want to sit down for some lemonade?" I motion toward the outdoor patio table where I've got drinks and snacks set up for me and the kids.

A slow and deliberate smile spreads over Sophia's face. "I'd love to. And maybe later we can have a glass of wine."

ach

THREE

The cork makes a satisfying little pop when I pull it from the bottle of Savennières. A dry white from the beautiful Loire Valley in France. I'm not much of a wine drinker, but Court is practically a sommelier. He carefully picks out all of the wine we keep in the house, usually from places we've vacationed or he's traveled for work. He's never said it, but I think he believes seeing the location makes the wine taste better. If he left it up to me, I'd come home with a case of cold beers and a pack of red Solo cups.

"Here you go."

Sophia's sitting across from me on the back deck and we are about to have that glass of wine I promised her yesterday. She tucks her dark hair behind her ear, swirls and smells the fragrance, then takes a long sip. "Mmmm... You can practically taste the Loire Valley honeysuckle. Lovely."

I smile and nod, sipping from my own glass. Truthfully, wine is wine on my palate. Court is out of town for a few days and the kids are upstairs in bed for the night, so I'm just happy to take a break and get a buzz.

Even if it is with the neighbor woman.

I'm still not sure how I feel about her.

"So, Sophia, you said yesterday you're in the art business? That must be interesting." I throw her a softball. People love talking about what they do for a living.

"I do, and it's alright, if you're into that sort of thing," she replies, as if her job is the most boring thing in the world, then takes another sip of her wine.

I wait the appropriate amount of time for her to elaborate. But she doesn't. She's too busy looking into my house. I left the sliding glass panels open to our living room, so I can hear the twins if they wake up.

"Oh, I see... I'm not."

"You're not what?" she asks, tearing herself away from staring at my living room. She makes direct eye contact with me. Her steely gaze looks—*amused.*

"I'm not into art." I smile and she shifts uncomfortably in her seat. I knew it. She's toying with me. She's aching to talk about her passion. "Don't get me wrong, art makes a room, wouldn't you say?"

Sophia quickly straightens up and leans forward. "Yes, actually, it does. A single piece can transform a space. Like that stunning Yayoi Kusama over your fireplace. It's playful, yet serious, and ties together everything else in the room. Did you pick it out?" Her eyebrows raise.

"God no, Court, that's my husband—he had an interior designer do it all when I was pregnant with the twins. I just put a Pinterest board together for the overall vibe I wanted, and they did everything."

She nods and tries to hide the smirk in her next sip.

My face is strained. I can already see how the rest of the evening will go. We'll sit here drinking this bottle of shitty-tasting, expensive wine, share a few anecdotes, and say our goodbyes. Then when I see her outside, we'll share pleasantries, and that's about it. Sophia is obviously more worldly than me and she knows it. I know her type. Chic, polished, well-bred with a trust fund, boarding school abroad, probably a Master's degree from Oxford. There's literally nothing we have in common. It doesn't matter that

I'm a business mogul in my own right, worth millions as an influencer and brand ambassador. She sees right through the version of me I've spent my entire adult life creating. I bet if she sniffs the air, she can smell the farm I grew up on.

"Twins run in my family. Three sets on my mother's side," she finally says, snapping me out of my spiraling thoughts.

"Oh yeah? Well, they don't run in mine. So it was a real shock when the doctor told us there were two heartbeats. I thought Court was gonna faint. He literally turned green during the ultrasound." I laugh, recalling the moment.

"I can only imagine," Sophia says, laughing with me. "That would be"—she pauses and picks an invisible speck of dust from her white pants—"a shock to any man's system. Twice as many diapers."

"I'm pretty sure Court is Pampers' number one shareholder." I giggle. "It might be hard to believe, but when they were babies, I barely had to lift a finger or change a diaper. Court was so hands-on." I don't know if it's the wine or talking about something I'm good at, being a mom and wife, but I'm feeling more relaxed. "Can I top you off?" I reach for the bottle.

Sophia looks at me funny, then reaches her glass out. "That's unusual... I mean, for an older husband to be so hands-on," she says. "Oh—I'm sorry, that was presumptuous of me to say. I'm not saying your husband is old. I mean, it's just that I saw him one day when I was outside."

I tilt my head. Something about making her uncomfortable is satisfying. Then I laugh, to lighten the mood. "Don't worry about it. Yeah, Court is nineteen years older than me. I wouldn't say he's old, by any means. But he's older than me for sure. He turns fifty in a few months. Which reminds me, I need to check on his gift."

There's a hint of natural blush rising in her cheeks.

"They say fifty is the new forty," she says and sets her glass down. "Can I use your restroom, or, uh, should I walk back home?"

"Oh please, of course you can use our bathroom. Come inside.

I was just going to pour a bowl of potato chips. It's my guilty pleasure when Court's out of town."

"Thank you, that sounds delicious."

I lead the way and point Sophia in the direction of the bathroom, before heading to the kitchen. I check the monitor to make sure the twins are still in their beds and asleep, before sneaking a bag of chips from my secret stash in the back of the pantry.

Sophia hasn't returned yet, so I decide to run upstairs quickly and use the bathroom there. I know I just checked the monitor, but I can't help but peek into the twins' room when I'm done, so I can listen for their little snores. I linger for a few seconds in their doorway. "I love you," I whisper.

When I get back downstairs, I spot Sophia inspecting our family pictures on the bookshelf in the living room. "That was our trip to London a few years ago," I say. She immediately sets the picture back down, as if she's been caught red-handed, sticking up a bank teller for cash. The glass frame clatters, knocking over a few of the other frames.

"I'm so sorry," she says and quickly tries to arrange them where they belong.

"No worries. I've knocked them over plenty. I'm always adding new ones." I approach her with a smile, so she knows I'm not upset. "I'm really into photography. I run a popular social page, but these ones, they are just for me." I pick up one of the frames and rub my thumb over our faces. I remember it like it was yesterday. Court and I with big grins on our faces, each holding a child on our hip, standing in front of one of London's famed red phone booths. "When Ruby and Rowen were that age, we traveled a lot. It was easy. Plop them in a stroller and off we'd go. But now, they are four and busy as bees."

"I've noticed you have your hands full," Sophia says. "I hope you have a nanny."

"God, no. Court works in crypto finance. He's way too paranoid to let me have a nanny."

Sophia nods once, then strides out of my living room and

reclaims her seat on the deck. "My husband is like that too. Not with a nanny, since we don't have children, but with help in general. No housekeeper or chef allowed in our house. Not that I mind—we are fine dining kind of people when he's around. He travels a lot for work." She tilts back her wine glass. Draining the contents, without making a face. If I did that, I'd have a sour look for an hour. She reaches for her handbag and pulls out a cigarette. "Do you mind?"

I shake my head. As soon as she lights it, Matt's face flashes in my mind's eye. It's still like this, when I meet a smoker. I hear his twangy country boy voice. *Hannah, don't be a chicken shit. Just jump.* My heart races, remembering the night we stood on the ledge of his dad's barn, in the light of a half-moon, taking turns jumping the two stories into a hay mound. Afterwards we smoked cigarettes in the field until the sun rose, talking about the life we were going to build together.

That was the night before he died.

I blink back the memories. "I didn't know you were married," I say, checking her hand for a ring. Empty. Now I'm curious. Maybe that's why she moved here... She's in the middle of a divorce, yet still refers to the man as her husband? Suddenly our night just got a whole lot more interesting, especially as she pours the rest of the bottle in her glass and sinks deeper into the chair, more relaxed and ready to spill the tea.

"I want to hear more. I'm gonna grab the chips and another bottle of wine. BRB."

FOUR

"I heard you and a lady laughing last night, Mommy," Rowen says at the breakfast table the next morning, between bites of syrupy pancakes.

Ruby scowls. "You were loud."

"Oh, sorry, sweets. Mommy had a guest over last night," I say and boop her nose, then pat Rowen's head on my way to the kitchen. I need ibuprofen, stat. I should not have drunk so much with Sophia. But once the floodgates opened, there was no closing them. We sat outside talking, drinking, and yes, laughing, until well after midnight. She's actually a lot more down-to-earth and funny than I first thought.

It just took a little bonding over our husbands' quirks to get the juices flowing. Her husband, Blake Carter, is also in finance, but on the real estate side. He's in Beijing right now, finishing up some big project. He bought their Florida house sight unseen and sent Sophia here to get it ready before he arrives in a few weeks. She said his next big land venture is in South America, so Florida seemed like a good home base.

"Typical man. Make the woman do all the heavy lifting," I teased.

"Right? Like, what is that all about? I mean, I travel the world buying and selling art worth billions. But, oh no, I have to put my career on hold to come play housewife. No offense." She reached in and took a handful of chips, setting them right down on those pristine white pants. Eating the chips two at a time. "God, these are good. I need to keep a secret stash in my kitchen too."

I didn't take any offense to her words.

I wasn't playing housewife. I was providing the life for my kids that I never had growing up—one with a full-time stay-at-home mom. Stability, security, and love. The things I'd longed for. Someone like Sophia would never understand that, but it didn't matter to me. I was happy.

We went from bonding over husbands, to our favorite places, to the latest styles, to pop culture, and rounded out the night by listening to music and singing songs from the musical *Wicked* and laugh-crying at how off-key we both sang.

Before she walked home, we even hugged and promised to do it all again soon. But the way my head is feeling this morning, I'm not sure I can keep up with Sophia. At least not very often. We'll have to start slow—maybe I'll ask her to get her nails done with me. A daytime hangout, without booze. I've had years here in Fort Myers to figure out all the best places to go, and if I can save her from a bad manicure, well—that makes me someone she'll want to stay friends with.

Friends.

The word rolls around, feeling foreign in my mouth. It's been a long time since I've had anything more than an acquaintance in my day-to-day life, besides Court of course. Don't get me wrong, I love my social media fans. But they aren't my friends. The last real friend I had was my college roommate, Cassie. At first, that was more of a forced proximity thing—especially our freshman year. By sophomore year we clicked and decided to keep rooming together rather than having to put up with someone new. By graduation, we were inseparable. But that was seven years ago, before her career took her to Las Vegas and my ambitions led me to Florida. Since then, we haven't seen each other much. She flew in to see me when the twins were born, but that's the last time I saw her in person.

I open my laptop and log on.

I know right where I can find Cassie, but I don't want to watch her work videos. She's CassieXOXO, one of the highest-earning models on OnlyFans. Not my cup of tea, but it works for her and she loves it.

I click to FaceTime her.

"Oh my god, if it isn't the trad wife queen herself. If you're calling for a recipe, I'm fresh out of those," Cassie says with a laugh when she answers.

"Bitch, you know I don't cook. Everything I plate comes from some gourmet food service I get delivered twice a week," I reply.

"Now, that's a smart cookie." She winks at me.

"What exactly are you doing right now?" I ask and squint. Cassie is lying down on a table, her platinum-blonde hair spread out around her. There's so many ways she could answer this question...

"Oh, you know, just an early morning pussy wax. You wanna watch? I can flip the screen," she says.

"NO!" I exclaim before she does. Because she will flip the screen and make me watch. And, sigh... it wouldn't be the first time I've seen her waxed. Countless times. That's how many. She hated going to the salon alone in college and made me hold her hand. Every. Single. Time. "Who's holding your hand?"

"No one. I just did that in college because I liked to watch you squirm." She laughs so much tears drip out of her eyes.

"You know, you suck."

"Oh yeah, I—" Cassie nods.

"MOMMY!" Rowen screams from the dining room, stopping Cassie mid foul-mouthed joke about sucking.

"Aw, take me in and let me see the little babies. I really need to get my ass back to Florida and see them in person again. I'm a terrible godmother." Her self-appointed title.

"You aren't their godmother, Cassie, but yes—you're welcome

anytime." I look over my shoulder knowing any second I'm going to have to tackle a sticky child before they wipe their hands on everything in sight.

"Hannah... I know you gotta run, but is everything alright?" she asks with genuine concern in her voice.

"Sunshine and roses." I smile. "I've got a new neighbor, and she was here last night for wine... I, uh, guess I wanted to talk to a real friend, make sure I still know how to do it. I know that sounds stupid."

"MOMMY."

"Hold your horses. I'll be there in a second."

Cassie flashes me one of her million-dollar smiles and winks. "Oh, babes. You were always the best of friends. Even if you didn't know it. When we met, you were still fucked in the head over Matt's death..." She lets out a deep breath. "As long as this new neighbor of yours isn't a bitch, have fun. But remember—don't shit where you eat."

"Got it." I blow her a kiss and close my laptop quickly. I wasn't prepared for her to mention Matt. I shake my head, not wanting to churn up any more of those old memories.

Thankfully, my ibuprofen is kicking in. After I clean up the kids and get them ready for a day at the beach, maybe I'll go knock on Sophia's door and see if she wants to come with us. I can't believe I didn't get her number last night.

"This beach is incredible. Thanks for inviting me." Sophia kicks out her legs and rubs them down with tanning oil. I make a face at her and shake my head.

"Skin cancer." I hand her one of the many bottles of SPF I keep in my beach bag. Then I check my watch. "Ruby, Rowen." They're busy building a sandcastle and ignore me. "Sunscreen time."

"Oh, leave them be. They're having so much fun—and look at them, slathered head to toe in SPF. I can see it from here."

Maybe she's right. They're both wearing bucket hats protecting their zinc-oxide-covered faces, long-sleeved rash guard shirts and shorts. Not to mention they've got on life vests. I'm not taking any chances with their safety. All it takes is a split second for one of them to wander down by the water alone, and a riptide to drag them under the surf. Even if the ocean looks peaceful and serene, it can be deadly.

"Some of my highest-rated posts are about sun and water safety for children," I tell Sophia. "You can never be too careful."

"Do you have a lot of followers?" she asks.

I lift my sunglasses and look at her. I could have sworn I told her I was an influencer last night, but—maybe that slipped my mind? I swear we talked about so much, how could I have forgotten to tell her? It's a huge part of my life.

"Five million," I reply.

"Five million what?" She smiles, then pulls a nail file from her bag and starts to shape the edges of her nails. "Seriously, five million what, Hannah?" she asks when I don't respond.

"Followers. I'm an influencer." And I suppose this is where she tells me she's above using social media. That she finds it all juvenile and attention seeking. Or that her trust fund forbids her from having an online presence.

Or worse. Maybe she has five million and one followers, and she's about to yawn, like it's so easy and not a big deal. Damn. Why didn't I look her up online?

"You're joking, right? You're a social media influencer? But what about your husband and his privacy rules?" She leans up from her beach chair. Suddenly she's much more interested in this conversation.

"He's fine with it. It's very curated. I'll send you a link to my page if you want to check it out. But if you aren't into that sort of thing, that's fine. And don't worry, I won't post you. I'm very partic-ular about my brand. I have a specific aesthetic." One that's taken me years to perfect. Not that I'm going to tell her just how much work I've put into it. Building the perfect algorithm is a highly guarded secret in the influencer world. I guess I'm like Court in that sense... Paranoid someone will steal my method.

"Hmmm. Yes, you'll have to send it to me." She pulls out her phone and AirDrops me her contact info.

I send her my page. Then I get up, leaving her to explore that part of my life, and sneak over to take a few pictures of the twins and their sandcastle, which has grown nearly as tall as they are. Very impressive. Now, this will make a great post. Especially with a warning about the dangers of skin cancer. I quickly tag my favorite sunscreen brand and DM their marketing department with information on how they can sponsor my post.

Within a few days, I'll earn tens of thousands on that one picture, and a lifetime supply of sunscreen. By the time I walk back and sit down next to Sophia, I've already been contacted by two major swimsuit brands with lucrative influencer offers.

"Hannah, this is—wow, I mean, I don't know what to say." Sophia keeps scrolling through my page.

I don't need her validation, but it still feels good.

FIVE

Over the next few weeks, Sophia and I fall into a comfortable rhythm of going shopping, taking the twins on walks, and having coffee. It's strange how easily she fits into my life without adding any extra strain or pressure. I almost can't believe how suspicious I was when we met. Now, instead of looking out the windows toward her house and imagining her shadow as some nefarious creature invading my peace, I smile and send her a text.

You wanna run to the store?

Sure, meet you in the driveway.

Her selfish husband, Blake, pushed his arrival date back another six weeks, and I hate that for her. All alone in that big, quiet house. If I didn't have Court and the kids... I shudder. I back my car out of the garage five minutes later and she hops in next to me. She doesn't ask which store. She didn't make me wait for her to get ready. She's just there when I need her. Which, I'm realizing— *is all the time.*

"Court watching the kids?" she asks. Her dark hair is smoothed into a ponytail, much like the one I'm wearing.

"Sort of, it's naptime. He's knee-deep in a spreadsheet—he just nodded and kept working when I said we were heading out. I figure we've got about an hour before the kids start wandering around the house."

"Perfect. Oh, can we swing through that little Italian market you took me to a couple days ago? I want to grab a few things," she says.

"Well, you're in luck, that's where I was headed. I need some marinated olives and those tiny mozzarella balls."

"Let me guess, charcuterie board post?"

"More of a charcuterie-bento-box-fusion thing." I slip on my shades and turn up the music. I've had so much fun teasing Sophia about music. Her taste ranges from symphony to Broadway and that's it. The beat pumps and I tap my fingers on the steering wheel. "You honestly can't tell me you don't know this one." I glance her way.

Lady Gaga belts out "Poker Face" and by the second chorus I'm singing along. I even move my hand around and wiggle spirit fingers.

Sophia smiles, but her lips never move a muscle to join in with the catchy tune. Oh my god. She really doesn't know this song.

"Pa-pa-pa-lease, at least tell me you've heard of Lady Gaga?" I ask, mimicking the song.

"How did such a big dork like you really get this far in life?" She resorts to name-calling.

I throw my head back and laugh as I turn into the parking lot at the Italian market. "Me? I'm not sure anyone has ever called me a dork in my life."

She rolls her eyes.

"You know what I'm going to do? Because I'm such a fabulous friend. I'm going to make you a Spotify playlist of all the songs you need to know to be a functioning modern adult."

"Oh goodie. I can't wait. At least it won't be filled with country music. I've noticed you never play country. Why is that?" she asks as we walk into the store.

I haven't listened to country music, at least not intentionally, since the night Matt died. It doesn't matter which band or singer, it all reminds me of him. That twang and guitar takes me right back to the night of the accident. A night that almost killed me too. But as close as Sophia and I have become, I'm not ready to share Matt with her. Sure, she knows I grew up in the Iowa countryside. But that's all she needs to know.

The old me, Hannah Price, is long gone.

Hannah McMillian, billionaire trad wife influencer, is here to stay.

"Oooh. Look at this." Sophia holds up a jar from the display at the front of the market. "They have truffle carpaccio." She's completely forgotten about my aversion to country music.

In our short but fast friendship, I've learned the best way to dodge something with Sophia is to ignore it. If she really wants to know, she'll ask again—in a sneakier way. Not that I blame her for being sneaky. I blame that on her upbringing.

I hit the nail on the head when I pegged her for a boarding school brat. Over several bottles of wine in the last few weeks, she's told me that she attended more than one elite boarding school across Europe. And wow, the stories she tells. The fighting. Lying. Stealing. Cheating. Sex. It all sounds more like an episode of a Netflix teen drama than real life.

All I can say is, Court better not get any crazy ideas about sending Rowen and Ruby to one of those places. I don't care if that's how billionaire nepo babies meet and befriend one another, making secret handshakes and plans to rule the universe together— Sophia's stories have scared me to my core.

After paying for our Italian goodies, we still have thirty minutes until I've got to get back to the house before the twins terrorize Court and he gets fed up and takes another business trip for a week. "One more quick stop—I just have to drop off some instructions at Tropical Prints."

"Sure thing, Captain," Sophia says, unconcerned, while scrolling on her phone.

"I don't know how you do that. I get carsick if I scroll in the car." I turn down the street and park in front of the shop.

Sophia looks up from her screen at our new location. "Oh my god, how cute. When you said Tropical Prints, I thought you meant some tacky tourist shop, not a local art gallery." She jumps out of her seat and is through the door before I'm halfway out of my seat.

"Well, okay, then." I laugh. I'd sort of forgotten that she might like this place. It's an adorable, family-run shop that specializes in signed prints and original pieces by Floridian artists. Six months ago I had a painting commissioned for Court's fiftieth birthday, which is right around the corner.

Sophia is bouncing from foot to foot—clearly she's excited to be in a room full of art. Even if it's mostly scenes of palm trees and beaches.

"What are we doing here?" she asks, looking in my general direction, but her eyes are darting from painting to painting.

"I took some measurements and wanted to drop them off. I commissioned a painting for Court's birthday, and they need to mat and frame it," I explain.

She narrows her gaze at me and takes a step closer.

"But you said you weren't into art." Her tone full of accusation.

"Yeah, because I'm not, but my husband is." Did that sound as annoyed as I feel? What's up with her all of a sudden? "He really developed an eye for it after helping our decorator with the house. I think he's going to love it."

Sophia snorts. "Really, Court is into art?" She turns and starts walking toward the back of the small gallery. "More like he was into banging your decorator," she says under her breath, but loud enough for me to hear.

I'm completely taken aback.

I can't tell if Sophia is joking around, or if she's trying to cause a scene. What a fucked-up thing to say. Of course my husband wasn't having sex with the decorator. Who, by the way, happens to be a sixty-year-old gentleman from LA and the top interior designer in the country. The only thing Court was into, was building our family a beautiful home.

Maybe this is a test.

Some kind of weird, boarding school, hazing thing. If I blow up on her, then I fail. But if I let it slide, I could fail too. What would Cassie do in this situation? She'd probably start laughing, walk out the door, get in her Rover, and leave Sophia in the dust.

Sigh... Sometimes I wish I could be more like Cassie. But I have an image to uphold. Storming out and leaving a friend stranded isn't what a trad wife would do. A trad wife is more like a girl scout, stopping to help when she sees trouble. Not the one who starts the trouble.

But I can't help myself, I have to say something. I stroll up behind Sophia and whisper, "Alfred D'Lane." Then I hold my head up high and walk to the counter to speak with the owner about the frame measurements.

When I'm done and turn around, I see Sophia through the front glass, talking on her phone and smoking. She's laughing and very animated, as if she's speaking with the most interesting man, or woman, in the world. I push open the doors, intending to just breeze past her, but when I check my watch, we've got ten minutes to get home. I tap on the watch to signal her and she waves me off. So I get into my car and start the engine. I watch her talking and the clock ticking down. Fifteen minutes goes by. My mozzarella balls are ruined for sure.

I consider honking the horn.

Instead, I text Court.

> Running a little behind in town.

> No problem babe, watching Bluey with kids.

> Aw, melt my heart.

> Love you, see you soon.

I smirk and sink into my seat, slide my shades down over my

eyes, then turn on some music and wait for Sophia to get in. Finally, after another ten minutes, she decides to get in the car.

"Ready?" I turn the music off and say cheerfully.

"If you are."

I back out of the spot and drive towards our neighborhood. Going unusually slow, coming to nice and easy stops. Neither of us says a word. The silence is rather refreshing.

"Well, aren't you going to ask who I was talking to?" Sophia finally asks once we're back in our gated neighborhood, rounding the last curve toward our houses.

"No." But ten bucks says she's going to tell me anyway.

"That was my good friend Alfred D'Lane. I can't believe I didn't recognize his fingerprint on your house. I had to tell him what a spectacular job he did," she says.

She called my interior decorator from five years ago? My skin crawls. I feel *violated*. Just when I thought everything was going so great and I'd finally found someone I could call a friend, she goes and pulls some weird shit like this. I keep smiling, willing my facial muscles to stay calm and relaxed, not tight and angry. If this was any other day, I'd pull into my driveway and invite her to come inside while I set up for my next series of posts.

But I'm pissed at her. So I drive past our houses, use the cul-de-sac and turn around in the other direction. Then I stop in front of her house, not even pulling into the long driveway.

She chuckles. "Oh, so this is how it's going to be?"

"I don't know what you mean, Sophia. I'm just dropping you off at your place before I head home." I refuse to look at her. I keep my eyes focused on something small and green on the hood of my car.

Without arguing, or saying anything else, Sophia gets out and I tap the gas pedal, pulling the passenger door shut as I drive the remaining fifty feet and turn into my driveway. By the time I get into the garage and close the door, I'm shaking. I'm so mad at her for suggesting Court was fucking the decorator, and then *calling* the decorator, no less. But I have to pull myself together. I can't let Rowen or Ruby see me upset.

Before I step into the house, I grab the green thing off the hood.

"Rowen! Ruby! Mommy's home, and look what I found," I yell once I'm inside. My right hand is holding something every four-year-old loves.

"Mommy!" they scream at the same time and come running from the living room. Court saunters in after them and grins.

"Hey, hon, everything okay?" He leans in and gives me a kiss.

"Much better now." *This* is what matters. My loving husband, my adoring, albeit hyper, kiddos, and this life we've built. Fuck the neighbor woman. She can go to hell.

"What is it, Mommy?" Rowen asks.

"What did you find?" Ruby is inspecting the bag and my purse.

I hold out my fists. "Pick one." They pick the left hand first and I flip it over, slowly opening my fingers. Revealing emptiness. They squeal with delight and anticipation for what might be in my other fist. I turn over my hand and open it, even slower. Rather than heading back to his office to work, Court is as fascinated as the children with what I might have in the palm of my hand.

As soon as my palm is open, the bright green sticky frog I plucked off the hood of my car jumps a foot in the air, landing right on Rowen's head, and we all scream and laugh until our sides hurt.

SIX

I'm not surprised the next morning when Court says he's heading to London for a few days. For two reasons.

First, he played outside in the yard with the kids for over an hour after my stunt with the frog. It was so cute—he pretended to be an explorer, leading Rowen and Ruby deep into our backyard jungle to discover "exotic creatures" (also known as lizards). After dinner and putting the kids to bed, we lounged on the couch watching a *National Geographic* special about Africa. He laid his head in my lap and I gently stroked his hair and rubbed his temples. I could tell he was exhausted from his dad duties.

And the second reason is that, exhausted as he was, he had that twinkle in his eye when we went up to bed. Like a lion on the Serengeti, stalking a female, ready to be king over his domain. I didn't marry Court for his love-making skills. If that was the case, we'd have broken up during our first month of dating. He was a selfish lover back then. His fantasies all revolved around telling me how to please him, like I was some sex robot. But over the last five years, I've turned the tide. Now he finds just as much pleasure and power in making me orgasm. Or, in the case of last night, making me orgasm three times.

A long day playing with the kids, followed by great sex.

Yep, two sure signs he was leaving.

"I wish you didn't have to go," I whine.

It's six a.m. I'm still in bed, my hair in a messy bun, no makeup, sitting against the pillows with my coffee in hand. Court's leaning casually in the doorframe, looking sharp in a slim-cut designer suit with a bag slung over one shoulder. His carefully packed travel suitcase stands next to him. I don't know why he bothers unpacking it when he comes home. He always travels with the same items and has the hotel concierge dry-clean his clothes.

"Take a later flight. I'll make you breakfast," I suggest, hoping to lure him into staying with food. I might be a terrible cook, but I scramble eggs just the way Court likes them.

"I'm securing a deal that dropped overnight. Crypto markets are volatile, so if I'm not there soon, another firm could swoop in." He glances at his watch. "My driver is here."

I drag myself from bed, throw my arms around his neck, and give him a kiss. "I love you, be safe."

"I love you too." He leaves without sticking his head in to check on the twins. When they were babies, he never would have walked past their room without whispering goodbye.

I know it won't be like this forever. Last night he talked about how much fun it will be to take Rowen on a hunting safari when he's a teenager. I didn't argue, because it's really more the thought that counts, but I'm not letting my son kill endangered species in Africa. I'm sure by then, we can come up with another, more appropriate, father-son activity. It's just nice to know Court is looking forward to bonding with Rowen as he grows up.

On my way for more coffee, I check on the twins. Both still sleeping—little bodies wrapped tightly around their favorite stuffies and tangled up in blankets. They won't be awake for at least another hour. I'd better use this time to my advantage.

I'm trying my hardest not to let my disappointment in Sophia's behavior yesterday interfere in my headspace. I just have to focus on what I can control, like my checklist. Almost everything I do is on my laptop or phone, except for my checklist, which I like to handwrite every morning to manage my day. I grab my trusty blue pen, flip to a new page in my pink notebook, and start writing my to-do list, drawing boxes next to each task. It's satisfying to check them off as I complete each one. *Proof scheduled posts.* Check. *Run analytics report.* Check. *Review influencer contracts.* Check. And lastly—I log on to my private bank account. Court and I have a joint account he puts money in for our living expenses, but the money I get from my social media accounts, I keep separate.

Court understands I'm an influencer. And he's smart enough to know that means I'm earning money. But I don't think he knows how many zeros come after the number in my account. It took about a year of hard work to build my trad wife brand before the money started pouring in. Then it all happened so fast, I wasn't sure what to do. And honestly, I was scared to tell Court about the money.

I have this vivid memory of my mom, with a wicked black eye —I must have been about five or six. She'd finally found a job and held on to it long enough to get paid and go shopping. I remember the brief joy of putting on new jeans and sneakers, something that didn't come from the second-hand store. But her junkie boyfriend was pissed. And I mean pissed. He said that money was his, since we were living in his house, and made my mom return the clothes and give him the money. Then he beat the shit out of her.

Thankfully, Cassie had some of her classic boss-bitch wisdom for me when I called in a panic over the money flooding my account.

"Hannah, he made you sign a prenup, so why the fuck would you tell him about your influencer money?"

"He didn't make me sign it, I offered." I corrected her.

"Semantics!" she shouted. "Men like him all have secrets. I know you say he's different and you're in love, but if something ever happens, you have to be able to protect yourself and those babies." Her logic wasn't wrong. "Get a PO box, hire an accountant and an attorney, and whatever you do, don't tell your husband."

So that's how I got here, checking on my private account. There's something soothing about looking at that number and knowing, no matter what happens, I can take care of myself and the twins. It's my security blanket. One I pray I never have to use.

I close my laptop, feeling content that I've completed my morning to-do list, when my phone buzzes.

Can we talk?

...

I start typing, and stop. No, I don't want to talk to Sophia. I don't even want to think about her.

Please, I'm sorry about yesterday. I need to explain myself.

"Ughhhh," I groan. Maybe it's a bad idea to give in and say yes, but what happened yesterday was so strange. I feel like I owe it to myself to at least hear her explanation face-to-face.

I'll come over after I take the kids to preschool.

Can I go with you? Then we can take a walk in that park you like.

Be here at 9:30.

At exactly 9:30 on the dot, the doorbell rings.

"I want to answer it!" Ruby screams and runs for the door with a giant stuffed animal in her arms, her pigtails bouncing from side to side, totally unaware that her new pal, Sophia, and I are in a fight. I follow close behind, just in case it isn't Sophia on the other side.

"Hey, kiddo." Sophia's dressed in a chic white blouse and black pencil skirt with heels. She dips her sunglasses down and says, "Who's that?"

"Oscar," Ruby replies and holds the giant pink stuffed frog in the air. A forgotten toy who recently got a new lease on life, thanks to our frog adventure yesterday.

"Hello, Oscar," Sophia says. She grabs its stuffed frog leg and shakes it.

Ruby giggles and runs away.

"Everyone to the car," I bark. I'm trying not to fume, but didn't she say she wanted to go for a walk in the park? I'm wearing lululemon from head to toe and Sophia is dressed for a freaking business date.

I take a deep breath and head to the kitchen for my phone and keys.

"I've got their bags." Fortunately, Sophia has been here for the morning preschool routine before, so she knows the drill.

Rowen howls, "Ouch! Too tight."

"What's too tight?" I look him up and down.

"Shoes." He points at his feet. I squat down and feel the toe. Yep, too small. Little man must be having a growth spurt.

"Sophia, can you help buckle Ruby in her car seat, while I see about these shoes?"

She nods, takes Ruby by the hand, and they go into the garage. Five minutes and three pairs of shoes later, I'm finally buckling Rowen into his car seat. My marketing brain is busy thinking up a way to turn this into a cute post. Growing boy, growing feet... No, that doesn't sound right. Hmmm... I'll have to spend some time this afternoon working on it. If Sophia wasn't with me, I'd open a voice memo and talk to myself while I drive. But with her in the car, that's out of the question.

"You kiddos want some music?" I don't wait for them to reply, I just turn on a song I know they'll both like. Saving me from having to speak with Sophia on the drive. This was such a stupid idea. I should have told her no. Every mile we drive further from our neighborhood, my blood pressure is rising, pounding in my ears. There's literally nothing she can say to excuse her behavior yesterday.

The preschool is packed for drop-off, so I have to park a ways away.

"I'll be right back," I say when I get out and start unbuckling Rowen.

But Sophia slides out and starts unbuckling Ruby's car seat straps on the other side. "I don't mind helping." She looks up at me and smiles. "Come on, Miss Ruby, let's get you and Oscar to class."

Ruby giggles and starts ribbiting like a frog. As soon as she's free from the harness and Sophia sets her on the ground, she hops to the sidewalk and grabs Rowen by the hand. They skip and make frog noises all the way to the front of the school.

I assume Sophia will just wait outside, but she follows closely behind, blending in with the sea of moms eager to sign the sheet. After signing my name, and ushering the kids to their class, then waiting for ten minutes while they show Sophia around the room and introduce her to their teacher as "Mommy's new best friend," we finally make it out of the building.

"You aren't dressed for a walk at the park," I accuse as soon as we get in the car.

"Yeah, sorry about that. I had an unexpected Zoom call with a former client that ran late, so all I could do was throw on some shoes and get to your place." She looks down at her feet. "I guess I could have put walking shoes on."

"With that skirt?" I laugh. Although it would have served her right—to look like a fool, walking around the park in a designer outfit, just like she made me look like a fool yesterday.

"Do you want to run back to the neighborhood? I could change?" she suggests.

But I have a better idea. I back the car out and turn in the other direction, heading toward a place I haven't been in ages. "Instead of a walk, let's grab a coffee and something sweet."

"That sounds amazing."

I glance over at her, and watch her shoulders relax against the passenger seat.

"Hannah, about yesterday, I am so sorry. I was—uh, projecting my own issues. Which is no excuse. But there's something about Blake that I haven't told you."

Oh god.

Was I right about this too?

Is she about to tell me that they actually are getting a divorce and she moved here on her own? I wonder why she lied about it. And if she lied about this, what else has she lied to me about? Ugh.

"Look, you don't owe me any sort of explanation. If you and Blake are getting a divorce, I'm not here to judge you. I just think what you said to me yesterday was very rude," I reply. We pull up to Duck Donuts and I put the car in park. Before I can get out, she reaches over and grabs my arm.

"No, that's not it. I, uh, Blake..." she stammers, very un-Sophia-like. "We aren't getting a divorce. It's just... He's not who, well, what I mean to say is..." She pauses to catch her breath.

I'm getting impatient. This is almost as bad as when the twins try to tell a story. Four-year-olds are notoriously awful at being coherent.

"Do you want coffee first?" I suggest.

She shakes her head, then blurts out, "Blake has a second wife and a family."

My jaw hits the floor.

"Wait? What?" That wasn't even close to what I thought she was going to say. Affair with his secretary, yes. A weird fetish, yes. Gambling, drinking, general billionaire debauchery, yes to all three. But *a second family*? Not in a million years would I have guessed that. The way she's described her husband, a savvy numbers guy and part of the stealth-wealth club, honestly reminded me of Court. I was kind of thinking this might be the chance for us to have "couple" friends. The guys could log off their computers, play golf, talk about something other than the stock market, while Sophia and I would pick nice restaurants for group dinners, you know—that sort of thing. But now, I don't want that man anywhere near my husband.

"Yeah, that's why it's taking him so long to join me. He doesn't want to leave them."

My head is spinning.

"So hold on, wait... What? No. I mean..." Now I'm the one stuttering. "I have so many questions. But first, does Blake know that you know about..." I look around nervously. *"Them?"* I whisper. I'm praying she says no.

I decide right then and there, I'll help her. I'll use my influencer money to get her the best divorce attorney money can buy. If that man has a second family, he's a fucking nut job. He probably doesn't let her have her own money. That's why she's still with him. She's trapped. My stomach is in knots waiting for her to answer; a bead of sweat forms at my hairline. The smell of sugar permeating the car is enough to make me vomit.

"Yes, he knows I know. We've... well, we've discussed it, at length," she says, tears forming in her eyes.

"Oh," is all I can manage to squeak out. There's a lump in my throat so big that if I swallow, I'll choke. She knows her husband has a second family.

He. Fucking. Discusses. It. With. Her.

My heart is shattered into a thousand pieces for my new friend.

The tears finally fall, cascading down her face. Her lips tremble when she tries to speak. "I'm so sorry about yesterday, I was projecting."

I lean across my seat and wrap my arms around her. "Shhhh... Stop apologizing." I feel like such a terrible friend, for not taking the time to ask Sophia what was really bothering her. Clearly she was triggered. She was crying out for help, and instead of giving it, I pulled up in front of her house and practically threw her out of my car and sped away.

Okay, so maybe I didn't speed away, I drove fifty feet to my driveway, but the intent was the same.

"Hannah, thank you, you don't know how much your friendship means to me. I sobbed all night. I can't lose you." She cries into my shoulder. Her hot, wet tears slide down my exposed skin and soak into my moisture-wicking tank top.

"You know what you need?"

She releases me and we sit back and dry our eyes.

"Tissue?" she says, and we burst out laughing.

"Well, yeah, but I was thinking we should have a sleepover at my house. Court went to London this morning, and who knows when he'll be back." Then I buckle my seatbelt, put the car in drive, and head somewhere I haven't taken her during our outings before. "But for a sleepover, we need supplies."

She's still sniffling and drying her eyes, but nods. After a few minutes, she looks out the windows, realizing we are in a part of town she's never been to with me. "Where are we going?"

I laugh. "Trad wife paradise, of course. Target."

SEVEN

"Oooh, I just had a brilliant idea," Sophia says through muffled lips.

We're lying together on my bed in matching pajamas. Target shopping spree for the win! Today is day three of Operation Save Sophia, which has consisted of a lot of wine, crying, pizza, beauty treatments, and rom-coms.

I blow gently to move the sheet mask flap off my lips. "What's your brilliant idea?" I ask.

"After we clean up, let's order Chinese food for dinner and have a dance party with the twins. I loved dancing with—uh... I mean, I love to dance."

I chuckle, picturing my rather uptight friend dancing with Ruby and Rowen. I'm sure the twins will love it. They've been so good, playing in their room while we've been giving each other facials all afternoon.

"That sounds fun." The timer on my phone goes off, signaling our treatment is done. "Don't get up yet," I say. Then I scoot closer to her on the bed, trying to keep my face steady so the mask doesn't slip off. I hold my phone up in the air and take a picture of us.

"Oh god, Hannah, that's like something from a horror movie."

She groans when I show her the picture. "It looks like we're wearing someone else's skin over our faces. Please don't post that."

I roll my eyes as I climb off my bed, heading to the bathroom to discard the masks and grab a couple of clean towels. "Here, to soak up any extra serum..." I pause when I see Sophia sitting on the edge of my bed crying. "Oh no, what's the matter? I thought you weren't going to cry about Blake anymore? He's an asshole, remember? And I'm going to help you get an apartment and an attorney." Last night I got her to admit he's basically holding her hostage, monitoring her bank account.

She sniffles and tries to smile, using the towel to wipe her face and eyes. "You're such a good friend, Hannah. I don't deserve it."

I wrap my arms around her. "Of course you deserve it. God, Blake really has done a number on you." How can I make her understand what I mean without coming off condescending? I take her by the hands. "Listen, you said your parents died and you practically grew up in boarding schools. So maybe you've never had anyone tell you how marriage works."

"No, I suppose I haven't." She sniffles.

"Not that I'm an expert by any means, but I do know it shouldn't be like this. Blake doesn't respect you—if he did, he wouldn't have put you in this situation. Love can conquer a lot of things, but not a second family."

"Even if I can't have children? And that's something he wants."

Infertility is such a touchy subject. I take a few moments before I respond. "So if you wanted something and he said no, would you go out and get it anyway?" I ask.

"What sort of something?" she asks.

"I don't know, a dog. It doesn't really matter what it is."

"I don't care for animals." She turns her nose up.

"That's not the point!" I cross my arms. "You wouldn't do it because you know it would piss him off and could hurt your marriage. Right? If having a family is important to him, then I'm sorry, but he should have asked you for a divorce when he found out you couldn't have children, so you could both move on with your lives. You deserve to have your own happiness."

"Do you really think so?" she asks.

"Of course I believe you deserve happiness, Sophia. You're a good person." I swear if I ever meet Blake in person, I'm going to throat punch him.

"Are *you* happy?" There's an edge to her voice.

I open my mouth to say yes, obviously, but then I close it. This isn't about me—this is supposed to be about helping Sophia get out of a toxic relationship.

"You know what would make us both happy right now? That dance party and Chinese food."

"Yeah, no more crying. You're right. I deserve to be happy."

I tap her on the arm. "Well, then, what are we waiting for? Tag, you're it." I run for my open bedroom door, throwing a quick glance over my shoulder.

"Hannah," Sophia whines, then she purses her lips. "Tag? Are you serious?"

I nod and smile.

"Oh what the hell." She sprints toward me.

I scream and run for the stairs.

"Me, me, chase me." Rowen charges out of his bedroom, like he's been waiting his entire life to play tag with us.

"No, me," Ruby squeals, joining in the chase.

I reach the bottom of the stairs before the twins or Sophia, then I quickly turn the music on in the living room. "Dance party!" I throw my arms up in the air and wave them around and twirl in a circle. The twins' faces light up and they both clap and jump and wiggle, dancing with the kind of freedom that only four-year-olds with very little self-awareness can.

Sophia stands on the edge of the room—watching. For a split second, I think she's going to turn around and walk out, because of the strange look on her face. But instead, she says, "Wait. I think it goes more like this..." She leaps forward, waving her arms and shaking her hips. Then she snatches the twins' hands. "Come on, Hannah, grab on."

"Wooooo!" I grab their hands and we all skip and boogie. Like one big goofy, ridiculously happy family. If this doesn't boost Sophia's spirits, I don't know what will.

Thank you, Sophia mouths after a few minutes.

I wink at her.

We dance until we're all panting and starting to break a sweat. I flop on the floor. The twins shriek and jump on me and start tickling me with their pudgy little fingers. Sophia drops to her knees and collapses next to me, laughing brightly as the twins pile on her too and tickle under her chin. This is a moment to treasure.

"Mommy, can Sophia live here forever?" Ruby asks later that night after we've stuffed our bellies with food and watched a movie.

"That would be fun, wouldn't it? But I'm not sure Daddy would like that," I reply, then give her a little nuzzle and kiss. "Thankfully, Sophia lives right next door so we can see her whenever we want."

Ruby smiles and yawns, content with my answer, before snuggling up with her stuffie and closing her eyes. Then I go over to tuck Rowen in. He's usually so angelic at night, but tonight he's got a scowl on his tired face.

"What's the matter, RoRo?" I tickle his tummy and he rolls away from me.

"I don't want Sophia to live here," he grumbles.

A pang of guilt settles in my gut and I sit on his bed and rub his back.

"Don't worry, sweetheart, Sophia's going home soon," I whisper. "And your daddy will be back tomorrow." Rowen rolls back toward me and flashes a grin before he lets out a big yawn. I lean down and give him a kiss, smoothing his hair from his eyes. "I love you."

Downstairs, I find Sophia sitting at the table. She's changed out of our matching puppy dog pajamas and is wearing the white blouse and pencil skirt from three days ago. I raise an eyebrow. "And what, pray tell, are you doing?"

"I figure I better head home—let the kids wake up to their normal routine with their mommy. You said Court is coming home tomorrow—I'm sure you have things to do tonight that don't involve another wine-soaked cry fest with me." She stands up and opens her arms.

I smile and nod, then wrap my arms around her. "I'm always here for you, no matter what, okay?"

"Don't worry, you can't get rid of me, I'm right next door." She laughs. Then she takes my hands and holds them tightly in hers. "I can't thank you enough for this. These have been the best three days I've had in a very long time."

"Matching pajamas have that effect on people," I tease.

"I'm serious. You've been like a sister to me, a real best friend." Then she heads for the front door. "I'll call you."

I wave, and just like that, she's gone.

I'm not really sure if anything I've said or done the last few days was enough to help her. But I tried. She was a woman on the brink of a complete mental health breakdown. If it was me, I know she would have done the same thing. Kept my head above water, as long as it took. But I do have to remember, my kiddos come first. My husband, our life, and the life I've worked so hard to build, it's meant for us. Not us and Sophia. And like I just told Ruby, Sophia lives next door. We can hang out anytime we want, unless she caves and that prick Blake moves in to split his time between her and his other family. Because I've already vowed to myself, I won't be part of that.

I know she'll have to make the hard decisions on her own. My influence isn't going to make Sophia choose the right path for her life. I already know that. Because of my mom. She stayed in toxic relationships, even when it hurt her, even when it hurt me. No amount of crying or begging as a child stopped her. The only thing it did was fuel her to leave me on my Great-Aunt Tippy's doorstep one night and never look back.

For a brief moment, I wonder if that's what Sophia will do.

Pack up a suitcase and never look back.

And then I think, *As much as I love my new best friend, maybe my life would be easier if everything went back to the way it was before she moved in next door.*

Thank god.

That's all I can say. Thank god Sophia didn't pack up a suitcase and leave town, because I would literally die without her. It started as an upset stomach and headache the day after Court returned home from London. I thought I might be pregnant. But it quickly evolved into something much worse—*the flu.*

I've never been this sick in my entire life. Every bone, muscle, and hair on my body aches. On top of the flu, I've also got a whopping case of viral strep throat. Which means high fevers (the hallucinating kind), teeth-chattering chills, drench-the-sheets night sweats, and a throat so sore I considered drinking bleach to burn the virus away.

"Achoo!" I sneeze, cough, wheeze, and start crying from the immediate searing pain. There's no one here to comfort me. I'm all alone in the lower-level guest bedroom, quarantined away from Court and the twins on the main two floors.

Sophia's my new hero, playing both housemaid and nurse. Taking care of me and my family. Seriously, without her, I'm not sure any of us would have survived.

"Knock, knock," she says and opens the door. "I picked up your meds and some stuff to make you more comfortable." She's wearing rubber gloves, an N95 mask, protective eye goggles, and carrying two huge bags. "Oh, Hannah, are you crying?" She drops everything and runs to my side.

I nod. I open my mouth to speak, but I've lost my voice.

"Don't try to talk." She pets my head. "Here, let me get you something for the pain." She rifles through the bags, removing various kinds of over-the-counter meds, lining them up on the dresser. "I wasn't sure what flavor you'd like, so I got them all." She puts a bunch of bottles of children's electrolyte drinks on the nightstand, where I can reach, before cracking one open and filling up my cup.

She hands me four pills. "I know it hurts to swallow, but you've got to take those. It says to take them with food, so I'll go grab you a yogurt. Maybe you can get a few bites down."

"Thank you," I manage to say, barely a croaky whisper. I sip the drink, choke down the pills, and lean on the stack of pillows, exhausted.

"I'll be right back with a yogurt. Don't worry about a thing... I've got everything covered." Sophia winks at me through her plastic lenses.

Before she returns, I fall back asleep.

When I wake up, I'm disoriented. The room is smoky, and my heart bangs in my chest as my pain-pill-dulled fight or flight response kicks in. Thankfully, I notice the smoke is actually mist coming from a dehumidifier before I leap from the bed and collapse. I'm so weak, my limbs like rubbery noodles, even if I tried, I'd probably fall flat on my face.

I check my phone.

Two a.m., but I'm wide awake and feeling restless from that little boost of adrenaline.

Everyone should be sound asleep in their beds upstairs. And I know it's a terrible idea, considering the rubber legs, but I desperately want to see the twins. I haven't seen them in days. This is the longest I've ever gone without them. One of Court's fears, besides having a regular nanny, is having anyone watch the children for an extended period of time. He likes to remind me that the children of billionaires are targets for kidnappings and ransom demands. Every time I suggest a romantic getaway, he emails me a news article reminiscent of the Denzel Washington movie *Man on Fire*.

Maybe if I take it slow. Clean myself up a bit. Sophia brought some of my clothes down, so I could take a bath and change out of these pajamas. If that goes well, then I could try walking upstairs to sneak a peek at my sleeping babies. And make sure Court actually went to bed, like he said he did around midnight, according to his texts. He loves to burn the late-night oil in his office—which makes him less able to tolerate the kids the next day. Let's face it, Sophia isn't going to be able to keep up her role as family caregiver forever.

The steamy hot water does wonders for my aching body and my spirits. When I finally get out of the bath, put on fresh clothes, brush my teeth and my long hair, I'm sure I'll be able to walk up the two flights of stairs without incident. I know it's terrible, but I kind of want to wake the twins for a quick Mommy hug. Just to feel their little arms wrap around me, however brief, would give my immune system the boost it needs.

As I tiptoe up the stairs toward their room, I glance over at Sophia's house. All the lights are off; I'm sure she's exhausted. Domestic life clearly isn't her thing—I know she's only doing this to repay me for our three-day pajama fest last week. But she doesn't need to repay me for doing what any decent friend would do.

Taking care of a sick woman and her family, now that's going above and beyond. I'm going to insist she lets me treat her to a full day at a resort spa. She deserves to be pampered. Not just for helping me, but for what she's been going through with her husband, Blake. I'm still devastated. She's a smart, intelligent, caring woman, and she does not deserve to be shit on. I know it's going to take time, but I swear, I'm going to help her leave that prick and start a new life.

My breathing is labored by the time I reach the top of the stairs, and I'm startled when I turn the corner and see Court leaning in the doorframe of the children's bedroom. His body is relaxed and he has a smile on his face.

"Are the twins alright?" I croak.

His head whips over and he straightens up. He looks confused for a split second when he sees me, but it is pretty dark with only ambient hall lighting to prevent nighttime falls, so maybe I'm misreading his look. He quickly walks toward me and puts his arms around me.

"What are you doing up? Shouldn't you be sleeping?" He sounds so worried. He kisses the top of my head and squeezes me. It hurts, but that's probably still from the flu. His heart is racing and I can feel it through his chest.

"I miss them," I say. "I had to come up and see you all, even if it's just for a few seconds."

He's holding onto me longer than he usually does. But this was probably pretty scary for him. I'm never sick. I think this is the first time since we've been together that I've had anything more than seasonal allergies. His mother was a sickly woman and died when he was a child. So this might have stirred up some unpleasant feelings.

"We missed you too. But your health is what's important. You really should go back to bed." He glances over his shoulder toward the twins' room. "Let me help you. I'm surprised you had the strength to walk up two flights of stairs," he says and guides me toward the stairs.

"But I just want to see them," I whisper. My throat throbs, from the talking, and I'm wheezing again. I plant my feet and try to turn around.

"Hannah, you might still be contagious, please. Let me take you back to bed." He's not taking no for an answer.

I let out a sigh and give in. It does make me feel better, knowing he stopped to look at the children before going to bed. He really is a great dad. I know sometimes I think the worst, that he's easily annoyed by them or doesn't put in as much effort as me. But that's my own insecurities, because every man in my childhood hated me. It wasn't until Mom dumped me at the farm with my Great-Aunt Tippy and her husband, Francisco, that I found a man I could trust. Fran isn't my relative by blood. But he's the closest thing to a father I've ever had.

Aunt Tippy was a no-nonsense kind of woman. But I never went hungry or worried about my safety with her, like I did when I lived with my mom. Uncle Fran was a kind and caring man. He wanted me to have nice things and was genuinely proud of me when I worked hard to get them. He'd give me twenty dollars for every A on my report card, much to Aunt Tippy's dismay. And he even helped me fill out my college applications and paid for my books all four years. Maybe that's why I was first drawn to Court. He's a lot like Fran. A hardworking, generous man, even if he's rather stoic and overprotective.

When we reach the guest bedroom, Court helps me crawl into the bed, tucks me in, and smooths out the blankets. He leans over to kiss me on the forehead but steps back the second his lips touch my flesh, his eyes wide.

"Hannah, baby, you're burning up," he says, his voice full of panic.

"But I'm feeling better," I lie.

He turns on the bedside light and looks around all the medical supplies Sophia's stocked, until he finds what he's searching for. A thermometer. I shake my head.

"Please, high fever in adults is dangerous. You don't want to go blind, or have organ failure." It seems like he's really panicking. Sweat forms at his hairline and he sticks the thermometer out. "Under the tongue, it only takes a few seconds."

I sit up, cross my arms, and open my mouth. It beeps and the digital readout is blinking red. Even I know that means a fever.

"103.8. Hannah, that's bad. I think I should take you to the ER."

"No, I'm fine. Just give me more of those meds over there, and I promise I won't overexert myself again. I'm sorry," I say. My throat is on fire. But I do not want to go to the hospital and take up a bed instead of someone who really needs it. I'll be fine if I just take my meds and sleep it off for a few more days. I was an idiot for thinking a bath would fix everything.

"Don't be sorry." He hands me several pills and something to drink before pulling out his phone. "I'm calling my doctor." He steps out of the room. I can't make out what he's saying, but he's out there for a long time. Finally he returns, looking calmer.

"Well?"

"Rest and fluids. If your temperature doesn't come down in a few hours, Dr. Addelson will meet us at the hospital. They have a private wing for VIP patients and—"

I put my hand up to stop him.

I am not leaving my home. I am not leaving the twins. I can't put my finger on it, but something in my gut is telling me not to go. Of course I believe in medicine and doctors. But maybe it's some of my cynical Aunt Tippy coming out through me. She's seventy, healthy as a horse, and can count the number of times she's been to a doctor on one hand. Including the day she was born. Or maybe this sudden paranoia is just fever-induced thoughts. But whatever it is, I'm not leaving this house.

"I'll recover here. I love you, go get some sleep." My voice comes out as normal-sounding as it's been in days.

Court tilts his head, stares at me, then leaves without so much as an *I love you too*.

EIGHT

Thankfully, I had enough pre-made content to cover the two weeks I've been recuperating from what the kids are calling "Sick-a-saurus Rex," thanks to their new obsession with dinosaurs. That was a Sophia twist I wasn't expecting. Who knew, the posh art buyer who grew up in European boarding schools has a thing for dinosaurs.

Every day while I was sick, she took them on an adventure. My only rule was not to the beach. Unless Court was with them. His fear of the children drowning is even worse than mine. He checks and triple-checks their life vests more than I do, and I've trained him in the art of sunscreen application. Because that's an area I know Sophia would blow off my rules. What's worse than a four-year-old with a sunburn? Two four-year-olds with sunburns.

I moved back into our bedroom late last night and I never want to see that guest room again. Until I start dismantling it to build a studio for the twins. A place they can throw on little smocks and be messy with clay, paint, or science experiments. On day five of my quarantine, I texted Court that I was going to redo the room once I was feeling better.

Sophia has even agreed to roll up her sleeves and help.

"I know being sick has been awful, and I'd never wish it on you again, but—if I'm being honest, these last few weeks have been the best distraction for me," she says, then takes a sip of her coffee. We are sitting at the kitchen island. She just returned from dropping the kids off at preschool. I could have easily done it myself, but Ruby and Rowen begged. And she offered. It did give me time to check on a few things around the house.

But every item on my list, well—Sophia had done it.

Laundry: Washed and folded.

Pantry: Stocked.

Fridge: Filled.

House: Clean.

And she hadn't just completed my trad wife duties. She'd knocked them out of the park. The children's clothes weren't just folded, every single item was ironed. The house wasn't just cleaned, but sparkling and reorganized. The pantry contents, shelved alphabetically and by size and shape.

I know it shouldn't bother me.

But it does.

"Sophia, before we start with the room downstairs, can we talk about something?" I ask. I don't want to put her on the spot, but it's eating me alive.

She shifts uncomfortably in her seat.

"Oh please, don't worry." This is such a touchy subject, I don't want to spook her. I reach a hand out and place it gently on her arm.

"I'm sorry if I moved stuff around, I can put things back," she blurts out. Her cheeks blush with embarrassment, like one of the twins caught doing something naughty.

"No, no, it's not that. Well, I mean, it is—but not how you think. I'm not mad. I appreciate it so much. You have way more of this trad wife and mom stuff in you than you think. Blake was a fool for thinking he had to go out and get another family to have it. You could have easily adopted."

She shakes her head a little.

"Hannah, it's not that easy. I do appreciate that you think I'd be good at this kind of life full time. But that's because it's been temporary. I could never do this every day, not like you. And Blake knew that. I'm not like you. I need to be out there, again." She stands up and I realize she's not in let's-rip-up-that-bedroom-and-get-dirty clothes, she's in a sleek business suit.

I'm confused. "You need to be out where again?"

"I've been meaning to tell you. Blake set up an incredible opportunity for me in Greece. I'll be meeting with a royal family, who are there vacationing, and hearing the history of several pieces that went missing a century ago from one of their country estates. I'm going to spend a few weeks traveling, meeting with my art dealer contacts across Europe, to hopefully locate the missing art pieces." Her face glows with this new adventure.

I want to be happy for her.

But did she really say what I think she said?

"Blake set this up for you? But, I mean, I thought…" I let the words dry up. Because it's just beating a dead horse. "Sorry, that came out wrong. What I meant to say is, I'm really happy for you. I'm sure you'll do a great job helping them locate their missing art."

This satisfies her enough. For now. But I knew as soon as I questioned Blake's involvement and watched her glow diminish, that she was going to hold this against me. Even though she's been constantly asking for my advice. I should know better.

"When do you leave?"

"In a few hours." She glances around my house. A strange look comes over her. Sadness, maybe. Or relief. Sometimes with Sophia it's hard to tell.

"A few hours? What the…" I stop, take a deep breath, remind myself that she probably needs a break from us. Even if it was Blake who planned this meeting for her. Just as long as that asshole isn't there with her. My heart sinks as soon as I think about it, because of course he's going to be there. Why would he go out of his way to set up some big meeting and job for her if it wasn't so he could see her? The job is the carrot. One he knew she'd never turn down. And he's going to weasel his way back into her life, so he can have his cake and eat it too.

"Well, then give me a hug. I'm sure you have a million things to do at your house before you go. Thank you for everything—I'll miss you. The kids and Court will too." I stand up and open my arms. She smiles and comes in for the hug.

"I'll miss you so much, Hannah. You're my best friend in the world."

"I'd tell you to call or text, but with the time difference, and how busy you'll be with traveling and meetings... Anyway, at least let me know you land safely."

"Yes, of course. It's only a few weeks, maybe a month, tops."

I walk her to the front door and wave goodbye as she walks down the stairs and turns left to cut through the yard to get to her house. After I shut the door and go back to my laptop and checklist in the kitchen, my motivation to start a home renovation project has fizzled. Court's gone for the day, a business meeting in Miami, so with the house to myself and nothing better to do, I plop on the living room couch and turn on the TV.

I'm probably not cut out to be both a trad wife influencer and a home renovation queen. I can still spin it that way on my social media with carefully curated pictures, but instead of breaking a nail or wearing down my immune system, I'll call a professional.

Sophia's been gone for four days.

Four days for me to simmer. I've noticed more of her changes around my house, and each one is making me angrier. The pantry organizing and ironing the kids' clothes, I chalked up to nervous energy. But reorganizing my husband's closet? Boxing up the twins' baby clothes I was saving, and putting them in the garage? Signing up to chaperone a field trip for the kids? That is crossing a line.

"I'm so sorry, Alice," I say to my manicurist. She's crying. Another one of Sophia's "improvements" to my life. Apparently, she told Alice my nails looked cheap, and if she didn't step up her game, I would never come back there. Then she cancelled my long-standing Tuesday appointment.

Alice wipes her nose with a tissue.

"All I asked was for her to phone and let you know I was sick and wouldn't be in for a few weeks, if you wanted to fill the spot with another client." I'm so pissed right now.

"So you don't hate your nails and think they're cheap?"

"Would I have kept coming here for four years if I thought that?" I reply. "Now, I know this isn't my normal time, but can you fit me in? Look. I need your help." I hold up my hands for her to see the tragic state of my nails.

With a fresh manicure, and Alice feeling better, I leave the nail salon with the assumption that Sophia has made a mess for me all over town. I decide to cancel the rest of my errands for the day and head home, too afraid to face any more crying service industry workers. What the hell was she thinking? I am so mad, I don't know what to do. I really need to get all this off my chest, but Court is busy prepping for some investor meeting in Québec. He's leaving for a week in the morning, and I know he'll only be half-listening to me.

But—there's no one else I can talk to.

If I call Cassie, she won't be afraid to say, *Bitch, I told you so.*

So Court it is.

Later that afternoon, once I've picked up the kids from preschool and fed them a snack, I tiptoe into Court's office. "Court, I know you're busy, but when you finish up, can we sit on the deck and talk for a while? Maybe have a glass of wine?"

"Of course, that sounds great. Is everything alright?" He looks up from a report he's highlighting and smiles at me.

"Yeah, well, no. It's just—there are some things Sophia did while I was sick, and I'd love to get your take on it. Maybe I'm over-reacting. But some of it hurts my feelings and—"

"Say no more. If you need a drink and to vent, I'm all ears, babe. Give me twenty minutes and I'll be done. We can have a little happy hour before dinner."

I rush to his side and give him a kiss. "Mmmm..." I moan into the kiss. His lips, soft and inviting. Sometimes I forget how lucky I am.

"Let me get this straight, she made your manicurist cry?" Court takes a swig from his drink, the ice cubes clanking against the cut crystal tumbler. Instead of wine, he mixed us each a Crown Royal with ginger and soda. A little nod to his upcoming trip to Canada.

"Uh-huh," I say and nod my head.

His eyes crinkle first, then the corners of his mouth turn up, then a chuckle rumbles up his chest, until he can't contain it and starts laughing.

"Court. This isn't funny." I set my drink down and cross my arms. But the more he laughs, the more foolish I feel, until I start laughing too.

"It's really rather sad, don't you think? She's so out of touch— she probably thought she was helping." He finishes his drink and stands. "You want another?"

"Oh, why not? Here, I'll come with you." I get up and trail after my husband to the bar cart off the living room. "You know she went to all these horrible boarding schools in Europe. The stories would even make you blush. Honestly, I don't think she's ever had a female friend before. She has no idea how to act around me."

He mixes the drinks and before he hands mine to me, he wraps his arms around my waist. He smells good and my body tingles for his touch. We haven't had sex in weeks, since the night he came home from London, just before I got sick.

"How occupied are the twins?" he asks and pulls my body in closer. Then he lifts my chin with his thumb and kisses me. His mouth is parted, and I accept the invitation.

"Occupied enough. Laundry room," I say and tug him in that direction. I've discovered the twins never go into the laundry room

—something about the monster that lives in the dryer and eats socks. If we're quiet, we have ten, maybe fifteen minutes before the kids come down hunting for dinner and shouting, *Mommy, Daddy, where are you?* Which is a surefire mood killer.

As soon as we get into the laundry room, which is nearly the size of a bedroom, complete with cupboards, shelves, and a table I use for folding, Court hikes my dress up over my head.

"My god, you are stunning, aren't you?"

I rip his shirt off and make quick work of his belt, getting his pants down while he kisses my neck, takes off my bra, and works his lips down to my breasts. Oh my god, I've needed this so badly. No wonder I've been a paranoid, obsessive freak show for days.

Court picks me up and sets me on the table. Thank god I put all the laundry away earlier. His body comes forward to meet me and I lean back, arching so he can put his hands around my waist as he thrusts into me. I moan quietly, afraid to get too loud and alert the twins where we are. I'm not sure even a laundry monster would keep them from barging in if they mistook my cries of pleasure for real ones.

"I fucking love you," Court says as he's slamming into me. I don't even care that he's making this mostly about him, because I'm so turned on, I'll orgasm even if he's not focusing on me.

"Harder," I beg.

He doesn't have to be told twice and after a few more glorious pumps, his eyes roll into the back of his head. I close my eyes and let my body relax enough to reach my own high. Goose bumps ripple across my bare flesh.

After a few minutes, letting our bodies come down naturally, we get dressed and go back out to the living room. Court grabs our drinks and gives me a wink. "Now, how about we talk about something happy for a while. How's the Disney trip planning coming? If I know my wife, I'm sure you have some matching shirts in the works?"

"Oh, you know me too well." And for the next twenty minutes

I tell him about the things I've planned for our trip, before the kids come down ready for dinner.

"I've got an idea... How about I order a pizza and we watch *The Lion King*?" Court says to the twins.

They both squeal with delight, run to where he's sitting, and throw their little arms around his neck. He looks over at me briefly, before shutting his eyes and hugging Ruby and Rowen with the most loving embrace. It's too bad he's so adamant that his face not be on my social page, because boy, this would be a post with a million views.

Oh, what's the harm?

I hold my phone up and take a picture.

Court's eyes open, his gaze narrows, as if he knows what I was about to do. I quickly drop the phone in my lap. Heat rises in my cheeks. "It's just for us, to remember this moment."

"I promise I won't forget," he says.

NINE

Everything is as normal as it can be around the house—laundry is folded, kids are watching cartoons, Court is still in Québec. It's just another Saturday morning in paradise, as I like to say.

I'm grabbing the pancake mix and a few other items from the pantry to make the kids breakfast, when I spot something near the back. I step closer, peering at several rows of cans organized by Sophia that I've forgotten to rearrange. Sure, maybe I appreciate her color-coded methods, but because I'm petty, I put the cans back how I had them before she came into my life.

I tap on the last one with my manicured nail and smile.

See if I ever let a friend spend time alone in my kitchen again.

Yes, I think to myself, Sophia is still my friend—even if it's complicated and she's on thin ice for her pretentious behavior around town. You don't mess with a woman's nail stylist, just like you don't mess with her man. That's not how friends behave, boarding school upbringing or not. As soon as she returns from Europe, I'm going to sit her down and just explain it. If she wants to stay in my life, there are rules. I blanch, thinking about what Cassie would do if it was her.

A laugh escapes my lips. I always imagine what Cassie would do in these kinds of situations. She's just so fearless. With her words, with her body. I'm not jealous, more like a light shade of green. There was a time when I was fearless—dancing with a beer in one hand around a bonfire with my hometown friends, singing at the top of my lungs, refusing to go home at the end of the party. There were so many nights Matt had to drag me home so Aunt Tippy wouldn't kill me when she woke up to find me gone. If I close my eyes, I can still see the flames and the little crackle of sparks floating up in the air, rising to greet the stars.

When I open them, it's not flames I see, but the glow of sunlight glimmering through the windows like a reflection on water. Maybe I'll take the kids to the beach later, but for now, they are still entertained in the living room by *Bluey*. The pancakes can wait a few more minutes... if I'm lucky.

Clasping a fresh cup of coffee, I sit down at the kitchen island, open my laptop, pull out my notebook, and look at my to-do list. Manageable. I write down a few notes for an idea I've been mulling over for some new posts.

I flip through the last couple of pages, then go back a few weeks to make sure I haven't missed anything. There are little reminders of Sophia everywhere. Things we'd done together. Or planned to do. I see a big circle around an activity I'd completely forgotten—we'd promised to take the kids to the zoo. Their faces had been bright with joy when we'd told them of the proposed adventure.

Sophia wasn't just part of *my* life. She'd integrated herself into the lives of my children, even before I was sick, even if she didn't mean to. She clearly made a strong impression, especially on Ruby, who has been quick to point out all of our parenting style differences. Sweet little Ruby doesn't understand the nuance of this thin-ice situation, that it grates on my nerves to have her compare me and Sophia.

All week I've been hearing things like, *But, Mommy, Sophia said peanut butter and jelly is bad for my teeth.* And, *I don't want to take a nap, Sophia said I'm too old for naps.* To which I have to respond with things like, *Yes, Sophia has a point—maybe you should brush your teeth after your sandwich* and *If you're too old for naps, why do you look so tired?* I don't want to let her know that my friendship with her favorite neighbor woman (the only one she knows) isn't as solid as her four-year-old mind might think.

Rowen, on the other hand, seems more reserved about the situation. He's not pointing out all the differences between me and Sophia. Maybe he's just extra tired. Hmmm. He was on the no-nap bandwagon with Ruby the last few days. But that still doesn't explain his current temperament.

"RoRo, is everything okay?" I ask him after he's finished eating his pancakes and I've cleared his plate. He's still sitting at the kitchen table, which is unlike him—usually he flies out of here ready to play with toys in his room. Ruby hightailed it for the bathroom as soon as she was done eating, probably brushing the syrup off her teeth.

"I'm okay, Mommy," he says, then sets his head down on the table.

I walk over and put my hand on his forehead. No fever. I take a different approach. "Do you want to talk about it?"

He lets out a very long, little-boy sigh. "I miss my daddy."

"Oh, sweetheart, Daddy will be back from Canada very soon." I ruffle his hair. "I know, why don't you go grab the tub of crayons and we can make Daddy a welcome home banner."

He lifts his head and his face lights up. He scurries from the table and heads for the cupboard with the crayons. Ruby comes out of the bathroom, wet handprints on the front of her shirt.

"What have I told you about using your shirt like a hand towel?" I narrow my gaze, crouch down, and creep toward her with my hands out like claws.

"The tickle monster will get me if I keep getting my shirt wet?"

"That's right. Rawrrrr!" I growl and run toward her. She laughs and squeals and goes tearing out of the hallway, shouting at Rowen for help.

"Rowen can't save you!" I exclaim and chase her up the stairs.

She's a fast little squirt, and evades my every attempt at grabbing her, even though I know she wants to be tickled. The chase is half the fun. I'm nearly to the top of the stairs when something catches the corner of my eye. I slow to turn my head and look out the window. There's a sleek black Mercedes 700 series parked in Sophia's driveway. That's odd. I stop chasing after Ruby, who's already made it to her bedroom and slammed the door shut. I stand on the stairs, watching the Mercedes for a few minutes, waiting to see if someone gets out or comes back when they realize Sophia isn't home. But no one does.

Sophia didn't mention anyone being at her house while she was gone.

I quickly run back down the stairs and grab my phone to see if she's called, texted, or emailed me any instructions. Whoever it is would need clearance to get in our gated neighborhood. So she must know there's someone at her house. Right?

I have no messages from Sophia.

Strange.

If I was going out of town, and she was at home, I'd let her know if there would be vehicles in my driveway or people in my home. Knowing her, she'd just walk over, bang on my door, and ask them what they were doing in my house. While me on the other hand, I'm not about to leave the kids alone to go snoop around next door. That feels like the start of a horror movie. My least favorite kind of movies.

Although... I should make sure someone isn't breaking into her house.

The expensive car means nothing.

Sophia has priceless art. The sorts of thieves that would target her collection don't drive around in junkers. They are professionals. My heart quickens. I rush back to the stairs, to look out the windows and see if the car is still there.

Yes.

I can't see anything in her house—the sun is reflecting off all the glass and she has the blackout shades drawn tightly. A purchase she made after I told her we could see her through the glass. After a few minutes of moving to various spots in my house to get different views, I've convinced myself there is an art thief scouting Sophia's home.

> Hey. Are you expecting someone at your house? There's a black 700 series parked in your driveway.

No response.

"Come on Sophia, look at your phone." I pace with my hands on my hips.

> If you don't respond, I'm going next door to investigate.

I wait for five very long minutes, all the while formulating a plan. I'll sneak around to the gate on the backside of our fence and go through her backyard. Her house has a similar layout to mine. There are big sliding doors along the west, facing the ocean. I can use the stairs, creep up to the deck, and if I stand on the edge, I think I can peer in without anyone noticing me.

I only know this, because I've been startled more than once by the twins, who were supposed to be waiting patiently for me to come back to the yard with snacks and drinks—and instead they scared the bejesus out of me, leaping out and making faces at me through the glass. I had no idea they were there.

A quick glance at my phone—still no reply from Sophia.

"Well, I've had enough of this. I'm not letting her home be pillaged." But before I can do anything, I'm intercepted by Rowen.

"What's pillaged mean, Mommy?" He has a fistful of crayons. Crap! I was supposed to help him make welcome home banners for Court.

"Uh... nothing. Mommy just has to go check on Sophia's house real fast."

"MOMMY!" Ruby screams, coming down the stairs. "The tickle monster never tickled me." She stomps her feet as she walks. Then she folds her arms over her chest and huffs and puffs as she approaches me.

Great.

With both kids right here, in need of attention, there's no way I can spy on whoever is in Sophia's house. It's going to drive me nuts every time I look out the window and see that car in her driveway without any answers. So I vow to myself, if it's still there when I get the kids down for a nap (I will reclaim naptime), then I'll walk next door. And maybe I'll be fearless and march up to the front door and ring the doorbell. I have a can of pepper spray in my purse that I'll take, just in case.

Buzz.

It's Sophia.

I exhale loudly. Oh thank god, I really didn't want to use the pepper spray today.

> Hey, thanks for the heads up. Just my contractor, he has a key, measuring for a new closet system

So the guy carrying out your Joan Miró? Should I stop him?

> What?! YES! Call the police!

jk

> Jerk!

Sorry, but maybe let me know next time so I don't worry.

> You worry about me?

I start typing that I'm worried and annoyed that Blake set up this trip for her, and she's fooling herself if she doesn't see how he's manipulating her. But then I delete that part and hit send.

well, yeah, duh. I worry about you all the time...

> Aww, well I worry about you too. Are you still feeling better? How are the twins?

I'm 100%. Twins are great, and both tugging on me for attention. I better go. Call me once you've fully settled in with your new job hunting art. I want to hear all about the royal family.

Of course. Hugs!

"Okay, where's my paper so I can color a picture for Daddy with you?" The twins are far too busy creating masterpieces to stop and answer me. I take a few candid photos of my Michelangelos in action and smile.

I decide I've had enough excitement for the morning and sit down to color with the twins for as long as this peace will last. Rather than making a banner for Court, I find myself sketching out a closet design. If her guy is driving a 700 series, those must be some nice closets. Maybe I'll get his number from Sophia—when he's done working at her house, of course.

TEN

Sophia's driveway has been a flurry of activity. There's been the contractor for the new closet. Then the woman to measure for new blinds. After that it was a florist—*strange*. Next was the other contractor for the upstairs bathroom. Then the downstairs bathroom.

I still don't understand why she's scheduled so many happenings at her home while she's halfway across the world. Even though she's been texting me before each person arrives, it hasn't stopped me from staring out my windows, watching with intrigue. The logistics alone are giving me a headache. Court would lose his shit if I had people in our home when one of us wasn't here to monitor their activity.

But maybe that's the point...

Maybe she's doing this as a big "eff you" to Blake.

At least, that's what I'm telling myself.

I suppose I could just ask her what the hell is going on. But I've been using any time we connect on text to have friendly, healthy conversations—to further and strengthen our friendship. It feels like the thing I can control while she's so far away. Plus, even though she's in a completely different time zone, she always seems to be online when I'm posting. Her insight on my recent activity has been invaluable.

> What if you broke down and actually baked something—we both know it won't end well, but maybe that's part of the allure. Mrs. Perfect—can't bake?

> OMG that's brilliant!

> Only brilliant if it works. And you don't burn the house down.

> How rude!

That sad, droopy cake with lumpy frosting picture (aka epic fail) is my most viral post to date. And I didn't burn my house down. I did however receive an influencer contract from Betty Crocker almost instantly—and a one-year supply of cake mixes delivered to my doorstep on a huge pallet.

I have no idea what I'm going to do with three hundred and fifty-six boxes of cake mix. Apparently that's the number of cakes they think one person can bake in a year. Yeah right! I'd really like to meet the woman who's baking one cake per day for an entire year ... and give her all this cake mix.

Court's been back from his Canada trip for a few weeks and doesn't seem impressed with all of the baking and mishaps I've been documenting in the kitchen. Even if my follower count has been skyrocketing, he doesn't seem to pay any attention to that part of my life. Unless it interferes with my wifely duties. Which, I suppose, have been lacking a little lately. I've just been so distracted by the goings-on at Sophia's house and all this goddamn cake mix.

"Do you really have to make more cupcakes today? What about that bakery you liked so much a few months ago?" he asks one morning as I'm setting up the eggs and oil on the kitchen island for another how-to video. This time I'm adding shredded vegetables into the batter in a trick-your-kids-into-eating-healthy video.

"What, didn't you hear, I'm trying to give Martha Stewart a run for her money?" I tease.

"Funny," he says without laughing.

"Is something wrong?" I ask.

He grabs a bottle of water from the fridge and takes a drink before answering. He's sweaty from working out, something we used to do together, but not so much lately.

"Don't get me wrong, I love domestic goddess Hannah." He approaches me and pushes the messy bit of hair from my face. "But sometimes I miss the well-polished you."

It takes every bit of self-control I have not to let my breath hitch in my throat.

Something stings about conditional love.

Girl, are you sure you want to get involved in the billionaire game? You know you have to put them first, no matter what, right? Cassie said as she gave me a hug goodbye after we'd graduated from Iowa State.

You worry too much. I laughed her warning off all the way to Florida.

But she was right.

I lean forward and give Court a kiss—gentle at first, just our lips. Then I use my lips, drag his mouth open, and my tongue slips in. My left hand reaches around and cups his ass cheek and squeezes, while my right hand grabs his dick through his flimsy workout shorts, softly, like I'm cradling one of the eggs I'm supposed to be cracking for this batch of healthy cupcakes. His hand reaches up and grabs my breast, and he's anything but gentle with it.

Jesus. If I wanted a mammogram, I'd have scheduled one. When I open my mouth to protest the squeezing, "I'm sorry," comes out instead. "Maybe I'll take a break from all this cake nonsense and go to the salon. I'll get my hair done the way you like, then swing by and let my personal shopper find me something sexy to wear tonight. Would you like that?" I muse.

"Yes, very much," he moans and kisses down my neck.

I'm disgusted with myself. Playing this game with my husband.

"I'm going to go shower," he finally says, his hand releasing my aching breast. "Until tonight, my love." He gives me a final passionate kiss.

As soon as he's done, I spin around on my heels, and grab my phone and keys. I make a beeline for the garage so Court can't see the tears in my eyes. Once I'm in my car and backing out of the driveway, I feel a sense of relief to be out of the house. I love my husband, but when he pulls that kind of crap with me, I can't help feeling sad and used.

I know there are a million women who would die to be me. To have this life. But if they really understood what that meant, the perfection required, not just for the posts, but for the man behind them—would they still envy me?

Would they think I'm perfect if they knew I'm basically fueled by the knowledge that all of this could come crashing down at any moment? I rub my aching breast. That's not the first time Court's manhandled me in a semi-sexual way—we both laugh it off, but I know it's about asserting his dominance.

I glance over at Sophia's house. I wish she was home. She's probably the one person who would understand how I feel right now. But it's just the 700 series in her driveway again. I wonder if he's there finishing the closets? I have no idea how all the contractors are managing to work on her house without work trucks full of supplies and equipment. Maybe they come and go when I'm not watching and offload the materials into her garage.

I let out a sigh and put on my sunglasses as I speed down the road. I've got to get my head in the game. I can't think about Sophia right now, or worry about what's happening at her house.

There should only be one worry on my mind. Reclaiming the undivided attention of my husband, who's decided he's jealous of my current domestication. He's done this before—shortly after the twins were born. He wanted so badly for me to be that same hyper-attentive-to-his-needs woman I was when we met, instead of the enamored-and-obsessed-with-Ruby-and-Rowen mom I'd become that it nearly broke us.

But I learned then, the solution... A visit to my hairstylist for fresh highlights and a blowout, followed by a trip to the lingerie department and the jeweler. There's nothing Court can resist less than me straddling him with gorgeous hair, satin-clad breasts, and dripping in diamonds—all at his expense. I don't often use his Amex Black, but when I do, I go hard.

It doesn't just turn him on.

If I'm being honest, spending his money turns me on too.

"Another glass of Dom Pérignon?" the salon concierge asks.

"No, thank you, I have other errands to run." I smile. My stylist is nearly done anyway. Plus, I've already texted my friend Sinclair that I'll be there in thirty minutes. He's a personal shopper extraordinaire and he's waiting with a delicious array of super sexy pieces for me to choose from. He'll wait all day if he has to, but I feel guilty. It always takes longer to do my hair than I expect. Matching my natural blonde highlights takes precision and detail.

On my way to meet Sinclair, I call the school.

"Hello, this is Mrs. McMillian. I was wondering if Ruby and Rowen could stay for the extended program today..." I pause, ready and armed with an excuse. I never, and I mean never, ask for them to stay late. I bite my lip, waiting for the administration to question my motives.

"Yes of course, late pickup is six p.m., Mrs. McMillian," the woman on the other end of the line says.

"Thank you," I reply. Well, that was easier than I expected. I let my body relax into the leather seat as I drive. I reach the Saks VIP entrance a few minutes later and whip my car into the valet spot in front.

"Mrs. McMillian," the young man says and nods his head when I toss him my keys.

I don't respond. I just march my yoga-pant-wearing self through the big glass doors, immediately greeted by Sinclair. He's wearing a slim-cut navy suit with a salmon-colored pocket square, thick-rimmed glasses, and is holding his trusty iPad. His assistant, Jamie, takes my bag and hands me an espresso. I follow them down the hall into one of the private VIP rooms lined with mirrors, black velvet curtains, and a tufted gray settee in the center.

"Hannah, it's been far too long," Sinclair says. We kiss on the cheeks, side to side, then he looks me up and down and says, "I know you said lingerie, but I've prepared an assortment of treasures. A full lineup of day and evening wear. I can only imagine what you have is..." He pauses and puts a finger up to his mouth as if he's thinking of a way to say it to me gently.

"You don't have to remind me, I'm at least one season—" I stop when I see his eyebrow raise. "Fine, two seasons out of fashion. What? I'm busy with the kids. I know you see me online. The trad wife thing is mostly lululemon and beige."

He doesn't say anything.

But I catch him giving Jamie a side glance.

"Ugh, don't be so fucking judgy, Sinclair."

"Me? Judgy?"

Jamie hides a snicker.

I'm not exactly sure what Sinclair considers me these days—a friend or a client—but I go with, "Friends don't judge friends for having fashion lulls."

"Friends?" he questions me.

"What would you rather I call you?"

He smirks, then waves his hand at Jamie to shoo him out of the room. As soon as we are alone, he wraps me up in a hug.

"Of course we are still friends, you big bitch." He releases me from his arms and clasps my shoulders. "You gotta go and get all internet famous on me and start ordering that trendy boring yoga shit for home delivery. I was starting to get a complex." He frowns. "God, you're too thin. The camera must really add ten pounds. I'm ordering food. The usual?"

I laugh and nod. Food sounds amazing. "I'm sorry. I keep meaning to come by and see you or invite you out to lunch. Time just gets away from me. Seriously though, why didn't anyone tell me having twins was so much work? I barely have a moment to myself these days," I complain.

"Yeah, well, at least your hair is fabulous," he says, examining my locks. Then he spins me around, giving me a full once-over. "I definitely picked the wrong size for you."

"I'm not that thin, relax."

"You are." He turns me again and grabs the fabric on my leggings under my butt and pulls. "This shouldn't be loose." Then he taps on his iPad. "I'm having Jamie bring in new athletic wear. And if these are loose, you probably need all new undergarments. You know what, just get naked—I'll have Danielle come in and do a full measurement."

"Is that really necessary?"

"DANIELLE!" Sinclair screams as he's exiting the room. "Hannah, honey, just let me do my job, okay? You might be an online diva, but I'm a personal-shopping diva."

So for the next three hours, I let Sinclair and his team measure me, fit me, dress me, and feed me. It reminds me of the first time I was here, seven years ago. I'd met Sinclair at a nightclub—and he told me I should come see him if I ever needed something posh to wear. I had no idea what that meant. But with a wad of cash I'd been saving from tips at the bar, I made an appointment that changed my life. He upped my clothing game and gave me the confidence I needed to land myself a man like Court.

Sinclair's taste has always been impeccable. By the time we are done, I've got a complete new wardrobe. Right down to my bras and underwear. He's even sending Jamie over to my house tomorrow to deliver everything and help me clear out all my old clothes. What a relief, because I really don't want to do that job all alone.

Now, if Court would let me hire a housekeeper, that's something she could do. Or if Sophia were around, I'm sure she'd get immense pleasure from organizing my new clothes—and underwear.

"Wait, so you're telling me, while you were sick, this Sophia woman organized your husband's clothes?" Sinclair gasps. I might have spent the last few hours spilling the tea about Sophia and her interesting style of friendship. "Girl, you have to bring her in. I love a devious, rich woman with no boundaries."

I roll my eyes. "I didn't say she was devious."

"Let's see, she took over your house when you were sick, trolled all your favorite places, tried to end naptime for your babies. If that's not devious, I don't know what is."

I laugh. I guess he's right. And I guess I told him a lot... I didn't realize I'd been going on and on about all the Sophia drama. Sinclair is just so easy to talk to.

"Sure, I'll bring her by when she gets back from Europe. I'm not really sure what kind of mood she'll be in. This whole will-they-won't-they divorce thing with Blake has got her in a frenzy," I explain.

"I work on commission, honey—a wealthy woman going through a divorce, she's my kind of client. And don't forget I've seen it all. When I'm done with her, she'll be ready for a new man in no time."

A smile spreads over my face.

Sinclair is right. Maybe all Sophia needs is a new look—to build up her confidence so she is empowered enough to really end things with Blake for good. Why didn't I think of it sooner? Maybe that's part of all the changes at her house. Not so much an "eff you" to Blake. But a way to redesign her home toward her personal tastes. I know she told me he monitors their bank account, but she seems too smart to me not to have her own secret bank account, like me.

I look at my phone. Shit. I have to go pick up the kids.

Sinclair gives me a final hug and I thank him for the wonderful afternoon, which is reflected in the very large tip I give him, on top of his commission. It was exactly what the doctor ordered to get me out of the funk I was in this morning after Court's behavior. So armed with a few of the new lingerie items for tonight, and arrangements for Jamie to deliver everything else tomorrow, I head out of the store on a high.

ELEVEN

Court is singing in the shower. I can't remember the last time the sex was so good that he was still singing the next morning. I solely focused on him—every move, every sound, all designed to give him the most pleasure possible—to feed his ego and remind him why he married me in the first place. After being a bachelor for so many years, he didn't have to marry me. Even after I found out I was pregnant, he could have just as easily provided financial support and nothing more. But he wanted to be a father, and a husband, and to be with me—which is what I thought about last night while I catered to his every fantasy and kink.

He chose me.

He could have had any woman, or stayed single.

But he wants me, and our life together, forever...

"I really wish I didn't have to go to Brazil today," he says. He's rubbing down his body with a towel.

I'm wrapped in my bathrobe, sitting on the bathroom counter, clutching my cup of coffee and watching him. My hair still looks fabulous, and I can see him eyeing my toned bare leg—which I have pulled up and out of the robe. I don't want him to go either, but I know that him leaving with last night still on his mind means he'll be eager to finish his work quickly and come home soon. Plus, it gives me and Jamie the entire day to tear my closet apart and install my new wardrobe.

I set my coffee down.

Climb off the counter and undo my robe, letting it fall to the floor. I know Court isn't going to want to have sex again, since he just showered, but I want the image of my naked body to be the anchor to his ship while he's away. I saunter to the shower, turn it on, and hit the steam feature. As I'm pulling my hair up to keep it dry, I feel Court's body behind me.

"I should get ready," he says, then he presses himself against me. He's hard. I'm rather surprised but not going to let on. If he wants to follow me into the shower, by all means, I'll let him.

So much for keeping my hair dry.

He pulls it down as soon as we are in the water.

Between the steam, the hot water, and his aggressive desire—I am gasping for air. I'm trying not to panic, but something about this feels like what I imagine drowning to be like, not knowing which way is up. But thankfully, almost as soon as we've started, I feel his body convulsing inside me, and he's done.

He grins.

"Okay, now I'll get ready. You take your time—sorry about your hair," he says and ruffles my wet mop, like I'm a puppy.

I just smile and nod until he gets out and grabs a fresh towel to dry off for a second time. Instead of singing, he's whistling what sounds like a sea shanty.

With him out of view, I slump down on the built-in tiled bench that I use when I shave my legs. I push my hair and the water out of my face, still gasping for breath. It takes me a few minutes to calm down, but my knees are shaky when I finally stand to wash my body. This wasn't how I wanted to start my day. I mean—I'm *happy* that Court is happy. Really, I am. I repeat the mantra over and over while I get ready. *I am happy*. Again, I chant it while I fix the kids breakfast, until I hear my husband yelling.

"Okay, family, I'm off to Rio de Janeiro," Court calls from the foyer. Odd. Normally he just pops in to let me know he's leaving, without any big gestures. But today seems to be a day of firsts.

"I'll miss you," I say to him as I approach. He's busy handing off his bags to the driver by the front door and I'm not sure if he heard me. But then he turns and looks at me, a sheepish grin on his face.

"That thing, in the shower, let's repeat that as soon as I get home," he whispers in my ear as he hugs me.

"Daddy!" Rowen and Ruby shout in unison as they come running.

Court bends down to give Rowen a handshake and Ruby a kiss on the tip of her nose. "Now, Rowen, you're the man of the house when I'm away. Take care of Mommy and Ruby."

Rowen nods but inches closer to my leg.

"I'll take care of Mommy too, with the sunscreen," Ruby adds.

Court stands up and laughs.

"Well, nothing is more important than proper sun protection," he says, still chuckling.

He leans in for one more kiss and says, "You've trained them well. I'll call you tonight from the hotel."

Then Court finally leaves us, his perfect adoring family—waving him farewell. As if this wasn't the tenth trip in so many months. As if he was some sort of hero sailing off to the wild blue yonder to conquer the great unknown.

"Well, kiddos, how about we—" I turn, but Ruby and Rowen are already gone. They seemed so needy not that long ago, but now they seem practically grown. Each slinking off to play on their own, or maybe they slunk together, I'm not entirely sure. I just know they've left the foyer for their own adventures.

Which means I have some time to myself.

I could run through my to-do list.

Or text Sophia.

I'm still waiting for all the juicy details about her exploits galli-vanting around Europe on the hunt for missing art. I know she probably signed twelve iron-clad NDAs, but still, you'd think she'd give me something. Out of habit, I take a peek out the windows to check her driveway. It's all clear, for now.

It's nine, so I have about an hour to kill before Jamie arrives. I decide to work on replies on my social page while I wait for my new wardrobe, even though I'm itching to go upstairs and start pulling all my old clothes out of the closet and heaping them in piles for the donation bin. But part of being authentic is engaging with my fans, not to mention it's great for my algorithm, which is constantly at risk if I don't babysit it.

Armed with my phone and laptop, I curl up on the sofa, turn on a Hallmark romance, and dive into the comment section. It's been fun talking about my epic baking fails. So many women have similar stories, sharing posts with their own goofy nailed-it moments. Those are the people I enjoy engaging with. Then there are the trolls. I never respond to negative comments. That was something I learned in marketing school. How to mitigate social media backlash.

Unfortunately today the trolls seem to be out in full force.

There's a slew of comments on my last few posts saying I look sickly.

I roll my eyes and move on to the fans who actually seem to care. Before I hit reply, I always click on the person to see if there are any red flags in their bios. It takes time and effort to do it my way, but I'd rather be safe than sorry. There are too many ways an influencer can find themselves in hot water.

After an hour, I've responded to fifteen fans with meaningful replies to my last few posts. I reach for my coffee cup on the side table but lean too far and my laptop slides from my lap.

"NO!" I scream. With lightning-fast reflexes, I use my left hand and grab it, pushing a slew of buttons in the process. Thankfully it doesn't hit the floor.

"Mommy, are you okay?" Rowen shouts from the top of the stairs.

"Thanks, RoRo. I'm fine. I just dropped something." I shout back. Aw, what a sweet boy—he wanted to check on his mommy.

Speaking of my sweet boy, when I look at my computer screen, I realize in my near-laptop-shattering moment, my social page has scrolled back four years to when the twins were born. I'm staring at a beautiful picture of baby Rowen, his tiny little newborn hand clasped around Court's finger. That's as much of Court as I can show on my page, his hands. Oh, melt my heart, it's so freaking cute.

Feeling nostalgic, I click on the comment section. A lot of congrats, how can baby hands be so small, and quotes about fathers and sons. I'm about to back out of the old photo and log off to get ready for Jamie, who should be here any second, when I spot a familiar profile picture and username near the very end of the comment thread. I squint and rub my eyes. The date is from three years ago.

"Well, that can't be." I click on it.

Sure enough—it's Sophia.

The comment is generic. A single word:

Cute.

But she acted like she didn't have any idea who I was when she moved in. She'd never heard of my online trad wife influencer status and was so surprised when I told her about it.

The hair on the back of my neck stands up. Why would she lie to me?

I put my computer down and stand up. My skin feels tight and itchy and my hands are trembling. I head to the kitchen for a glass of water. Standing at the sink, I look out the window at Sophia's house. I gulp down the cool water, then hold the glass to my forehead.

"Stop spinning," I say to myself. I'm sure there is a perfectly good explanation for her commenting on one of my pictures years ago. My content probably just showed up randomly in her feed... Someone she follows must follow me too. The more I think about it, the more I calm down. It's not like I remember every random picture I comment on—let alone one from three years ago. I laugh. Why did I let my imagination run away from me?

Ding-dong.

"Jamie!" I exclaim. I set my cup down and head for the door.

Little feet come pounding down the stairs.

"Is Sophia here?" Ruby screams.

"Maybe Daddy's back!" Rowen yells.

"It's just my friend Jamie. He's here with Mommy's new clothes. We are gonna be organizing my closet today."

The twins both moan and groan, then turn around and run back to their room and slam the door. I really need to break them of this new habit before Court gets home. He'll go bananas if he comes back from a long trip to a couple of door-slamming four-year-olds.

I expect to see Jamie with an armful of garment bags when I swing open the front door—but it's Sinclair, holding a tray with three cups of coffee. He's got his big black shades on and he's wearing Bermuda shorts and a pink polo shirt.

Jamie comes strolling up behind him, with bags filled with clothes slung over each shoulder. "Thanks for the help, babe," he grumbles.

"I have the coffee." Sinclair scoffs. "Hannah, be a dear, and take these."

"Sinclair. I didn't expect to see you. And wait, 'babe'? Are you two an item?" I reach out and take the coffees from Sinclair and lead the way into my house. They follow, oohing and aahing with one another over the art and decor.

"Oh, we've been an item for years," Sinclair finally says after he takes off his sunglasses and puts his stuff down on the kitchen island. "Jamie's my rock."

Jamie blushes.

I put my hand on his arm. "I'm so happy for you guys, that's amazing. I had no idea."

"We keep it private. Because of work."

"Well, you had me fooled. I would never have guessed and I spent all day with you yesterday."

"We've had years of practice," Sinclair says. He pulls the coffees from the tray and hands me one. I'm not sure if I can handle any more caffeine, but I take it anyway. As if he knew, the label says *chai tea*. I take a sip and think about Sinclair and Jamie having to hide their relationship. It makes me a little sad for them—no one should have to hide the person they love, for work, or any other reason. But I guess it's no different than Court not wanting to be on my social page. For privacy.

"Enough about us—show me this house. I want the full tour while Jamie brings in everything." Sinclair doesn't wait for me but heads for the living room, lobbing questions at me about the architecture, designer, and other decor choices.

"Jamie, why don't you join the tour? I'll help you bring in everything when we are done," I suggest.

"Thanks, that sounds great." He smiles. As we walk into the living room to catch up with Sinclair, Jamie leans closer and says softly, "And now that you know Sinclair and I are together, I promise—next time you come in, you'll notice. The signs are subtle, but they are there."

Aw, that makes me happy, thinking that the next time I go in for clothes, I'll know their little secret. Not that I'll need more clothes again anytime soon. Considering I just purchased an entire new wardrobe.

If anything, I'll be shopping for Ruby and Rowen. Those two have grown so fast, they both need a new wardrobe. Actually—

"Sinclair, do you style children?" I ask when I come up beside him. He's staring at the painting over the mantel.

"Not unusually, but for your little influencers, it would be an honor." He smiles. "Have Jamie set up measurements with Danielle, then I'll need a week to prepare before we do a fitting. And, sweets?"

"Yes?"

"One child at a time."

I laugh. "Deal."

After showing off the house, I help Sinclair and Jamie bring in all the new clothes. Then I make Jamie play photographer, hoping to catch some nice candids while Sinclair and I empty all the drawers, take everything off hangers. Then we get down to the business of unpacking and reorganizing the new items. I feel fresher, lighter, and more in style than I have in a very long time. Maybe Court was right, I needed a little refresh.

While we work, Sinclair, that sneaky man, asks more questions about Sophia and keeps going over to the window to look out at her house.

He's such a snoop.

And I'm getting a kick out of it. Court tends to be so formal, same with Sophia—which I attribute to her not being American. Being with Jamie and Sinclair is more like what it was like hanging out with Cassie back in college—I can relax.

"Okay, you wanna hear something strange?" I take an item from one of the many garment bags, a pale blue sundress, and hang it in the closet.

"Always!" Jamie and Sinclair shout at the same time. So I tell them about the "Cute" comment on Rowen's baby picture. I know it's silly, and it means nothing because I've already debunked it, but I still want their hot take.

"Hannah, Hannah, Hannah." Sinclair shakes his head as he says my name. "Girl, how do you not know if you and Sophia have mutuals? That should have been the first thing you did when you met her and invited her into your world. A basic internet search. And what about comments on other pictures? Did you go through the rest of them?"

"No, I uh, well... It just happened this morning—right before you got here." I wasn't expecting Sinclair to respond this way. I thought he'd tell me I was being paranoid and we could laugh it off together. My cheeks feel warm; I'm sure I'm blushing.

"Oh, stop filling her picture-perfect head up with nonsense," Jamie says. "Hannah, you're fine. I'm sure it's just a random coincidence." He puts his hand on my shoulder for comfort.

Sinclair chuckles, very slow and deliberate. "Oh, Jamie, you sweet, innocent, forgetful man. Did you forget what I told you about my stalker of '08?"

Jamie knits his brows. Then he bends over and picks up another garment bag and sets it on my bed. There's silence for a half a second too long and when I open my mouth to say something, Jamie blurts out, "Maybe Sinclair is right, go get your laptop. We'll finish the rest of this while you search."

"Down the rabbit hole you must go," Sinclair says, like he's a spiritual guide and he's helping me reach enlightenment.

I roll my eyes.

But who am I to argue with two stylish men organizing my closet?

"Fine, but I bet I won't find anything else."

Except... *I do*.

For the next hour, while Jamie and Sinclair argue over the best way to organize my clothes—by style, season or color—I sit on my bed with my laptop in front of me. I discover six old posts of the twins with single-word comments from Sophia.

Adorable.

Precious.

Lovely.

Each comment blends in with the thousands of others from fans. Nothing that would have triggered me to even give it a second look at the time they were posted. I don't tell Sinclair and Jamie what I've uncovered—not because I care about losing a superficial bet, but because I'm shaking. If I open my mouth to say something, my voice will crack.

I click on Sophia's profile. I need this to make sense.

We have three mutuals, which as far as I can tell are bots and shouldn't affect the algorithm, causing my posts to show up on her page. It's the first time I've paid any real attention to her page. You'd think as an influencer, I'd spend hours and hours online—which maybe I do, but it's only to curate my own materials. Not to deep dive on anyone else's page. After a quick scroll, I've learned three things about Sophia.

First, she doesn't post very often. Second, when she does, it's almost exclusively pictures of her standing alone in front of some piece of art or a nature scene. And third, her last post was the week before she moved in next door and she's not in the picture—it's a large Chinese statue carved in stone. The way the sunlight streams from behind, there's a shadow outline of Sophia with a man standing next to her. They are holding hands. That must be Blake...

"Find anything juicy?" Sinclair pops his head out of the closet and asks.

"Umm... I'm not sure." I bite my tongue. "Unless—is it strange that Sophia is an art dealer and doesn't have a very active social page?"

"YES!" they yell from my closet.

"Does she have a website?" Jamie asks.

"I don't know. I'll search..." But before I can open Google, I hear little giggles in the hallway. The twins have been so good today, playing on their own.

"Hey, babies, you wanna come in and see what Mr. Sinclair and Mr. Jamie have done to Mommy's closet?" I ask.

"No, we wanna go outside." Rowen jumps into the doorframe. He's wearing his swim trunks and swim shirt and a superhero cape. Then Ruby comes racing in, wearing a tutu and tiara over her own swimsuit.

"Fighting crime and performing ballet at the beach?" I ask.

They both start laughing and zooming around the piles of my old clothes on the floor.

Sinclair and Jamie see the kids and say, "Aww," at the same time. Ruby and Rowen squeal with delight and race out of the room, charging down the stairs like a herd of wild animals.

I close my laptop. "You guys wouldn't want to call it a day and go have a glass of wine in the backyard while those two run off their energy before naptime, would you?"

"I thought you'd never ask." Sinclair beelines for the door and heads down the stairs nearly as fast as the twins.

TWELVE

"Bye. Thanks again for everything." I wave goodbye to Sinclair and Jamie. After a bottle of wine in the backyard, kid-friendly snacks, and watching the twins run themselves ragged, my personal shopper and his assistant-boyfriend are finally leaving. I suggested they stay for dinner, but they'd already promised some friends they'd meet them at some new bar and grill downtown. However, we vowed to do this again and not wait until I need a new wardrobe again in two years.

The twins are asleep on the couch... I'd prefer naptime be in their beds, but I won't argue: at least I've reclaimed the nap. I'm so excited about it, I'm literally thinking of turning it into its own brand: "Reclaim Naptime." I can already see the cute T-shirts for sale on the e-commerce site I've been designing in my free time.

A yawn escapes my lips. It's been such a busy day—I'm completely exhausted. Probably a good thing Sinclair and Jamie had to leave. Their energy is amazing, even if they've got my head spinning over the Sophia posts. Sinclair made me promise to ask Sophia why she lied. But he doesn't know her like I do. Hell, he doesn't know her at all. You don't just ask someone like her something like that—she'll have a sophisticated answer why she commented on my pictures years ago. And I'll feel foolish for asking in the first place.

But I can't help this nagging feeling in my gut.

I'm mad at myself for not taking a bigger interest in her online presence before today. But online is just not Sophia's vibe. She doesn't check her phone, she doesn't take a bunch of pictures. I think about all the times we've hung out, and it doesn't fit her personality at all, to be a social media stalker.

Maybe I just need to let all of this go.

Who cares if she commented on pictures of my kids three years ago before I knew her? It doesn't change anything. We are still friends.

I snap a picture of my sleeping babies, deciding to lean into this "Reclaim Naptime" idea, and head upstairs to get my laptop. On the way up the stairs, I look over and see a light on in Sophia's house. The blackout blinds must be open, if I can see a light. Strange. There isn't a car in the driveway. I check my phone—no text or email alerting me of more work in her house today.

> There's a light on in your house. Did you have someone working there today?

No reply.

After grabbing my laptop and heading back downstairs to wake up the twins so they don't sleep the entire evening away, my phone buzzes. Court.

> I want you.

My mind flashes to the shower scene this morning, the urgency with which he wanted me. Even so, I suspect he really meant to text, *I miss you.*

> I miss you too. Are you already done for the day?

> No, heading to a dinner meeting.

I send him a picture of the twins sleeping.

Naptime this late?

Yes, but naptime. I have reclaimed naptime… I'm about to wake them up and order a pizza.

Have a nice night.

I start typing my standard sign off. *I love you more.* To which he will reply with, *Not possible.* That's when I realize he didn't say, *Have a nice night, I love you.* He only said, *Have a nice night.* I wait a few seconds to see if he's going to say it. But he doesn't.

I love you.

Nothing.

He probably arrived at the restaurant. Or his business associates called. Something to distract him from finishing his text. I laugh it off. I don't know what's wrong with me lately. Look at this beautiful life he's given me. The twins, the house, the new wardrobe. Of course he loves me. More than anything in this world.

But something gnaws at me—the sex last night.

All about him.

The sex this morning.

All about him.

Why is he being so needy? But at the same time—emotionally distant?

Buzz. I look at my phone. It's Sophia, replying to my message.

Actually, I'm home.

What?

Surprise! But there's a problem. I came down with severe bronchitis and had to come home early.

Oh no. Did you find the missing art?

It's complicated… I'll tell you about it later.

I can't wait to hear everything. Let me come over and take care of you, it's the least I can do.

No, I don't want you to get sick or give it to the kids or Court.

He's in Brazil for a few days. I'll wear a mask. You took care of me when I was sick. I want to help you.

Hannah, I'll be fine. I've had groceries delivered. I'll just lie low for a few days. Once I get my voice back, we'll hang out. I have so much to tell you.

Promise if you need anything, you'll let me know. I can leave medical supplies, food, dry-cleaning, whatever you need, on your porch.

You're such a good friend.

You too. Get some rest. Message me tomorrow.

I'm so excited Sophia is home. I've missed her, and it's only been two weeks—wait, no, that can't be right. I check my phone. Has it really been four weeks? I think about everything I've done in the last month. Did it actually take me this long to get the kids back on naptime?

"Oh shit!" I exclaim and run out to the living room. Ruby and Rowen are both still sleeping, curled up in their blankies and clutching stuffies. Damn. If I wake them up now, they are gonna be awake until midnight or later. But they haven't eaten dinner, or taken a bath, or brushed their teeth…

I let out a long sigh, then I open my phone, quickly order a pizza and prepare myself for a late night.

"RoRo, time to wake up from your nap," I whisper and gently nudge my little man. He stretches and yawns and sits up. Ruby, on the other hand, makes groaning sounds and rolls away from me.

I turn on the TV for the kids to watch, then head into the

dining room to wait for the pizza to arrive. My laptop is sitting on the table. Might as well get some work done—there's all the pictures and videos from the closet makeover to upload and process. But as soon as I sit down, my eyes catch more lights on next door. Sophia's home.

Why didn't she tell me when she got on the plane?

Or when she landed?

I shake my head. I'm not sure I'll ever understand her.

THIRTEEN

I'm glad Sophia is home and I don't have to keep checking my phone for her text alerts about contractors and deliveries. Or stare out the window nervously every time a random vehicle pulls into her driveway. I started feeling like a nosey neighbor, which is the last thing I want to be. However, I am anxious for her to feel better so I can go next door and see all the changes to her home. I'm especially excited to see the work on her closet. After my big clothing overhaul, I am fully convinced mine needs a complete gut and remodel.

I've only been inside Sophia's house a couple of times. It's just easier to hang out at my house, because of the twins. Her home is *not* four-year-old proof. We figured that out quickly, when Ruby ran smack into a giant vase, knocking it against the wall. The rim shattered. Thank god she wasn't hurt, but I was embarrassed as hell. I used some of my influencer money to cover the cost to replace it, so I didn't have to tell Court. He wouldn't have been pleased to write Sophia a five-thousand-dollar check.

Sophia's voice still hasn't returned, so we've been texting, but not much—sounds like the bronchitis turned into a mild case of pneumonia. I begged her to go to the hospital for an X-ray, but she said her private physician diagnosed her on video chat. I just hope she's going to start feeling better soon, because Ruby and Rowen overheard me telling Court that Sophia was home—and they haven't let me hear the end of it.

"Mommy, when can we see Sophia?" Ruby asks, for the tenth time in the last week.

"Remember, we have to wait until she's feeling better." I slather the sunscreen on Ruby's legs. We are sitting on the beach, getting ready to have a seashell-hunting party.

"I want to see the dinosaurs with Sophia," Rowen says. Then he waves a stick in my face. "Look, it's like a bone. I bet Sophia would like it."

"Yep, I bet she would like it. Why don't you set it over there, and when we walk home, you can run up and leave it on her porch."

"How 'bout shells and other stuff too, Mommy?" Rowen jumps up and down. "Come on, Ruby, let's find presents for Sophia." He grabs Ruby's hand and they sprint toward a chunk of driftwood before I can respond.

After a few hours of treasure hunting, the twins collapse on their beach towels. They've collected more treasures than we can carry... Not to mention Sophia isn't going to want all of this stuff on her porch.

Once I've whittled the haul down to five items max, we trudge across the sandy trail from the beach that leads behind our house. I drop off the beach chairs along the back fence, then I take the kids over to Sophia's house. Much to my surprise, there is a large wrapped present sitting near the front door. I wonder if she's left something for the twins. Maybe a gift from her trip? She didn't tell me she'd brought them anything. Hmmm...

"Is that for us?" Ruby shrieks.

Rowen picks up the box and starts shaking it.

"Put that down," I hiss. "Set your shells over there." I point, then I carefully look for any card or tag to indicate who the gift is for.

I spot a card tied under the big silver bow with a note that reads:

Sophia, my darling, you're more beautiful now than the day we met.

"Oops, uh, nope. This is not for you kids, it's a gift for Sophia from—" I assume it's from Blake. Which makes me want to vomit. But on the off chance it's not, I say, "It's from an admirer."

"What's an admir?" Ruby asks.

I laugh. "Not admir, *admirer*... It means someone that likes her."

Rowen is still poking around the present. "RoRo. Stop that. Now, shoo, run home before I get crabby." I wave my hands at him, like he's a stray chicken on Aunt Tippy's farm. I had plenty of run-ins with those clucky hens. The trick is using both hands in an outward motion.

"Betty!" Ruby shouts when she spots a giant orange-and-black Monarch butterfly. She leaps off the porch to chase it across the yard toward our house. Rowen is hot on her heels, waving his hands like a little maniac.

Ruby screams at him, "Stop scaring Betty!"

But Rowen doesn't care and whoops and hollers even louder.

"Betty the butterfly." I chuckle at the pet name Ruby uses for all butterflies. I meander back to our house and text Sophia. As if she could have missed our delivery—the kids were loud enough to wake the dead.

> Someone left you a present on your porch.

> Tell Ruby and Rowen thank you.

> No, not the twins. I mean, yes, the twins left some seashells and a coconut husk. But there's a real present sitting out there. If you're not feeling well, I can bring it inside for you.

> No, that's okay, I can get it. Thanks.

I really want to know if it's from Blake. Ugh, I hate that I've become so nosey. But it was such a strange way to deliver a gift—it wasn't in a cardboard box or bag or anything. Just a wrapped box with a bow sitting on her porch. So it must have been a local delivery. Shouldn't the driver have rung her doorbell? I guess she could have been asleep or in the shower. Still, if she didn't answer, the driver should have scheduled it for redelivery. What if it's chocolates? Or something else perishable. Sitting outside in this swampy Florida heat, it will be ruined.

Serves Blake right if it is ruined.

He really needs to leave her alone.

And what does he mean by that awful note in the card? She's more beautiful now than the day they met. Has he seen here recently? And in what way? Because I am very sure Sophia has always been beautiful on the outside. If he's referring to her inside beauty, well, then he's just trying to manipulate her—he's got to know their divorce is imminent. That's when a lightbulb goes off in my head. I text Sophia to confirm my suspicion.

> Was Blake in Europe with you?

Um. Will you be mad at me if I say yes?

> It's your life.

If it makes you feel any better, I got sick right after he arrived, so we didn't spend much time together.

Yes, it does make me feel better. I smirk. Even her body rejects him. But I'm not going to say that to her.

> Well, I wish you'd get better soon. I really want to introduce you to my friend and personal shopper, Sinclair. He has impeccable taste.

I'm looking forward to it.

Speaking of Sinclair, I should see what he and Jamie are up to tonight. We promised to get together again soon, for drinks or dinner or something. I could sure use a few hours away from the house. And since Court got home a couple days ago, there's no reason I can't go out with some friends. It really is his turn to watch the kids. It's only fair.

After getting the twins cleaned up from the beach and settled in their room with popcorn and an episode of *Bluey*, I head to Court's office. I'd better ask him if he minds watching the kids before I call Sinclair and get anyone's hopes up. Specifically mine.

"Hey, babe, how's work going?" I walk up behind him and rub his shoulders. He's hunched over a stack of spreadsheets. He's wearing his glasses—so I know he's hyper-focused on whatever numbers he's reviewing.

"You have fun at the beach?" he asks, circling something, then takes his glasses off and sets them on his desk. He leans back in his chair, giving enough room for me to sit on his lap. I haven't done this in a while, but it used to be his favorite.

"We had a great time—maybe tomorrow you can come hunting with us. You know this is the best time of year for shells."

"Hmmm, maybe." He leans toward me for a kiss. "You smell like coconuts."

A laugh escapes my lips.

"What's so funny?" he asks.

"Oh, your son left a coconut husk on Sophia's porch after our beach trip. He can be such a handful."

Court laughs. "Have I told you what a great job you're doing lately?"

"What do you mean?"

"As a mom, a wife, all of it. We'd all be lost without you, Hannah." He kisses me again. I melt into his arms. That's about the nicest thing he's said to me in a long time.

"Soooo..." I draw out the sound. "Would you still be lost, if it was just one evening? For a few hours?"

The corners of his mouth curl and he raises an eyebrow. "Girls' night? I thought you said Sophia was still sick."

"She is. I was thinking more along the lines of Sinclair and Jamie. They really wanted to hang out again," I explain.

"So, girls' night." He chuckles.

I play-slap at him. "Oh, stop it. Gay doesn't mean girl... So is that a yes, you'll watch the kids tonight?"

"I've been meaning to watch *Moana*," he teases.

"Thanks, babe." I give him a hug and a big kiss before leaping off his lap. Now I just have to pray Sinclair and Jamie are free.

"Oh, and, Hannah—"

I turn around and look at him. He has a big grin across his face. He's about to say something he thinks is clever...

"Just promise to wash off the body glitter when you come home." He throws his head back and laughs.

I roll my eyes.

FOURTEEN

SOPHIA

My fingers pinch the bridge of my nose, then slide down as I look right, then left, in the mirror. It's definitely thinner, more refined. The bruises around my eyes are almost gone. And with a little makeup, they'll disappear entirely. I touch my cheeks—they're higher, but it's subtle. My lips, on the other hand. Waaaay too Kylie Jenner. At least lip filler isn't permanent.

I really hated lying to Hannah about the trip to Europe. But I knew she'd get mad and try to talk me out of it if I told her the truth. And the truth is, I needed a change.

I did play out the scenario in my head first. Telling Hannah that I was going under the knife and I'd be home recovering for six weeks. But all I could hear was her trying to talk me out of it. *Sophia, you're perfect just like you are. You don't need plastic surgery.*

But there's no way she, of all people, can understand how I feel. She has this amazing life, with Court and the twins, and I'm jealous. So jealous I almost couldn't see straight after spending two weeks helping out while she was sick. Playing with Ruby and Rowen, cooking, organizing, having a glass of wine with Court in the evenings—it all just reminded me of what I don't have.

"By choice," I tell myself, "You don't have that kind of life for a reason."

But still, it was eating at me while I was at Hannah's house. That's when I thought if I could look a little more like her, *be* a little more like her, it might fill the pain and ache and longing in my chest. If I could just figure out how she does it all—being the perfect wife, mother, and online celebrity—then I might win Blake back.

So far, the plastic surgery hasn't helped.

The pain has been excruciating, and if I'm being completely honest, I miss my old look. But there's no magic pill to reverse a nose job. What I've done to my face is forever. I suppose being cooped up in my house for the last six weeks hasn't been great for my mental health either. I've had way too much time alone to think. At least my doctor has come by to check on me multiple times. For what I paid him, he should have moved in. I also called in a hair stylist, manicurist, and yoga teacher to help pass the time.

"Hannah's going to freak out when she sees you," I say to my reflection after I finish putting on my makeup. I pick up the curling iron and fix my new hair just like the stylist showed me. Is this what it feels like when Hannah styles her long hair every day?

"Ouch!" I burn the tip of my finger, too busy thinking about Hannah. I slam the hot iron down on my bathroom counter and run my hand under cold water.

I'm always thinking about Hannah. What would she do? What would she say? She's consuming me, and I'm disgusted with myself. I deserve this blistered skin. I never should have gotten so involved in Hannah's life when I moved here. I should have been focused on my situation with Blake... But even if I take Hannah up on her offer to pay for a divorce attorney and an apartment so I can start a new life, I know I'll still be trapped. Blake will never let me go, he's said so on more than one occasion.

So for now, it looks like I'm stuck with Blake.

Just like I'm stuck with this new face.

I take a quick selfie and compare it to Hannah's profile picture. We could easily pass for sisters. Which is a little satisfying, since my own sister and I never looked this similar. But it also makes me feel overwhelmed. Why did I think having surgery to look like her was going to fix anything in my life? God, this is all such a mess. I need to get out of here, have a drink, meet some new people. Stop obsessing over Hannah and Blake and my fucking face.

And then, because I can't help myself, I text the selfie to Blake, just to see what he'll say. I told him I was having surgery, but he hasn't seen a picture of me all done up yet.

Wow, you look… stunning.

Thanks. I'm thinking of going out tonight.

I brace myself for an argument. Ever since I arrived in Florida, Blake has been paranoid and jealous. He wants me to check in with him constantly and tell him if I'm going out to do anything around town. It was different when I was in Beijing… He hardly cared. Which is why all of this is so fucked-up. If he wants me so badly, then he just needs to be with me.

Sounds fun.

You aren't mad?

Don't be an idiot. Go out, make some friends, have fun.

His WhatsApp status changes to *Do Not Disturb* and I know our conversation is over.

"'Don't be an idiot, Sophia,'" I mimic his voice. "Piss off, you arrogant prick." I throw my phone on the bed before slipping into a new dress. It's not really my style, but it goes nicely with the new color of my hair. Maybe tonight I'll discover if blondes really do have more fun. Maybe I'll even meet a man, bring him back here, and fuck him in Blake's bed.

I wish I could FaceTime Hannah and ask for her advice.
But I'm scared.
She's going to know I lied when she sees me.
God, I ruin everything.

FIFTEEN
HANNAH

Three hours, two outfit changes, and one twin-sized "why is Mommy leaving" meltdown later, my driver finally drops me off in front of a bar. Sinclair gave me an address on the far side of town, close to where I used to bartend at night for extra cash when I moved to Florida after college. Being back in this area stirs up all kinds of memories and emotions for me.

But this is where I met Court. The best day of my life, besides the day the twins were born. Looking around, a lot has changed. There are several new restaurants and bars, a new hotel is going up behind the strip, and there are more people than I ever remember seeing here on a Saturday night. According to Sinclair, this is the new hot spot in town. I would've been happy going somewhere quieter and closer to home, but I kind of invited myself, so who am I to argue about location.

I'm just excited to be out for some adult company.

"Sorry for making you wait, took me longer than I thought to get the kids and Court set up for an evening without Mommy." I try not to sound too exasperated when I find Sinclair and Jamie in the bar.

"Of course it did," Sinclair says. "I can't get over your billionaire husband denying you a nanny and housekeeper. What a—"

He pauses when Jamie elbows him. "Never mind that, come on, let's get you a drink."

After a couple of tangy margaritas, a basket of chips, and tons of gossip and laughs, we step outside into the humid evening air. I grin at the vibrant scene in front of us. The street is packed with people arriving to go bar hopping. Fairy lights shimmer along the length of the avenue, and music pours out of a new night club. I pull out my phone to call my driver, but then I have a wild idea.

"How about one more drink and a little dancing before I go home?" I expect them to say no. Sinclair said they have a busy day tomorrow at work. Some oligarch's wife is in town and it sounds like she's extra demanding.

But they don't say no. Instead, Jamie grabs me by the hand and we run down the block toward the music. My hair swings side to side and I laugh as I try to keep up.

Inside the club, I pull Jamie and Sinclair close to me. "Take a group selfie, for my friend Cassie."

"That's your porn star friend, right?" Jamie asks over the music.

I laugh. "She's not a porn star! OnlyFans."

Sinclair rolls his eyes. "Po-tay-to, Po-tah-to."

I want to remind him that what he does—catering to the rich— isn't all that different to what Cassie does. Sinclair uses his personality as much as his impeccable taste in fashion to keep his clients coming back for more. Same with Cassie. She's not just selling her banging hot body, but the witty personality that goes with it.

"Should we take a break?" I ask after we've danced for a while. I'm sweating and the dance floor is really starting to fill up.

"Yes, a break," Jamie says and Sinclair nods.

We weave through the crowd and collapse on the couches at our VIP table. Our server comes to take our drink order—waters and a bottle of champagne, because what the hell. Sinclair laughs at me before he excuses himself to go to the men's room.

"Hannah, I am having such a good time." Jamie smiles, then chugs the entire glass of water as soon as the waitress sets it in front of him.

I sip on the champagne. "Thank you again for letting me go out with you guys tonight. It's been ages since I went anywhere dressed up without the kids."

Jamie leans in, looks side to side, as if what he's about to say is completely taboo. "Is he cheap? Is that it? Doesn't want to fork over the cash for a nanny?"

"If only. Then I could just pay for it with my own money. No, he's paranoid. Scared some crypto hackers will infiltrate us through the hired help."

"Ohhhhh, I get that. Crypto guys. They are all super secretive and usually pretty sketchy." Jamie purses his lips and nods.

Before I can ask Jamie how many crypto guys he knows, Sinclair comes back to the table, but he's not his usual charming-albeit-snarky self. He looks like he's seen a ghost. Uh-oh, maybe all the drinking and dancing didn't agree with his stomach. I get that. Mine is feeling a little queasy—so I switch from the champagne to water.

"You look like you're ready to go. Will you guys wait with me until my driver arrives?" I look at my phone to call, when Sinclair puts his hand on mine. I glance up and he's shaking his head.

"No, it's not that. I mean, yes, we can go if you want. But I just had the weirdest experience," he says.

"Oh my god, were you assaulted in the bathroom?" Jamie freaks out.

"No, nothing like that." Sinclair puffs up his chest a little and shakes himself out. "No, I was coming back from the bathroom when I saw someone..."

"Who? Who did you see? Was it Gaga?" Jamie stands up and peers around frantically.

"No! Not her. Sit down, Jamie." Sinclair grabs Jamie by the pant leg and jerks him back into his seat.

"Then who?" His eyes are still darting around in search of his diva queen.

"I saw Hannah."

I'm confused. "What?"

"I saw you. Well, I thought it was you. From behind, an exact replica. The hair, the body, the green dress." He's insistent.

"Wait, so you saw a woman that looks just like me from behind?" I ask. "Half the town probably looks like me from behind."

"I'm so embarrassed. I walked right up to her and asked, 'Did you send my man for more drinks?' But when she turned around and smiled, I think I scared her. I said, 'Oh, honey, you aren't Hannah, but damn if you don't look like her.' And then—this is the weird part—she went completely white as a ghost and said, 'Hannah?' Like she knew you. Then she bolted for the door!"

The hair on the back of my neck stands up and goose bumps ripple my flesh. I jump off the velvet couch and sprint. I have to see the woman who looks like me and ran away when Sinclair said my name. Maybe there's a chance she's waiting for the valet or a driver to pick her up.

When I get outside, I look right, then left. There! A blonde woman, waiting for her car at the valet. "Excuse me!" I shout in her direction, hoping she'll turn around. But a car pulls up and the valet gets out and hands her the keys. Wait, that car, I recognize it...

It can't be. Can it?

"Sophia?" I call her name. The woman turns around and looks at me before sliding into her car. My heart leaps from my chest into my throat and I gasp.

"Hannah, Jesus Christ, you're fast," Jamie says, out of breath, putting his hand on my shoulder.

"Did you find her?" Sinclair rushes up next to us.

I turn around to look at my friends. I open my mouth to say something, but I can't speak, so I throw my hands up in the air. Then I pace around in a circle.

"Hannah, sweetheart, it's okay—so what? Another blonde in this zip code looks like you. Who cares?"

"That wasn't just another blonde... *I know that woman*." I raise my hand and point at the taillights on her car as she drives away. "That... was Sophia."

SIXTEEN

Day 2: Still no sign of Sophia. No reply to my calls or texts. I thought I saw the curtains peek open, so I went and knocked on her door for twenty minutes. No answer.

Day 5: I was at the Italian market checking out, and the woman behind the counter was confused. She said, "Didn't you just check out?" I ran out of the store and saw Sophia's car driving off.

Day 7: I feel like I'm going crazy... Maybe that wasn't her at the club. Or at the store. Why would Sophia go around town looking like me anyway?

Day 10: I've called her at least 100 times. Why doesn't she answer? This is getting ridiculous. I think I should call the police and file a missing persons report.

Day 12: She must be dead.

It's been almost two weeks and I haven't seen or heard from Sophia, which is really starting to freak me out. I've been keeping notes in the margin of my to-do list notebook. Today's entry was a little dramatic. I'm sure she's not dead, but what the hell is she up to? Why won't she just answer my calls or send me a text or open up the door when I knock? What is she so afraid of?

I check her social page again, to see if she's posted any updates. Nothing.

My phone rings, startling me. I forgot I turned the ringer on. "Finally—I've been trying to get a hold of you for days. Have you even read any of my texts?" I snap at Cassie.

"Sorry, hon—I've been in the zone filming for a few days at this house I rented at Lake Tahoe."

"It's fine." I can taste the bitterness in my words.

"Hannah, that bitch is gone, why do you even care so much?" Cassie asks me. Okay, so she did read all my texts. My shoulders relax.

The kids race past me, like little maniacs.

"Hold on a sec—" I put the phone down. "RUBY, ROWEN, stop all that running around right now. Go sit by the door and wait for me to take you to school!" I shout.

"Yes, Mommy," they say at the same time and walk with their heads hanging in defeat.

"Sorry. And I dunno, Cassie, I'm just freaked out. What if that wasn't her at the club? It really could have just been a random lookalike. I'd been drinking. It might not have been her car. The real Sophia might be hurt or missing."

"Oh please. She's the wife of an international billionaire. If she was dead in that house—there'd have been cops there by now. Men like that don't let go of their possessions easily. He's keeping tabs on her, monitoring her phone, tracking her location, that kind of stuff. I promise you. She's alive."

That's when a lightbulb goes off in my head. Maybe I need to find Blake. I could explain what's going on and ask him if he's talked to Sophia.

Ding-dong.

"Ugh, someone's at the door. I have to go."

"I'm home now. Call me later." Cassie hangs up.

"Can I answer it?" Rowen shouts.

"NO."

I reach the door and find Ruby and Rowen sitting patiently, like I asked, with their little backpacks on, and I feel all kinds of bad for yelling at them.

When I open the door, no one is there. Just a bottle of wine with a bow and a tag on it that reads:

Sorry I've been MIA. Let's catch up soon. xo Sophia.

"Oh, the nerve of that woman." I want to throw the bottle of wine off the porch and let it smash all over the walkway.

"Everything okay out here? A lot of commotion," Court says as he comes strolling down the hallway from his office. I hand the bottle of wine to him. He doesn't know everything that's been going on, specifically Sophia's transformation to look like me—it would just upset him. But he does know Sophia has been avoiding me. That much I've told him.

"See, I told you she was ignoring me."

"I don't know why you've got yourself so worked up over all this." He's turning the bottle over in his hands. "She has impeccable taste in wine. This is a bottle of Château Margaux."

"Ughhhh." I don't have time for this. Court shrugs and whistles a little tune as he takes the bottle to his collection. Sometimes he is so dense. "Kids, let's go. Time for school."

I'm fuming the entire drive to the kids' preschool.

They must know it, because they are whispering to each other. They've always been able to communicate with one another in a way I don't understand. They call it their twin language. Right now, I just call it annoying. But I can't snap at them again—it's not their fault I'm stressing.

I park the car, get them out of their car seats, and hold their hands on the way to the front door. "Sorry I was grouchy this morning," I say when I squat down to give them each a kiss before they run into their classroom.

"It's okay, Mommy," Ruby says and hugs me.

"I love you," Rowen adds and gives me a kiss on the cheek.

"Hannah, your kids are precious," someone behind me says. I stand up and watch the kids rush into the classroom before I turn around. I recognize the woman's voice, but I'm trying to remember her name... Sarah, Stephie, Sadie...

I spin and when I see her, I say, "Sandy. Hey, thanks, yeah, they are pretty cute." I smile. Phew. I'm not great with names. Sandy has a daughter in Ruby and Rowen's class. Shit. What's her daughter's name? Ruby doesn't like her, that's all I can recall. "So is yours." I pretend to peer around like I want to see her child.

"Adrianna's already in the classroom. I was actually hoping to run into you today. I follow you on social media. I'm so impressed with everything you do, like the brands you work with," she says.

"Oh well, thank you," I reply.

"So, I was talking to your neighbor Sophia the other day. Oh my gosh, she's such a sweetheart. Anyway, see, I'm starting a 'Mommy and me' hair and makeup studio. She suggested I invite you and Ruby to join us at the launch party. Maybe if you enjoy it, you could post about it, to boost visibility," Sandy explains.

"Uh-huh." I nod. She said Sophia. She said that she was talking to Sophia the other day. Now—does she actually mean the other day, as in two or three days ago? Or does she mean a few weeks or months ago? I'm trying to smile and feign interest in her crappy idea that she keeps droning on about, all the while I'm screaming on the inside.

When Sandy pauses for breath, I'm finally able to ask, "When did you say you were talking to Sophia?"

She looks a bit surprised that, out of everything she's said, that's the one thing I'm asking about. "Oh, um, Tuesday, I think—we've both been volunteering here a few times a week during art time. They always need extra hands."

Sophia's been volunteering here? So wait, she hasn't been answering my calls, but she's been coming to the twins' school? "Oh, um, I didn't realize she was volunteering." My voice cracks.

"She's been coming for months. I'm surprised she didn't tell you, considering she's your best friend," Sandy says. She looks a little confused.

Quick—I don't want her to think I don't know who's around my kids. And best friends? Hardly. "I meant *still* volunteering."

"Oh right, because of her nose job. Yeah, she took some time off for that, but she's back. She's really embracing the Florida look. I'm loving her blonde hair. She must be using your stylist. It's a perfect match."

Sweat beads at my hairline. I finally have confirmation Sophia has altered her face and hair. So that *was* her at the club. My hands shake.

"I, um, I have to go," I whisper and back up slowly.

"Hannah, are you alright? You don't look well," Sandy says. She reaches an arm out to me, but I turn on my heels and run for the administration office.

"Mrs. McMillian, you can't just walk in—" the secretary scolds me as I barge into the administrator's office.

"What kind of fucking place are you running here?" I shout.

Mrs. Hubbard is holding a phone to her ear. "I'll have to call you back." She places it in the cradle. "Mrs. McMillian, would you like to sit down and explain why you're so upset? Or should I call security?"

I laugh. Did she really just threaten to call security on me? I point my finger at her. "I want to know why you allowed my next-door neighbor to volunteer in Ruby and Rowen's class without asking for my permission."

"I'm not sure what you're talking about." She looks around nervously and starts thumbing through folders on her desk.

"Sophia Carter. My neighbor. She's been volunteering here." I can feel the steam coming out of my ears as I'm losing patience.

"Yes, yes, I understand that. But we all thought that's what you wanted—your husband sent this note." She hands me a piece of paper.

It looks like a glowing endorsement from Court, claiming I

want Sophia to volunteer in Ruby and Rowen's classroom. But why would he write this and not tell me? I look at the date—it's from when I was sick. I stare at the words. It does look like my husband's handwriting and signature, but until I speak with him, I can't be sure. Sophia might have forged this. I'm not willing to put anything past her after today.

"Can I have a copy of this?" I hand the supposed note from my husband back to Mrs. Hubbard.

"Yes, of course, I'm sorry, I, uh..." she stutters.

"Can I just get a copy of that so I can leave?" I feel like I can't breathe.

She makes a copy of the letter and hands it to me. "I should have called you."

I wave her off and leave the office. As I walk down the hall, I realize, it's not just Sophia that's lying to me. It's also my husband, if he truly wrote this. And my children! Why didn't they tell me Sophia's been coming to their school?

Instead of leaving, I make a beeline for their classroom.

"Mrs. McMillian, is everything okay?" Their teacher looks confused when I walk in, interrupting storytime. She gets up and comes to my side.

"No, it's not okay," I hiss. "You should have told me my neighbor Sophia was volunteering in your classroom."

"But I, uh..."

"Ruby, Rowen, grab your backpacks."

They don't argue, but I can tell by the way they are looking at one another and whispering that they think they're in trouble. As soon as we're in the hallway, I growl under my breath, "Why didn't you tell me Sophia was coming to your school?"

"I'm sorry, Mommy, she said it was a secret," Ruby says.

I squat down and look at her, then at Rowen. "You never keep secrets from Mommy. Do you understand me? It's dangerous to keep secrets. Something bad might have happened to you." They start crying and I feel awful, but it's the truth. I have no idea what Sophia's up to. But asking my kids to lie is a huge red flag.

"Shhh... Please don't cry," I beg them. "I didn't mean to scare you." But it's no use. They don't understand. How could they? I'm not even sure what the hell is going on.

My blood is boiling as I'm driving home. It's one thing if Sophia wants to behave strangely with me. I'm an adult. I can handle it. But it's entirely different when she wants to involve my children. Telling them to keep secrets from me? She's got to be out of her fucking mind if she thinks I'm going to let this slide. I'll march next door and throw a brick through her window. I'm done with knocking, texting, calling, DMing... If she wants to play this game, well then, I hope she's ready.

I'll play. And I will win.

She might have grown up in boarding schools—where the over-the-top teen drama sounds more like a best-selling novel than a real childhood. But I grew up in Sioux City, Iowa, living on food stamps and fighting for everything I had. Even after Mom dumped me at Aunt Tippy's farm, I still had to fight and work my ass off to prove I deserved the roof over my head. I had to learn to kill a chicken with my bare hands when I was nine. Shoot a badger through the eye with a rifle at eleven. And jumped in the corral with an angry bull during castration season when I was thirteen. Which means I'm not fucking scared of anything, let alone Sophia. And that's what I'm about to say to her when I smash her face with my fist. *I'm not scared of you.*

But first, I'm going to get to the bottom of this note from my husband. What would possess him to write such a thing and not tell me? Too bad his car is gone when I pull into the garage. As soon as I get the kids in the house and settled down, I text him.

Where are you? There's a problem. You need to come home.

Are you okay?

Did you write this?

I take a picture of the note and send it to him.

No.

Are you sure?

He doesn't respond. I try calling him, but he doesn't answer. He's the one person that might keep me grounded right now, and the fact that he's not responding only fuels my rage even more.

"I have to go next door. Stay here," I tell the twins. They've stopped crying and are engrossed in their show and don't respond. Probably ignoring me too. Just like their father.

Instead of walking down my driveway and over on the sidewalk to Sophia's house, I stomp across our manicured lawn and cut between the bushes. Before I know what I'm doing, I'm banging on Sophia's door.

"SOPHIA!" I scream. "OPEN THIS FUCKING DOOR!"

No answer.

My fists pound on the wood.

Then I turn around and walk around the side of her house and up the backstairs on the deck, so I can see inside the glass windows along the back of the house. I pound my fists on the glass. God, I really wish I had that brick right about now.

"SOPHIA, OPEN UP!"

Nothing.

I have my phone with me—and I want to do something reckless, like livestream me trying to speak with the woman who has altered her appearance to look like me and infiltrated my children's school. Next thing you know, she'll be trying to steal my husband. Arghhh. I'm so fucking pissed right now. But instead of livestreaming, I text her.

Open your fucking door right now and show me your NEW face. Or should I say, MY FACE.

I know you've been at my kids' school.

I'm going to hire an attorney and sue the shit out of you.

WHAT IS YOUR FUCKING PROBLEM???

I'm having a massage. There seems to be some confusion here… give me a chance to explain myself before you keep stressing out. I'll be home in a few hours.

BITE ME

I walk home. I'm physically shaking. Does she really think she can explain this away? My breathing is labored, struggling to leave my lungs, and I think I'm going to be sick. I barely make it to the bathroom before I start throwing up.

"Mommy!" Rowen yells and comes to my aid. He holds my hair back and whimpers. "Are you sick again? Is Sophia going to spend the night in our room like last time?"

In our room… Hot yellow bile rises up and floods my mouth and nose. I heave a few times before I can respond to my son.

"No, baby, Sophia is not coming over here. She asked you and your sister to lie to me. To keep secrets. She's not allowed in our house anymore." I stand up and flush the toilet watching the vomit water swirl down the drain and wonder what the hell went on in my house while I was sick. I glance over at my son, who's gone quiet and still.

His bottom lip quivers.

"Hannah, I got home as fast as I could, what's going on?" Court's voice calls out from the hallway.

"Thank you for holding my hair," I say to Rowen and give him a hug. "Now, go play while I talk to Daddy. Everything's okay, I promise." Then I boop his nose and he perks up and smiles before running out of the bathroom. I use some toilet paper and blow my nose.

Court comes in, looking confused. "What's happening? Are you sick again?"

"Why didn't you pick up your phone?" I throw the wad of toilet paper in the trash and glare at him.

"Hannah, clearly you're upset."

"You think?" I walk past Court and head for the stairs. I just want to go up to my room and clean myself up and try to calm down. But as soon as I'm halfway up the stairs, my head turns automatically to look next door. I fall to my knees and start sobbing.

"Hannah, baby, please..." Court runs up behind me. "You have to talk to me." He rubs my back in a soft circular pattern.

All I can do is cry.

SEVENTEEN

Court hoists my limp body off the stairs and helps me walk to our bedroom. My limbs feel like they weigh a thousand pounds and I collapse in a heap on our bed. I'm still crying—now that I've started, I'm not sure I can stop.

"Hannah, sweetheart, I didn't write that note. Sophia must have done it when you were sick so she could help out at the school. It's not the end of the world." He kicks off his shoes and climbs on the bed next to me, and holds me and strokes my hair. I let myself melt into the warmth of his embrace. But I can't stop shaking.

"Babe, please, what else is going on? Why are you so upset?"

Sniffle.

"Hannah, I'm right here, talk to me."

I really want to tell him, but I'm scared he's going to think I'm crazy. Because it sounds crazy! It's madness to think that Sophia underwent some kind of physical transformation in order to look like me. But I know what I saw that night at the club. And I know what happened at the school today.

But I also know my husband. He's going to ask, *Why would Sophia change her appearance to look like you? What's her end game?* And I'm racking my brain to figure it out. She is avoiding me. But she's still going to see the kids at school. She is trying to look like me. She's befriending moms from the preschool. She's getting the twins to lie for her. And something Rowen said downstairs... About Sophia spending the night with them, like she did when I was sick. Which I was unaware of. I thought she'd been going home every night, not sleeping in the room with my kids.

And that's when it dawns on me. It's the children. That's what Sophia wants—she wants my children.

I sit up and look at my husband.

He props himself up on an elbow, staring deep into my eyes. His hair is freshly cut and his skin looks smooth and soft. I lean over and kiss him. "What I'm about to say is going to sound bizarre."

Then he sits up all the way, takes my hands in his and squeezes. I catch his eyes glancing at his watch. He's probably wondering how long this is going to take, so he can go back to work.

"I think Sophia is trying to steal *your children*." That gets his undivided attention. His jaw twitches and the warmth in his eyes flicks to something more like fear or anger.

"What does that mean?" he asks.

I take a deep breath, and then I tell him what happened at the club two weeks ago, with Sinclair and Jamie and the doppelgänger. Then I tell him about today. Speaking with that mom and her saying Sophia's hair was the perfect match to mine, and what happened in Mrs. Hubbard's office when I confronted her about Sophia volunteering in the twins' classroom. Stress lines form around his eyes as he considers everything I've said.

"Hannah, this is unbelievable." He rubs his palms over his face then pinches the bridge of his nose. "So what you're saying is you think our neighbor had plastic surgery to look like you, so she can eventually steal our children?"

"Yes!" I'm too wound up to sit on the bed anymore. I climb off and start pacing around the room. "What other explanation is there?"

"Well, I can think of a few, but—"

I shoot him a nasty look. "She must have had the plastic surgery done in Europe..." But then I remember all the cars coming and going when she was supposed to be away. "Or maybe she had it here. Maybe she never even left town."

"Hannah..." Court walks over and puts his arm around me. "You've been under too much stress, with your social media work, and the kids. Not to mention I've been out of town a lot the last few months." His voice has softened, like he's talking to a scared cat he's trying to coax out from under a bed.

"Wait, so you just think I'm stressed out? That I'm imagining all of this?" I knew he wouldn't understand.

"Now, don't put words in my mouth. I never said you're imagining it, but you haven't even seen Sophia since she got home from Europe. You're making a lot of assumptions," he defends his position.

"So if you look at her, with your own two eyes, and see that she has my hair and my nose and lips, then will you believe me?" I ask.

"Imitation is the sincerest form of flattery, Hannah. Who cares if Sophia did her hair to look like you, or even if she had a nose job? Has she really done something so terrible to you—"

"She's been going to the twins' school behind our backs. She forged a letter with your signature. She told the kids to keep it a secret from me. Why don't you find that more upsetting?" I throw my hands up in disgust.

"No, you're right. She crossed a line. Sophia had no right to ask our kids to keep her volunteering a secret from us."

"Thank you." Finally he understands. "Now, call your attorney. I want a restraining order against her. And we should start looking at new houses. I don't want to spend one more night living next door to her."

I lean down and pull my suitcase out from under the bed.

"What are you doing?" Court asks.

"Packing, obviously. You can rent us a house somewhere until we can sell this place—"

Court puts his hand up. "Hannah, slow down. We aren't moving."

"Umm... yes we are." I walk to my dresser and scoop up the contents of one of the drawers and dump it in the suitcase.

"I will call my attorney and get him to file a restraining order against her, if that makes you feel better, but we need to sleep on this and decide what's best for our family, and—"

"What's best for our family is us not living next door to a woman who could charm her way into our kids' school and skip town with them."

"Look, I've got to go back to Québec for a week. Why don't you and the kids come with me? Time away might do everyone some good," he suggests. Now, that's the first logical thing he's said. It would be great to get away from here for a week or two. But Québec? Stuck in a hotel with the twins while Court is working? That sounds more like torture than a relaxing time away from home while we figure this out.

That's when a better idea pops into my head.

EIGHTEEN

Court leans down and gives me one more kiss. "I'm going to miss you," he says. He has that satisfied twinkle in his eye, from an evening of amazing sex. I made sure to give it to him good last night, since I knew it would be the last time for a few weeks.

"I'm going to miss you too. But this is for the best," I remind him.

"I know." He nods. "Okay, hands up if you're excited to go live on a real farm," he says to Ruby and Rowen. They raise their hands up in the air and squeal. He uses the opportunity to check their seatbelts one more time. "Be good for Mommy, and helpful around the farm, and use your best manners with Aunt Tippy and Uncle Fran."

"Yes, Daddy!" they shout.

Then Court walks over and says a few things to the flight attendant and pilot of the private charter jet before he gets off and walks across the tarmac toward another private jet. The one that will take him to Québec. Ours is destined for Sioux City, Iowa.

After a quick call to Aunt Tippy last night, to make sure it was okay for me and the kids to spend a few weeks on the farm, I got busy packing everything we'd need for an extended trip. I'm really hoping while we are away, Sophia uses the time to clear out of her place. Court has had his attorney drawing up a strongly worded cease and desist letter, urging her to relocate away from me and the children, or else we will get the authorities involved.

He said doing it this way is better than going straight to the police and filing a restraining order, because that might be seen as an act of aggression and put her on the defensive. She might do something reckless to retaliate. This way, he said, we are giving her the opportunity to leave peacefully with some of her dignity intact.

Not that that bitch deserves any dignity. You don't come into my neighborhood, take advantage of my friendship, and then try to *become* me. And you don't mess with my kids.

Although, I thought about it a lot this morning while I was staring in the mirror doing my makeup. Maybe I am partially to blame for letting it go this far. There were so many red flags. Like when she told me her husband had a second family, and her first response wasn't to divorce him, I should have known she had some screws loose. But what did I do? I invited her to spend a week inside my home.

Then, when I was sick, she felt comfortable and took over my entire house. I had a bad feeling afterwards, but again, I brushed it off and gave her the benefit of the doubt and continued to be her friend.

I shake my head. Well, I won't make that mistake again.

I don't want to keep thinking about Sophia for the next two weeks. I want to think about me and Court and the kids and what our future holds. I'm going to focus on our picture-perfect life.

So for the next three hours, that's what I do. I work on my computer, coming up with some great ideas for posts on the farm and how I can leverage some of my current influencer contracts. I'm deep in thought when I feel the altitude shift. I look out of the window as we approach the ground. The Midwest landscape looks like a patchwork blanket of green and brown squares. Farmland as far as the eye can see. I bet Rowen and Ruby would love this view, but they are both sound asleep.

I was so determined to grow up and prove myself, that I never really appreciated this place when I lived here. But now I can appreciate this view, and having a place to come home to, as sanctuary from... I stop myself from thinking her name.

After landing and loading up the suitcases and twins into a rental car, we get onto the interstate, driving north past the city—which looks like a relic from another time. Old brick buildings, stock yards, and trains. The river runs along the west side of the interstate and memories of going boating in the summer with Matt flit across my mind. I frown—his is another name I am going to try my best not to linger on while I'm here. A few miles past the city, I veer the car onto the exit ramp, taking a long country highway, before turning down the dirt lane toward the farm.

"Are we almost there?" Ruby asks.

"I have to go potty," Rowen says.

I knew I should have forced him to go at the airport. But he was grossed out by the bathroom. I can't really blame him—it was disgusting. "Can you hold it?"

"No. Pleeeeease, Mommy."

I look in the rearview mirror. He's squirming in his car seat. Shit. It's still another fifteen minutes to the farm. Which could be the difference between having a dry or wet four-year-old when we arrive. So I pull over and quickly get him out of the car.

"Okay, RoRo, I want you to pee in the grass right there by that fence."

"Huh?" His little face twists.

"Oh, don't 'huh' me, mister, I've seen you pee in the backyard at home. Just point it and aim at the fence post," I say.

He giggles and runs to the post, pulls his little pants down, and makes a satisfied "Ahhhh" sound when he lets loose. "Make sure no one can see me!" he shouts.

"Yep, all clear, nothing but us and the cows."

"Cows?" His head whips left, then right, and he screams when he sees a big brown Jersey cow meandering toward us at a very slow pace.

"Relax, just finish peeing. The cow can't hurt you. It's on the other side of the fence."

Even so, Rowen's jumpy. He hurries and comes running back to me, crying that he has pee-pee on his hands. But I'm prepared with a wet wipe and get him cleaned up and loaded back into the car.

Rowen tells Ruby all about the cow that wanted to watch him pee. I chuckle. I'm sure it was a pretty bright moment in his young life. Hopefully the twins are about to have a lot of bright moments over the next couple of weeks. I can already see it in my mind—them chasing chickens, collecting eggs, climbing trees, playing with barn cats, wearing rubber boots and stomping in puddles. All the things I used to do when I was a kid.

"Look, there's the farm," I say as I veer the car around the bend. A giant weeping willow tree that Uncle Fran planted marks the edge of the barnyard. The farmhouse is tucked back a ways from the dirt lane, and surrounded by outbuildings. The big red barn has a huge white smiley face painted on one side.

"See that smiley face on the barn?" I ask, pointing.

"I see it!" Ruby screams.

"Happy Barn," Rowen chimes.

"Exactly. Not just Happy Barn, but Happy Farm. That's what Uncle Fran named this place," I explain. Which I'd always thought was some kind of sick joke when I was a kid, because Aunt Tippy never seemed happy, unless I was outside working my tail off.

I'm glad to see the new tractor in the barnyard, the one I sent them as a gift last year, to replace the sixty-year-old one Fran was always fighting with. And the new green roof on the farmhouse really makes the place shine. Another gift. Even if it was tough growing up here, I still appreciate everything they did for me.

I park the car, unbuckle the kids, and they clamber out of their seats, racing toward the barn like wild animals. I put my hand up to shout at them. A variety of parent-sized warnings bubble at my lips, like *be careful, don't get dirty, slow down*. But I see Uncle Fran and a couple of his farmhands exit the barn, so I know the kids will be safe. I stand and watch for a minute just to make sure. Uncle Fran pulls something from behind his back and holds it out for Ruby and Rowen.

"Mommy, it's a kitten!" Ruby shouts, turning to look at me.

I wave. "Have fun." Now that the twins have discovered the barn cats, they'll be entertained for hours. I walk slowly up to the front porch, sucking in the sweet smell of flowers mixed with barnyard, and tug open the old screen door. As I cross the threshold, I'm swept away by a thousand memories of my childhood.

PART TWO

NINETEEN

HANNAH

Seventeen years old

"Matt, shut up, you'll wake up Aunt Tippy," I hiss at my boyfriend as I sneak him into the house. He's drunk as a skunk. What an idiot. I told him to stop drinking hours ago, but does he ever listen to me? Noooooo.

"I love you, Hannah," he slurs.

"I love you too... Now *be quiet*." I guide him to the couch so he can sleep it off. His dad will punch his lights out if he goes home drunk. Aunt Tippy won't be thrilled to see Matt snoring on her couch in the morning, but she won't be mad, and she won't tell his dad. She always says the farm is a safe place for wayward strays.

Like me.

Like half the cats in the barnyard.

Like her two little yappy dogs, George and Ringo.

We were all dumped here over the years—by people who didn't want us anymore.

Aunt Tippy might be cold, but she's protective.

After flopping Matt on the couch, giving him a kiss, and throwing a blanket over him, I creep up the stairs to my bedroom. I step over the boxes. It's been torture trying to decide what to pack for college. I can't believe graduation is only a week away.

Everyone else has all summer to pack.

I pick up the flyer off my desk.

Earn money and credits. Summer work-study program for incoming freshmen.

I'm so glad they chose me for the program. Not only do I get to move into my dorm early, but I get to spend the summer working in student services. By the time school starts, I'm gonna know everything there is to know about the campus and won't have any of those weird first-day jitters. Plus, I'll earn credits so I can graduate sooner.

I take off my clothes, crawl into my bed, and look up at the plastic stars on the ceiling. Someday it won't be plastic stars I'm staring at, it will be real ones, through a huge glass window in the ceiling of the dream house Matt is going to build for us. We have our perfect future planned out. Once I finish college, we're going to buy our own land and do things our way...

As I close my eyes, about to drift off to sleep, my door cracks open.

"I'm home," I whisper. But it's not Aunt Tippy or Uncle Fran in the doorway. Matt comes in, somehow navigating the boxes without crashing into them. He stands at the edge of my bed, strips down to his boxers, and crawls in next to me.

"I know your Aunt Tip will kill me if she catches me in your room. But would you hold me? I'm scared," he says.

"What are you scared of?" I ask, wrapping myself around him. He's warm and muscular and my body tingles.

"I'm gonna lose you. I can feel it."

"Matt, you'll never lose me. I love you." I squeeze him closer to me.

"But you're leaving," he whispers.

"I'll come home all the time on weekends and holidays. You'll hardly notice I'm gone." I stroke his hair and wipe a stray tear from his eye.

He doesn't say anything else, and after a few minutes I can tell he's asleep by his heavy breathing. I know he's gonna miss me, but it will be worth it if I can use what I learn at school to help us build our own empire. I'm so mad at his dad for not letting him go to college with me and for guilting him into staying. It's so unfair. Matt is smart. He deserves to go to college and get a degree in agriculture with me. Times are different now; to be a successful farmer, you have to be educated. His dad knows our plan is to buy the old Thompson place and turn it into an organic farm.

Aunt Tippy said it doesn't matter. She said Matt's dad is possessive and, since his mom died, the only person he has to control is Matt. She said the best thing for me to do is go to college and let Matt figure it out on his own. And if he loves me as much as he says, he'll be here waiting when I get home.

I believe her.

When I wake up the next morning, the bed is cold. Matt's gone, but there's a note on my desk.

Hannah,

I woke up in your arms. Best feeling ever. Someday that will be our everyday.

Gotta go home and help Dad in the field. But I promise I'll be round as soon as I'm finished, so I can spend every last second I can with you dreaming about our future.

I love you always,
Matt

My heart flutters. There's just something about Matt—his

green eyes, the way he smiles, his laugh. I look at all the boxes in my room. Maybe it's stupid for me to go and leave him here, all alone. What if Jaelynn Papish starts dropping by to see him—she's always staring at him in school like some lovesick puppy.

But if I stay here, there's nothing for me to do. If Matt and I are going to have the life of our dreams—with enough money to buy the old Thompson place and start our own organic farm—it starts with me going to college.

TWENTY

Present day

"You just gonna stand in the doorway, letting the flies in, or you gonna come give me a hug?" Aunt Tippy demands.

"Sorry, just thinking about when I was a kid..." My voice trails off.

"What'd I always tell you?" she interrupts.

"Don't look back, keep moving forward," I reply as I walk across the original hardwood floors, stepping over the boards that squeak. Aunt Tippy started saying that to me when I first moved in and I kept bringing up my mom. Probably not the best advice for helping a nine-year-old cope with abandonment issues. But that's Aunt Tippy, ever the pragmatist.

Like, after Matt died, she gave me a week to stay home and cry, and then loaded me up in the farm truck and drove me to college to start my work-study program as scheduled. I hardly remember that summer. I was like a zombie, just going through the motions. At the time I was so angry with Aunt Tippy. I felt like she deserted me in my time of need. It regurgitated a lot of childhood trauma. But looking back on it now, I know she was doing what she thought was best. Trying to keep me moving forward.

"Thanks again for letting me and the kids come spend a few weeks," I say when I give her a hug. She feels the same and my shoulders relax. I always worry that at her age she might be starting to decline. But she looks and feels as sturdy as she ever did.

"You know you're welcome here anytime you want. This will always be your home." Her voice wavers, ever so slightly, and she pulls the dish towel off her shoulder and dabs at her face. "Oh nonsense, what am I crying for?"

"I missed you too."

It takes me about an hour to bring in the suitcases and get our things unpacked and organized in my old room. The walls and furniture are clean and refreshed. There's even matching twin beds for Ruby and Rowen in the bedroom across the hall. Ever since my accounts started generating income, I've been sending Aunt Tippy and Fran money to help with the upkeep on the farm. It was sweet of her to use some to make a room for the kids.

She must have known we'd need a place to land at some point.

"You gonna tell me what has you so spooked?" Tippy says from behind me as I'm bending over to put the suitcases under the bed.

"Jesus! Don't you know you shouldn't sneak up on people like that?" I stand up and push the hair out of my face. "Have you seen the twins yet?"

"Fran's got them out in the chicken coop, collecting eggs."

"I apologize for any broken ones now."

Aunt Tippy waves it off. "Them hens lay more than we can eat. A few broken ain't gonna hurt. Now, you wanna sit on the bed and tell me? Or should we get a glass of iced tea and sit on the patio?"

"Tea on the patio, please." I follow Aunt Tippy down the stairs. She's already got the tea set up. She really is sneaky.

I carry the tray and she holds the back door open. The back patio looks great. The old wicker furniture from my youth has been replaced with a new set made from weatherproof materials.

They're adorned with lovely green tufted cushions and positioned to take in the best view of Aunt Tippy's prized rose garden. The vegetable patch in the distance has been freshly plowed and is ready for planting. It's so perfect, I take a quick picture. We sit, and Aunt Tippy waits patiently for me to tell her why we are here. She isn't a gossip. She'll just want the facts of the matter and then she'll give me her honest opinion.

"It's my new neighbor. She's..." What exactly do I say? Weird? Strange? Obsessed with me?

"You hightailed it here because of a neighbor?" Her brows raise with disbelief and she shakes her head.

"Let me finish before you assume I'm overreacting," I whine.

She purses her lips and sits back, both hands clasped around her glass of tea. "Well?"

"Well, she..." What exactly is it that Sophia's done that has me so upset? I hear Court's voice in my head, making Sophia's actions sound almost trivial. How can I explain everything in a way that Aunt Tippy will understand? "She scared me. I guess that's what it boils down to. She scared me, and I have a family to protect. I'm tired of feeling like I'm always looking over my shoulder in my own home."

Aunt Tippy takes a long sip of her tea.

"You tried talking sense into this woman?"

"Kind of." Which isn't really true. I've sent angry texts. I've left her an insane amount of irate voicemails. I've pounded on her door. Which, as I say it all like that, kind of makes me feel like the one doing the scaring, not the other way around.

"You get the law involved?"

"I'm not sure there's anything they can do."

Before Aunt Tippy can ask any more questions, I hear Ruby.

"Mommy! Eggs!" Ruby screams. She's holding up a little basket and running.

"Be care—" But before I can get it out, she trips and goes careening into the grass. The basket flies out of her hand and eggs crash down onto the ground. As quickly as they splatter, three cats come running to lap up the creamy yellow yolks.

Ruby stands up and starts crying. I want to go to her, to scoop her up, and snuggle her and tell her everything will be okay. But Aunt Tippy grabs my arm and shakes her head. She goes to Ruby in my place. "Now, don't cry, child, them cats need feeding too. You just saved me from having to crack all the eggs."

Ruby isn't sure what to think. She looks at me, then at Aunt Tippy, then at the cats. "Kitties eat eggs?"

"Oh yes. And while you're here, feeding the kitties will be your job. Go on, pick up your basket. I'll show you where to hook it by the front door." Aunt Tippy starts walking. Ruby quickly grabs the basket and follows, all the tears evaporated.

For years, I've thought Aunt Tippy was a cold, unloving woman. But watching her now, I realize, she is showing love in her own way—by teaching Ruby resilience.

A skill she worked hard teaching me growing up.

One that maybe I've taken for granted. I don't need Aunt Tippy's six-shooter to protect me from Sophia. I just need to live my best life and not let her get under my skin. Plus, Court said the attorney's cease and desist letter would be delivered by a process server sometime today. And those guys are relentless.

"Rowen!" I put my hand to my mouth and yell. I spot him standing on the railing of the corral, watching the men and cows. Someone has given him a red handkerchief and he's got it tied around his neck. My little cowboy. Two weeks of this life and he'll be begging me and Court to buy a farm. I wouldn't mind a piece of property with a farmhouse, a place to spend the summers—with fresh air, a swimming hole, a place to relax. Maybe I can convince Court. Somewhere in Montana, maybe?

Just as I'm heading inside to check on Ruby, my phone rings. It's Cassie.

"Bitch, you're never gonna guess what I just did."

"Hmmm... A threesome?"

"Oh please, I was doing those in our dorm room while you slept. No. I just talked to your favorite neighbor, Sophia."

I practically drop my phone. "What?"

"Are you sitting down? I feel like you should sit down for this."

Somehow I stumble to the patio furniture, even though I can't feel my body. I knock over the tea and a glass shatters. My breathing is wild and erratic. But at least now I'm sitting. Or I think I'm sitting. I look around—yes, I'm in a chair.

"Who called who?" I ask. Which is stupid. Why would Cassie call Sophia?

"You know, I almost didn't pick up, but you'd just sent me that text saying you were flying to Iowa with the kids and I thought maybe it was you, from the plane's phone," she explains. "Honestly, at first, I did think it was you! The way she said hello and my name, it was uncanny."

"The nerve." I'm shaking my head.

"But once she started talking, I knew who it was, because of her accent. I kept thinking, how did this bitch get my number? But then I remembered, billionaire wife, she can get anything for a price. Anyway, she said she was calling because you'd had a falling out and she was embarrassed by her behavior and wanted to explain everything—"

"Embarrassed my ass. That woman has no shame."

"Clearly. You should have heard her fake crying. But don't worry, I wasn't buying any of it," Cassie says.

"What did you say?" I'm on pins and needles. My constant *What would Cassie do?* mind-game is happening in real time.

"Well, babes, I figured she must've done something super fucked-up for you to be taking the twins to your Aunt Tippy's house. So I called her a sad, tragic little bitch who needed to get a life."

"You didn't!" I squeal with delight.

"I did. And that shut off her waterworks."

"Did she hang up on you?" Which is what I would do if a stranger yelled at me.

"Nope. She started laughing. She said you were right, I'm feisty, and she could see why we're friends. Then she said she'd subscribed to my OnlyFans and if I ever wanted any tips, she'd be happy to give me a few."

"No. She. Didn't."

"I know. The balls on that one. I just laughed and said thanks for the money. Then I asked her what the hell she'd know about it anyway, and she said a lot more than I might think. Finally she said she had to go, and to tell you she was sorry."

I'm... I'm... in a state of disbelief. The audacity of this woman. So what, now she's trying to bond with Cassie? What does she want?

"God, Cass, I'm so sorry you've gotten caught up in this mess."

"Girl, please. This isn't the first time, and it won't be the last. I have more stalkers than you can count. Most of them are women, you know."

"Really?"

"Well, yeah, it's a jealousy thing. To be honest, I'm surprised this is your first stalker. The Perfect Wife and Mommy industry seems like it'd be ripe for obsessive wannabes."

"I do have some superfans. But they're cute, harmless fangirls." I think about some of the comments from my followers. They share every picture I post, comment on everything, vow to buy every brand I promote. Then I think about Sophia, commenting on my old posts, inserting herself into my life.

"Cute until they're holding a knife over you because they want to know what it's like to wear your skin." Cassie laughs, then snorts because she laughs so hard.

"Jesus Christ. I hope no one has done that to you?"

"Oh, not me, babes, I'm talking about Sophia. That one would love to snuggle up inside of your body."

"Ugh, shut up." But I start laughing too. Who would have guessed this is where we'd end up, when Cassie strolled into our dorm room all those years ago at Iowa State and said, *Tell me if you're a lame ass right now so I can switch rooms*, to which I replied, *You wanna get drunk? I know a party.* I didn't really, because zombie summer, but I knew where Greek Row was from working in student services.

When I met Sophia, I thought I needed a local best friend. Someone to hang out with every day. But I was wrong... Cassie is just a phone call away and she's always been there for me, since the beginning.

"Hannah, I wish I didn't have to say goodbye, but I've got dinner plans with my agent. Can we talk tomorrow? I feel like there's so much to unpack with this Sophia stuff," she says.

"I have a better idea. Why don't you fly out here and stay for a few days? I'm sure Aunt Tippy and Uncle Fran would be happy to see you. It's been ages since we got into trouble on the farm."

"Oh my god, you remember that Christmas, what was it, junior year? When we crashed Fran's farm truck in the snow?" Cassie laughs.

"And he had to use the tractor to pull us out!" I exclaim. God, Cassie and I used to have so much fun when she came home with me to the farm for holidays. Her childhood was even more fucked-up than mine. There was no way in hell she was spending the holiday breaks with any of her former foster families. "Seriously, I'd love to see you."

"Yes, absolutely. I just have to move a few things around on my schedule. I should be there in a few days."

"Great! I can't wait."

"Love you." She hangs up.

I'm not feeling shaky anymore. I've got backup coming. My girl Cassie will be under the same roof as me. No matter what kind of crap Sophia's been putting me through or might try and pull, I'm with my people.

TWENTY-ONE

Court's in and out of business meetings for days and hasn't had time to call the attorney to check if the process server did his job. I ask him for the number, so I can follow up myself. He says he'll text it to me but never does, and because I'm so busy chasing the twins, feeding cows, and riding tractors, you'd think I'd forget. But I can't stop thinking about it. I figure maybe I'll message one of our drivers and have them go over to the house and check. It's as easy as a quick drive-by to see if there's a moving truck in Sophia's driveway.

My phone buzzes.

Cassie just landed, which means she should be here within the hour.

Aunt Tippy is outside with the twins, and it's quiet in the house. Almost too quiet. I throw in a load of laundry—the creaking sound of the old washing machine is loud and soothing. Learning to use the washing machine was a bright moment when I was a kid. After bouncing around with Mom, and not always having clean clothes, I instantly loved this machine. And the fact that Aunt Tippy was more than happy for me to do my own laundry. But it's definitely seen better days. I'll add a new washer and dryer to my growing list of things I want to buy for the farm.

I sit on the couch with my laptop and notebook. I check my socials, type some notes on the analytics, schedule a couple posts, and write "washer and dryer" on my list. I'm sure Court won't mind if I use our joint funds—since the kids and I are staying here for a couple of weeks. Usually I use my influencer money to buy Aunt Tippy things for the farm, but knowing my husband, he would insist... He'd probably get a kick out of it too. On one of our first dates he asked, in a very romantic way, if I could have anything in the world, what would it be? Without thinking I blurted out, "A new washing machine," because the one in my apartment was terrible. We both had a good laugh.

And the very next day a delivery driver showed up at my apartment with a brand-new washing machine. That's when I knew I would become the future *Mrs. Court McBillionaire.*

I often tell Court it's fate that we met.

Which is true.

I could have never planned for him to walk into the bar where I was working. But the part that wasn't fate, was my desire to meet a man like Court. It's why I was in Florida in the first place. Cassie, who seemed to know a lot about rich men, said that's where they all hung out. Or as she liked to say, *Where they can show off their yachts like a dick-measuring contest.*

So on my days off I'd go to the beach club at the marina, where all the mega yachts were moored. I'd order a drink and sit at a table alone on the veranda and take notes.

I studied them. The wealthy men and their trophy wives.

I started noticing a pattern: the way they dressed, the way they talked, their stolen glances, the secret whispers.

The bar where I worked wasn't the kind of place to attract an upscale clientele. Mostly tourists out for drinks on the weekend and the local regulars during the week. Which was why Court stood out to me when he walked in one late, balmy September afternoon. He had the same air about him as the wealthy men at the beach club. He ordered a Scotch and sat alone at the end of the bar, working on some paperwork and sipping on his drink.

By his third visit, we'd started chatting. But rather than use my normal routine, asking "Where ya from?" and offering up info on local haunts, I took a more calculated approach. I acted like one of those trophy wives. Skillfully seductive with him—making direct eye contact, ignoring everyone else at the bar, gently touching his arm, leaning in to whisper minor details about myself. Every movement designed to lure him in.

Even so, it took him a month of visits before he worked up the courage to ask me out. I remember telling Cassie all about him after our first date. She told me, *Be careful—billionaires can't be trusted. All that money makes them think they are goddamn Zeus.*

But Court felt safe and warm. I thought he was just some tech nerd, a Zuckerberg type, not some muscle-bound narcissist with a god complex. Not to mention, he had a way of making me feel like the only person in the room—his eyes never left me—and he was so generous, like sending me the washing machine.

He was the perfect mark.

"Knock, knock." Cassie's voice echoes from the mudroom off the porch.

"Oh my gosh, I didn't even hear your car pull up," I shriek and jump to my feet, running to give my friend a hug. She's got her hair in braids and a tight-fitting blue jean dress over her curvy body. Underneath she's wearing her old brown cowgirl boots and, honestly, she looks just like the character Beth Dutton from the show *Yellowstone.* It wouldn't surprise me to learn Taylor Sheridan and Cassie had met somewhere along the way.

"Hannah." Cassie throws her arms around me and squeezes. "Jesus, when was the last time you ate? You're wasting away. I'm all for skinny girl vibes, but honey!"

First Sinclair, now Cassie. Maybe I really should step on a scale and try to eat more.

"I'm not doing it on purpose, I swear to god. I think it's just all the stress lately and chasing the twins around." I offer a quick explanation so she won't worry. She eyeballs me but nods once.

Cassie has a sixth sense and can always tell when I'm lying. And I'm *not* lying. Any weight loss has been entirely unintentional.

"Yeah, well, I'll be here for a few days and I expect to see you eating." She puts her hands on her hips and looks around the room. "Well, this place hasn't changed."

"Like a time capsule." I nod. "They did do some renovations upstairs—a new bathroom, fresh paint, and furniture," I tell her. "But we can look at that later. Let me help you get your bags in and we can find the twins."

A few hours later, Cassie's settled in and we are all sitting around the big dining room table for lunch. Aunt Tippy's set out sandwich fixings, potato salad, Jell-O and Rice Krispies Treats. It's a Midwestern feast. Cassie helps me dish up plates for the twins, who are jabber-jawing about their morning adventures collecting eggs, feeding cats, and riding in a wagon filled with hay.

I look at them with pride. My little farm babies with sunkissed faces and a smattering of new freckles across the bridges of their noses. Then I have a moment of panic. How could I be so stupid? I haven't been putting sunscreen on them, or sun hats to protect their tender skin.

"After lunch, I need to go to town for sunscreen. Do you need anything, Aunt Tippy?" I ask. I cannot believe I forgot to pack the Coppertone. I literally have a lifetime supply.

"There's a list on the fridge you can take," she says.

"Rowen, sandwich first," I snap at my son, who's busy shoving a second Rice Krispies Treat in his mouth.

Aunt Tippy shoots me a dirty look. "Let the child eat in peace. Food is food on a farm."

Cassie and I look at one another and laugh. Aunt Tippy's famous line. *Food is food on a farm.*

"Remember the three-day-old lasagna for Christmas breakfast?" Cassie asks with a glow in her eye.

"Food is food on a farm," I tease, using Aunt Tippy's stern voice.

"I don't recall either of you hooligans complaining at the time." Aunt Tippy huffs. She picks up a Rice Krispies Treat and takes an exaggerated bite.

That sets Uncle Fran off and he throws his head back and laughs. We all join in the laughter, even the twins, although I'm not sure they know what they are laughing about.

When we finish eating, I offer to take the kids to town with us, but they are too excited about going up in the hayloft with Uncle Fran. He thinks one of the mama cats has a batch of kittens old enough to be held.

After multiple warnings about keeping the kids away from the edge of the hayloft, and plenty of reassurance that the railing was replaced last summer, I finally wave goodbye and climb into Cassie's rental car. She prefers to drive. Always has.

She puts on her sunglasses, grips the wheel, and steps on the gas. She drives the rental like it's a race car, drifting around the corners of the long dirt road. It feels like we are flying. Like we are teenagers again...

"Okay, I can't wait a second longer. What's going on with Sophia? Did she get served?"

"I think so. Court's been busy and hasn't connected with the attorney to confirm."

"Why don't you just call the attorney?" she asks.

"I don't have his number. I asked Court to send it to me, but—"

"Let me guess, he's busy?" Cassie looks over at me. I can tell her eyes are judging me, even through the dark lenses. "Call him right now. I'm so nosey, I have to know."

I groan. Court hates when I ask him things over and over. But there's no way Cassie is going to let this one go. I pull out my phone and dial Court. It goes straight to voicemail.

"Hey babe, it's me. Just checking on the process server. Call or text me when you're free." I hang up and say, "There, happy?"

"No, I'm not happy. Why the fuck did his phone go directly to voicemail?"

"It must be turned off. He's probably... *busy*," I defend my husband.

"Sweetheart, your husband is a billionaire crypto mogul. He's always fucking busy. That's no excuse to turn off his phone. I haven't turned off my phone in six years. Do not disturb, sure, but off? Never."

I don't know why Cassie's harping on it. She doesn't understand Court—he's probably giving a presentation and can't be bothered to look at his phone right now. Whatever the reason, it doesn't matter. What matters is finding out if Sophia received the letter and is leaving.

Because until she's gone, I can't go home.

"What if I call one of our drivers? They could go over and check. *If* Sophia got the letter, there should be a moving truck or some other sign that she's leaving."

Cassie makes a sound. "Babes, think about it, Sophia isn't going to worry about packing. She can buy new wherever she goes."

Yeah, that's true. Why would she hire movers? She bought everything when she moved in. It would be just as easy to sell the house fully furnished. All she really needs to do is pack a suitcase and get on a plane.

Ugh, this is all so frustrating. I just want Sophia gone and out of my life.

Cassie pulls the car into a spot at Bomgaars.

"What are we doing at the farm supply store?" I ask.

"You said sunscreen, but what I heard was cowboy hats for those little munchkins. Plus, I'm picturing an epic bonfire tonight after the kids go to bed. Which means we need some tight-ass bedazzled jeans and matching plaid shirts."

"Ooooh, beer in red Solo cups, and a little Tim McGraw?" I can't believe I'm suggesting we listen to country music.

"Not a little, *a lot* of that sexy man. Move over, Faith Hill, CassieXOXO is in town."

"Oh please, like you could get Tim McGraw." I laugh.

She raises an eyebrow. "How do you know I haven't already had him?"

I elbow her, then grab her hand and run toward the entrance. We act like teenagers with our Friday paycheck burning a hole in our pockets. We each push a green cart around the store, racing up and down the aisles, tossing in a mishmash of items. Bomgaars has everything from live baby chicks to fishing gear to clothes. They even have an entire glorious section filled with vintage candy. Yes, I'll have the bright orange circus peanuts and gummy worms.

"Shut up. Shut up!" Cassie shrieks when she pushes her cart around a corner. "Hannah, get that skinny ass over here right now and check this out."

I laugh. I can only imagine what has Cassie so excited. When I turn the corner, I spy the big display that has her panties in a twist. It's a mechanical bull surrounded by cowboy hats and lasso ropes. It's being used as a display, to lure customers, but Cassie couldn't care less. She's hiking up her dress and climbing on the big brown beast.

"Yee-haw." She grabs the cowboy hat off the horns and holds it up in the air and swings her arm around, pretending she's really riding the bull.

Before the store manager can yell at her to get off, I take a few pictures.

"Hey, you. Yeah, you—boy with the broom, come here." Cassie points at some pimple-faced teen lazily pushing a mop. "Hannah, give him your phone and get on this bull with me."

"What? No." I shy away.

But Cassie is relentless. "Kid, I'll give you twenty bucks. Take our picture. Hannah. Bull, now." She snaps her fingers.

I groan. She'll keep making a scene until I give in. Suddenly I remember all our years together in college. Cassie was wild. Always wanting—no, *needing*—more and more attention... The only way to stop her was giving in. So I hand my phone to the teenager, whose face is as red as one of Aunt Tippy's garden toma-toes, then awkwardly climb onto the bull behind Cassie.

I throw my own arm up in the air, give a big fake smile to the boy holding my phone and yell, "Take the picture."

Cassie claps with delight.

"There, pictures taken, are you happy?"

"Almost," she says. "Now, let's see what this baby can do." She leans over and pushes a button on the bull.

I scream, "NO!"

She starts laughing and the bull lurches forward very slowly, then back even slower, then forward again.

"Uh, it doesn't really work," the boy says, the tomato blush gone from his face. "Oh, lady, your phone is ringing. You want me to answer it for you?" He walks toward me. "It's Sophia."

As the bull lurches back again, I lose my grip and slide right off its butt in a heap on the floor. Cassie swings her leg over gracefully and grabs my phone from the boy, answering it as I'm shouting, "Don't answer!"

"Hey, Sophia, did you get the letter from Hannah's attorney?" Cassie says when she answers my phone.

I scramble off the floor and rush to Cassie's side so I can listen in.

"Ohhhh really," Cassie replies to whatever Sophia just said. Her eyes roll. "Well, here, why don't you talk to Hannah yourself." Cassie hands me my phone.

My hand is shaking.

I don't want to talk to Sophia.

I just want her out of my life. But Cassie narrows her eyes and mouths, *Talk to her.*

As soon as I put the phone to my ear, I can hear Sophia's pleading voice. "Hannah, please, don't hang up, I just wanted to call and say I'm sorry and let you know I'm moving—home to the UK actually. This whole thing has been an eye-opener for me... I, uh, well, I overstepped and I'm sorry if I ruined our friendship."

My voice catches in my throat. My vision blurs. I nod and manage to squeak out an unconvincing, "Okay."

"I wish you all the best," she says and hangs up.

"What a bitch. Come on, we need beers. Stat." Cassie grabs my arm. "You, kid, push our carts to the register."

TWENTY-TWO
SOPHIA

Let's see. I've royally fucked up my friendship with Hannah by lying to her face, ignoring her, having plastic surgery to look like her, and my favorite, asking her children to lie about me volunteering at their school. If I could just tell her the truth about everything... If she really knew what I'm going through with Blake and my sister. Maybe she'd understand I haven't done any of it to hurt her. Maybe she'd find a way to forgive me.

But that's a long shot. And I'm feeling emotionally drained. It's probably best if I leave Florida.

Which is what I just said when I called her.

I was a little surprised when her friend Cassie answered the phone. She must have hopped on the first flight to Iowa after I called her a few days ago. That wasn't my best decision either. Calling Hannah's best friend from college. But since I knew I couldn't come out and tell Hannah everything without her freaking out, I thought I could tell Cassie and let her relay it all instead. But I was crying and having a hard time trying to articulate my thoughts. She called me a sad, tragic little bitch. Which actually made me laugh.

Because she's right.

I am.

I set my suitcase on the bed. I don't need much—I can buy new wherever I land. "It's time. A fresh start," I say to myself as I pack a few things. I told Hannah I was moving home to the UK, but maybe I'll go to New York. I've always wanted to live there. Plus, the art scene is one of the best in the world.

After I zip up my suitcase and lug it downstairs, I take a quick look around. Fuck this house. It's been my prison, not some tropical sanctuary like I'd dreamed it would be. I glance at some of the paintings. I hate to leave them, but they aren't going anywhere. I own the place, nothing is going to happen to the house if it sits empty—it's not like it's going to disappear. I can always come back someday, if I really want to.

My hand closes around the front doorknob. It feels symbolic as I turn it, like I'm opening the door to a new life.

"Hello, Sophia."

"Blake!" I gasp when I see my husband standing on the other side. "What the hell are you doing here?"

He sees my suitcase and cocks his head. "Are you going somewhere?"

"Oh well, I mean, I was. But, um, not anymore—now that you're here." My heart sinks. I'd convinced myself I could leave him. I could walk away from this life and start over. But like the devil sitting on my shoulder tempting me, there stands Blake. The man who ruined my fucking life. The man who's had control over me for a decade. He still sees me as that sad, pathetic girl at Oxford, clamoring for his attention. Even with my new nose and hair and contoured cheekbones. I can see it in his eyes.

Disappointment.

TWENTY-THREE

HANNAH

Cassie smooths her palms over her bedazzled jean-covered hips and looks at herself in the mirror. "Damn, I look good in some country girl bling."

"I feel so cheesy." I walk up next to her, wearing my own pair of blinged-out Bomgaars-buy jeans. We match from head to toe, from the jeans to the pink plaid button-down shirts over tank tops and tied at the middle.

"Quick, let's take a picture."

"Oh god, you want proof of this? Sinclair will kill me if he sees me in this getup." But who am I to deny my friend a photo-op? We're back at the farm, several red Solo cups in, standing in front of the big mirror. The number of times I stood here as a teenager, looking at myself, picturing the woman I wanted to be someday. I'm not sure if I've become her yet—I'm not sure if I'll ever become her.

Cassie snaps some pictures and laughs.

"Shhhh... We'd better go outside, the twins just fell asleep," I remind her.

"Oh shit, sorry. Yes, let's go outside and dance around the bonfire." Cassie holds up her cup and wiggles her hips as she walks out of the room. Aunt Tippy already said she'd listen for the twins, so Cassie and I can stay up late. It's overly generous and totally unlike her. But who am I to look a gift horse in the mouth.

As Cassie and I walk across the backyard toward the blazing fire pit, Uncle Fran heads toward us. "You girls have fun now. There's a big stack of logs next to the pit—use up as much as you want."

I throw my arms around him. "Thanks, Frannie." Then I give him a kiss on his sun-weathered cheek.

"It's good to have you home, Hannah. We've missed you somethin' fierce." His eyes twinkle. "Now, go have fun with that one. She's a spitfire."

"Hell yeah, I am!" Cassie yells, then she tips back her cup and drains her beer. "Hannah, do you know what time it is?"

I don't have to check my watch. Because I know what time it is. "Tim McGraw time?"

"Winner, winner, catfish dinner." She points at me, then turns some music on her phone, grabs another beer from the cooler, and holds it up above her head. "Here's to real friends. Not fucked-up neighbors trying to steal our lives."

I hold my cup high over my head. "Cheers!"

The rest of the night isn't just a blur... it's a hot mess. I vaguely remember dancing semi-naked around the fire. Cassie was definitely naked. Ohhhh god, my head hurts. I need water and aspirin.

"Mommy," Ruby whispers.

I groan.

"I can see Cassie's boobies," Rowen says and snickers.

I sit up in bed, my arms instinctively covering my chest, just to make sure I'm not topless. Thankfully, I feel a shirt. Phew.

"Scoot. Go find Aunt Tippy." I wave the kids out of the room before looking over at Cassie. I pull the sheet over her giant silicone breasts as the twins giggle and run away, their little feet scampering down the stairs.

Jesus, I haven't partied that hard... well, since the last time I was with Cassie here at the farm, before I got married to Court. I'm getting too old for this crap... But, a sheepish grin spreading over my face, we did have fuuuuun.

I reach for my phone.

My unread text count is unhinged.

SINCLAIR:

Girl, you are a maniac.

JAMIE:

Hannah. Stop texting me pictures of Cassie's boobs.

COURT:

I miss you.

SOPHIA:

Sorry again…

Jesus. I scroll through to see what the fuck I was doing last night. A video of me and Cassie singing, sent to Sinclair. Boob pics to Jamie. Crying and heart emojis to Court. And nothing to Sophia. Just her unprovoked text. I roll my eyes.

Then, because I'm hungover, or maybe still a little drunk, I decide I'm going to snoop on Sophia's social media. As I click on her profile, something rings a bell from last night—Cassie berating me for not being more of a spy.

"But what's the point?" I moaned at the time.

"So you can protect yourself!" Cassie yelled in my face, before pulling a cigarette from her pocket and lighting up.

"Smoking now, are we?" I teased.

"I don't inhale." She coughed, trying to blow a smoke ring.

I laughed and pointed. "Epic fail."

"Bitch, as if you could do it better," she accused and handed me the cigarette. The smell, the taste—it all reminded me of Matt. And I sat down in the grass and started crying.

"Oh, honey, don't cry, I'm sorry. Give it back." She plunked down next to me. But I didn't want to give it back. So we sat there crying and smoking until somehow we ended up half-naked in my bed.

I look at my phone.

If I waste time deep diving on Sophia's posts, tracking her likes and followers, that makes me the stalker. Not the other way around. But if I don't, am I not doing everything I can to protect myself and my family?

And I would do anything to protect my family.

So I scoot myself up, wipe the sleep from my eyes, and look at her profile. She's added a bunch of pictures since the last time I looked. Surprisingly she's in a lot of the pictures, but not direct shots. Her hand holding a fork, diving into a five-star dish. The back of her, staring at a painting. I grit my teeth—her hair is longer and blonde. Extensions—that much is certain. But the color, goddamn her. Did she call my stylist? Because if I didn't know better, I'd think that was a picture of the back of me.

I slam my phone down in my lap.

I can't keep looking—it's only going to drive me crazy.

What does any of it matter? She said she was moving back to the UK. Which I find a little funny, since she said she'd never move back, after her horrible upbringing.

"Ughhhh... Why'd you make me drink so much?" Cassie rolls over, groaning.

"Go back to sleep." I pat her head.

She's snoring within a few seconds. I slide out of the bed and head to the bathroom for that aspirin and a shower. I'm glad Aunt Tippy kept the claw-foot tub when she redid the bathroom. Because lying down in it, with the shower head spraying my face, is helping my headache and washing away all my tears. I couldn't say exactly why I'm crying—maybe because I'm still upset by Sophia. Maybe because I miss Court. Maybe because I miss Matt. Maybe because I'm tired...

The last six days have flown by.

With Cassie leaving town, and the spring calving and planting consuming Aunt Tippy and Uncle Fran's time—I've decided to take the kids home early. Plus, Sophia's gone dark. No calls. No emails. Her social accounts have been quiet for days. I can only assume she got on a plane to the UK and is rebuilding or rebranding her life. Or maybe she's back together with Blake. Or finding a new neighbor to obsess over. Whatever it is, doesn't concern me anymore. The only thing that matters is I'm going home with my kids to see my husband.

TWENTY-FOUR

After a cramped, smelly, I'm-never-flying-domestic-again flight, I put myself and the kids in an Uber. The entire ride home I picture Court rushing out to greet us, but since I didn't tell him we were coming home early, that's not going to happen. Somehow I get the suitcases, twins, and car seats out of the Uber by myself. Sweat beads at my hairline. Damn, it's humid. I already miss the cooler Midwestern air.

"Go knock on the door so Daddy will come help us," I tell Rowen.

This was so stupid. I should have just told Court we were coming home early. How do people travel this way? It's terrible. I will never take private cars and charter flights for granted.

Rowen bangs on the door, but Court doesn't answer.

"Let me do it," Ruby says and runs up to help, first banging on the door with Rowen, then ringing the doorbell.

"I guess Daddy's not home." Figures. "Scoot over, kiddos, I'll use my key to let us inside." I set down the suitcases, dig the keys out of my bag, and just as I'm about to stick the key into the lock, the door opens up. Court is standing on the other side with a very strange look on his face. His hair is disheveled and kinda wet, and he's wearing nothing but swim trunks.

"Out for a swim in the ocean?" I ask and smile. "I hope you put on sunscreen."

"Daddy!" the twins cry out and throw themselves at Court's legs.

"Hannah, I uh, well... I, um..." He's stuttering and patting the kids on their heads.

My husband is never tongue-tied. My spidey-senses kick in and I narrow my gaze. "Is everything okay?" I ask.

"I wasn't expecting you home today," he manages to say.

"Who's at the door?" a woman asks as she rounds the corner from the kitchen. She's wearing a low-cut bright red swimsuit wrapped with a sheer white sarong. Her blonde hair is pulled up into a bun on top of her head. As soon as she sees us, she drops the wine glass she was holding and it crashes to the floor and shatters.

"Sophia," I whisper.

"Now, Hannah, it's not what it looks like." Court holds his hands up to surrender.

"Ruby, Rowen, bedroom—NOW!" I scream. They look terrified but don't argue, and run through the dining room for the stairs, avoiding Sophia entirely.

"I'll get a broom..." Sophia turns around and leaves.

"What the fuck is that bitch doing inside our home?" I spit the words at my bastard husband. How could he do this to me?

"Well, now, it's actually a funny story..."

I scoff and cross my arms over my chest.

But Court isn't deterred. "See, I was out having a swim when I saw someone walking on the beach—and honestly, I thought it was you so I got out of the water and ran to her..." He pauses ever so slightly to slow his breathing. I can tell he's trying very hard not to paint himself in a bad light. "I was caught off guard. You told me Sophia left for the UK."

"That's what she said," I growl through gritted teeth. Obviously the bitch was lying.

"Anyway, I demanded to know why she was still in town, and

she said there'd been some issues with her travel arrangements, and we got to talking, and—"

"And then you invited her into our home for a fucking glass of wine?" I drop my arms. My fists ball up at my side. This is unbelievable. I'm so angry I could punch my husband in the face.

Court is nervous. A vein throbs on the side of his neck. He shakes his head. "No, not exactly. I came home after the beach and was sitting on the patio to dry off, when Sophia showed up with a bottle of wine, wanting to apologize again for the trouble. What was I supposed to do?" he asks. His tone becomes defensive.

"Ummm, how about tell her to get the fuck off our property?"

"Hannah, don't you think you're being a little hard on the woman? She didn't mean to upset you with her makeover."

I'm about to lose my shit and scream at my husband that he's a fucking idiot, then I remember that Sophia is still in my house. My house. Of which I'm still standing in the entryway, like I'm the one who doesn't belong here. I shove Court out of the way, surprising him, and march across the shattered glass into the kitchen. I don't see Sophia anywhere.

"SOPHIA!" I shout her name. "WHERE ARE YOU?" Then I notice the glass backdoor panels are open to the deck. I walk out and look across the yard to Sophia's house. She must have fled the scene of the crime when she said she was getting a broom. There's an empty bottle of wine on the table and a bowl of my secret-stash potato chips sitting next to it. That snake.

"Is the yelling really necessary?" Court walks in behind me.

My face contorts. I'm seeing red. If I don't walk away from Court right now, I'm going to say something I regret. Or I really am going to assault him. So I take a deep breath, then say, "I'm going upstairs to freshen up. Why don't you clean up that glass?" I grab the broom, shove it at Court, then storm out of the room. I'm absolutely fuming as I walk up the stairs.

I peek my head into the twins' room to check on them. I'm sure it scared them when we walked in and I shouted at them to go to their room. I expect to see one or both of them crying. But Ruby is curled up on her bed holding her stuffie—she looks like she might be asleep. Rowen is playing Legos quietly on the floor near the toy kitchen. God, I'm so lucky—look at my perfect angels. Before Rowen sees me, I close the door gently and go to my room, to continue freaking out... in private.

I cannot believe my husband sat outside on the deck drinking wine with the enemy. And then he let her in my house to steal my chips.

Don't be stupid, Hannah. Do you really think that's all they did? I can practically hear Cassie's voice in my head.

No. I'm not stupid. I look around my room for any evidence of Sophia. I check my closet, the bathroom, even under the bed. But I don't notice anything out of place. I desperately want to call someone and vent, but how can I burden Cassie or Sinclair with this kind of information? Especially when I'm not entirely sure what happened. Should I believe my husband? It makes sense, his version of events. I can picture him swimming in the ocean, stopping to catch his breath, and looking up to see a woman he thought was me standing on the shore. He probably waved at her, then swam at full speed, and was surprised when he realized it was Sophia and not me.

Or maybe he's full of shit.

Maybe they've been having sex all morning at Sophia's house, then went for a refreshing swim afterwards. Or maybe it was here, in our home, on our bed. Images flash in my mind, playing out every sick and twisted possibility.

I grab a pillow off the bed and scream into it.

It has a faint smell of perfume, but I can't tell if it's mine. I throw it as hard as I can at the wall, knocking off a picture of me and Court in Paris on our honeymoon. My skin is crawling. I can't stop picturing them here, together, in my room.

Up against the wall.

His hand at her throat.

Taking her hard and violently.

Fulfilling some twisted fantasy together. Her longing for a

husband who's abandoned her for his second family. Luring my husband into her arms. Telling him how much they have in common. That he's alone because I abandoned him for my other family in Iowa.

They comfort one another with their naked flesh.

I'm panting, the room is spinning, and I think I'm having a panic attack. I splash some cold water on my face in the bathroom and put my hands on the side of the sink. I can hardly bear to look at my reflection in the mirror. When I do, I see a woman I hardly recognize. My friends are right. I'm thin. The light in my eyes is gone. This perfect world I've built is crumbling down around me. What the fuck am I going to do?

Even if nothing inappropriate happened between Court and Sophia, how can I ever get the images I've conjured out of my head? I'm so mad at him for putting me in this situation. But I'm even more mad at myself. I let this happen. I opened the door by inviting her into our lives. This is my fault. Tears stream down my face.

"Babe, can I come in?" Court slowly opens the bedroom door. He sees me in the bathroom and comes to my side. Normally I'd hate for him to see me like this. Frazzled, crying, weak. All character traits he hates in a woman. But it's not like I can hide it. "Oh, Hannah, honey, please don't cry. Nothing happened." He puts his arms around me.

I want to shove him away from me.

And call him a lying son of a bitch.

But I'm tired and I slump against his bare chest. He's warm and smells salty. I guess the swimming part of his story was true.

"Why don't you take a nice hot bath? When you're done, we can order dinner and watch a movie. I'm sure you've had a long day —you should have just told me you wanted to come home sooner. I would have made private-travel arrangements." He pets my hair, then guides me toward the tub. I don't reply or make any moves to undress myself.

I'm numb.

"What did you say?" I'm dazed. I find it hard to concentrate on anything he says.

"Here, let me help you," he says. He turns on the faucet, then picks up a bottle of lavender bath salts and pours some in. The room fills with a calming, steamy aroma. Then he stands in front of me, unbuttons my shirt, and discards it to the floor. He carefully unfastens my bra before moving to my pants. He slips them down my hips and helps me step out of them.

I'm naked.

Exposed.

Weak in his presence.

I can tell he's getting aroused. I should stop him before he takes this any further—but his mouth finds my neck and his hand slips between my legs. I want to tell him no. I'm angry with him. So fucking angry that I want to bite down on his tongue as it glides into my mouth. But my body betrays me as it comes alive under his touch. My hips and shoulders relax.

I want him. Right now, I'll have him. He's mine.

My frantic hands tug at his swim trunks, until they come loose and drop to the ground. I wrap my palm around his cock and pump it while his fingers go deeper inside of me.

"I missed you so much," he mumbles, moving from my lips down to my breasts. He kisses my tender flesh, then puts my nipple in his mouth and suckles and bites. I moan with pleasure and I hate myself for it.

"Don't you ever, ever betray me like that again." My grip tightens around his cock and his body trembles in response.

"Hannah, not too hard."

"You are mine." I squeeze. "Say it."

He gulps. "I'm yours." But something in the tone of his voice makes me angry—I don't believe him. I release his cock and shove him away from me.

His nostrils flare and he wraps his arms around me in a bear hug before I can push him again. "Shhhh... Babe, it's okay. Nothing happened."

My breathing is heavy and erratic.

"I'm yours," he says again. "Shhhh... I'm yours." His lips find my mouth. I don't fight it, how can I, when my body is trembling with this bizarre desire to fuck him and kill him at the same time? His arms finally loosen and instead of pushing him away again, I pull him in closer.

"I need to fuck you," I growl. "Get on the bed."

He doesn't argue. He lies down on our bed and I climb on top of him. He's as hard as a rock—must be all the adrenaline. I move my body slowly at first, up and down. He reaches his hands out to touch me and I smack them away.

"Don't fucking touch me. I'm still mad at you," I hiss.

"Babe... please," he begs.

"Fine."

His hands squeeze, rub, and grope all of me. I reach my high just as his eyes roll into the back of his head.

"That was..." He sucks in a breath.

"I know." I climb off his lap and go crawl into the bathtub. The water is teetering at the edge, fully consuming me. I put my gel-infused mask on, close my eyes, and lay my head back. I don't want to look at Court. He might have given me an orgasm, but that doesn't replace this giant hole in my heart.

He's betrayed me.

And we both know it.

I just have to figure out if I'm going to let it ruin our marriage.

TWENTY-FIVE

Sophia's still at her house days later. I'm not watching her out the windows, like I used to, but I do see her car coming and going. I try not to let it bother me. At this point, what can I do about her? I can't force someone to move, no matter how much they fucking irritate me.

Then there's my husband.

He's been so strange. Instead of his usual workaholic, somewhat dry self, he's extra attentive and romantic. Flowers, candies, candlelit dinners when the twins go to bed. Not to mention we've had sex at least twice a day, if not more.

But what I find most odd is that he's so distant around the twins.

He's hardly speaking to them, sending them to their room when they want to play with him. Which is worrisome. I wish he'd give my body a break and take them to the park or teach them to ride their bikes without training wheels, like he's been promising since last summer. That would be the best gift he could give me.

I suspect he's trying to dote on me to deflect from the whole Sophia situation when we got home, but it's having the complete opposite effect. I'm even more suspicious now than I was the day I walked in on him and Sophia having wine in their swimsuits.

I'm sitting at the table, sipping on my coffee, and working on some new picture-perfect-happy-family-style posts—which feels like such a lie, when Court strolls in whistling. He's got a blue Tiffany box in his hands and sets it in front of me.

"What's this for?" I ask and close my computer. But I already know what it's for—our anniversary.

"Our anniversary is next week," he exclaims. "I was going to wait and surprise you with it. But then I thought you might like to wear it now." He smiles.

"That's so sweet. Thank you," I gush when I open the box and see a diamond necklace. What I really want to say is, *Are you trying to buy my forgiveness?* And it's not a surprise at all. Every year he gives me a Tiffany necklace on our anniversary; it's become a tradition. But getting it a week early on a random Tuesday morning while I'm trying to work makes it feel like a cheap trick. Even though I know these jewels were anything but cheap.

Something is seriously off with Court.

It's guilt. It's got to be. But I just can't tell if it's because he knows he screwed up by having wine with the enemy, or because he was fucking the enemy.

"Babe, you know what would be amazing?" I say.

"Hmmm?" He pulls the hair back from my neck and starts kissing it.

Oh my god. What has come over my husband? I seriously cannot have any more sex. Is that what the necklace is for? Because he knows I'm all sexed out and he wants it again? I need to get him out of the house so I can rifle through his hygiene products—he must be taking Viagra. That's the only conclusion I can come up with. And it would explain away a lot of this weird behavior.

"It would be amazing if you took Ruby and RoRo to the park. The city sent out a notice that the new park on Fourth Street opened. It's got a carousel, food trucks, and a new million-dollar play yard."

He keeps kissing my neck. Immune to my suggestion.

His hand reaches over my shoulder and down the front of my

shirt to my breast. Ughhhh. He's too amped up to even hear what I just said about the park. I'm going to have to fuck him again if I want him to leave and give me some alone time.

"Let's go to your office and lock the door—I'm wearing the royal blue thong you like." I stand up, take his hand, and walk toward his office. I want to make this quick so he will take the kids to the park.

"Oooh, feisty Hannah." He sounds like a schoolgirl. My god, why? Why is he acting like this? It's complete overkill, if the story he told me about running into Sophia by accident that day on the beach is true. What he's doing is behaving like a man guilty of an affair.

And I'm going to get to the bottom of it once and for all.

As soon as we get into his office and lock the door, I attack. I know every move he likes—some of which I've been saving up the last few days for just this kind of occasion, where I need him to blow his load in under ten minutes.

I could care less if I orgasm.

I honestly don't even want him to touch my clit.

Thankfully, he doesn't notice—he's ultra-turned on by my aggressive takeover of his body. When I check my watch as we leave the office, I got him off in under five minutes. That might be a new record for me.

"Thank you again for the beautiful necklace." I give him a final kiss, so he doesn't question my motives for the fast and furious sexcapade.

"Anything for you, my love." He smiles. "Well, I should probably get some work done."

"But, honey, you said you'd take the kids to that new park."

"What new park?" He looks confused. He grabs a bottle of water from the fridge and offers me one too.

"Remember, on Fourth Street? You said you'd take the twins to play so I can get some work done. I really appreciate it."

His face twists as he tries to recall when he told me he'd take the kids to the park. But I've got him by the balls. He can't say no now, not after what I just did to him.

"I'll drop you a pin. The kids are ready—you can go now." I smile. Then I walk out of the kitchen at a regular speed, before running up the stairs. "Ruby, Rowen, Daddy's gonna take you to that new park with the carousel and cotton candy. Hurry, hurry," I say as I bust into their bedroom.

They're sitting at the little table, having a tea party with their stuffies.

"Yay!" they both exclaim and jump up. There's no time to change their clothes or fix Ruby's hair. I want them to leave and spend time with Court so I can snoop around the house. I have to get to the bottom of things once and for all.

I grab the sunscreen off the shelf, give them each a quick spray, tie their shoes, and they are ready.

"Run. Daddy's ready to go." I hurry them out of the bedroom.

"Daddy!" Ruby shouts as she runs down the stairs.

But Rowen hesitates in the hallway.

"What's wrong, buddy?" I squat down and ask.

"Can you come too?"

"I'm sorry. Mommy has some things to do, but I promise you'll have fun with Daddy." I give him a hug.

"I, um, Mommy... I don't want to see Sophia," he says.

"Oh, honey, you won't, I promise." I give him a squeeze and then let go.

"But Daddy likes her." He twists his hands together nervously. "He kissed her."

My heart races. Did my son really just say what I think he said?

"Rowen, let's go, bud, the park's waiting. They have cotton candy!" Court bellows up the stairs.

I feign a smile. For my son's sake. But my blood is boiling. I fucking knew it. I knew something was going on between Court and Sophia. Was it when I was sick and she was here? My mind flashes back to the night I climbed the stairs in a fever-delirious state. I was right here in the hallway. I wanted to go in to see my kids—and Court wouldn't let me. He steered me away. Because Sophia was in there... And Court was standing there admiring her as she pretended to be their mommy, giving them a kiss goodnight. And after that, she probably went and crawled into my bed, pretending to be Court's wife.

I want to vomit.

But I need to get Court out of the house.

"Go on, Daddy and Ruby are waiting. You'll have fun, I promise," I croak.

"You're sad. Why are you sad, Mommy?" Rowen puts his chubby hand on my cheek.

"I'm fine, RoRo, please, go with Daddy."

So with my reassurance, my son walks down the stairs. I stand up, shake myself off, plaster a big fake happy smile on my face and rush down to say farewell to my family.

"Have fun at the park." I wave from the door to the garage as Court is backing out his car. As soon as the garage door closes—I scream once, at the top of my lungs. I let out all the pent-up rage that's been filling me for days.

"I'm going to find out what you've been up to, Court, even if it kills me," I announce to the empty house.

TWENTY-SIX

I know it's only ten in the morning, but I toss back a shot of mint-infused vodka with a very shaky left hand. Then I call Cassie on speakerphone while I walk around the house trying to decide where to search first.

"Hey, babes." She's awfully perky, considering she's three hours behind me. Which is a good thing, because I need her fully awake for what I'm about to tell her.

"I think Court's having an affair with Sophia."

"Nooooo!" she screams, eeeks, and gasps, all at the same time. "How did you find out? Tell me everything."

"I caught them when we came home."

"What? Wait... hold on... But that bitch said she was leaving for the UK."

"She lied. When the kids and I walked into the house, I found them sharing a bottle of wine. In their swimsuits."

"What. The. Fuck." She's genuinely shocked. "That was days ago. Why are you just telling me about this now?"

"Wait, it gets worse."

"Worse than finding them drinking wine in their swimsuits?" she squeaks.

"Uh-huh. So I haven't had a second to myself because Court's been sex bombing me for three days, so I finally convinced him to take the twins to the park for a few hours so I can get some work done. But as I was getting the kids ready, Rowen said he saw Court kiss Sophia."

Cassie screams and I drop the phone.

"Jesus, Cass."

"Oh my god, that fucking bastard. What are you going to do?" Cassie asks.

"I'm about to tear my house apart to look for evidence."

"He's smart, Hannah. You've gotta look everywhere," she encourages me.

I look through his dresser, nightstand, closet, the pockets of his pants, even the shoe boxes where he stores his Italian leather mules.

"Try his luggage," Cassie suggests.

"Yes! He always keeps a packed suitcase." I open it and pull out every item, even feeling around for a false bottom or hidden compartment, but come up empty-handed.

"This is stupid. I can't find anything." Shouldn't I be happy there's no evidence of an affair? But instead I just feel hollow inside.

"Hannah, it's not stupid. Your husband is up to something. You know he is. Now, go, check his office. Hurry."

Her encouragement gives me a renewed burst of energy. "Will you stay on the phone with me while I look?"

"Like I'd go anywhere, babes. I'm half-tempted to get on a flight... Oh, wait, shit... Let me call you back in ten minutes. I need to move a producer meeting to tomorrow. Seriously, ten minutes or less."

"Sure, no problem..." I feel kind of guilty. What if she has a meeting with some huge producer for a movie deal, and she's blowing it off to be on the phone with me? "No, Cassie, don't. Don't change your meeting for me. I'll search his office and if I find anything suspicious, I'll text you."

"Are you sure?"

And even though I need her, or I might break down, crawl under the covers in my bed and never come out again, I can't ruin her opportunities.

"Yes, I'll be fine."

But after ten minutes in Court's office, I regret letting Cassie go. Because I'm staring at a suspicious file folder on Court's desktop. He doesn't know I have his password. I only know it because I was standing behind him one day, rubbing his shoulders, and I watched him type it in. I don't have a photographic memory or anything like that, but it was pretty obvious he'd used the twins' birthday followed by my birthday.

He's a neat freak and his computer files are ultra-organized with color-coded labeled folders all lined up in a row. That's why the random folder on the opposite side of the screen, without a label, catches my eye. My hands are shaking and I look around. I'm scared to double-click and open the file. I have no idea what I might find. It's probably nothing more than a bunch of financial statements and business documents, but what if—*what if it's something else?* What if it's proof?

"Aghhhh," I groan and click.

My eyes instinctively close, because I'm terrified.

After a few deep breaths, and a pep talk with myself, I crack one eye open and take a look at the screen. The only thing in the folder is a bunch of documents and PDFs with dates ranging back ten to twelve years ago, long before Court and I ever met.

I move the mouse arrow to exit the folder, when something in my gut says to open one of the documents.

Click.

I choose a PDF. It's an image of a scanned handwritten bill of sale. Before I can really take a good look at it, I hear the garage door opening.

"Shit!" I yell. The last thing I want is to get caught snooping around Court's computer.

I quickly take a picture of the screen, then log off and rush out of his office. They've only been gone for an hour. That means he spent like ten minutes at the park with the kids by the time he got there, unbuckled them, let them play, and then loaded them back up in the car.

What an asshole. Doesn't he know I need more time than that to uncover what the fuck he's up to? Or maybe that's exactly it. He doesn't trust me to be in our home alone for more than an hour. Because he knows I'm going to find something. My heart beats wildly in my chest. I have to calm down.

I throw myself on the couch and turn the TV on just as the door opens.

"Mommy." Rowen comes running at full speed, holding a stick of blue cotton candy.

"RoRo, slow down before you—"

But it's too late. He takes a nose dive on the living room floor. His body lands on top of the blue sugar, smearing it into the carpet. He bursts into tears and I'm so frazzled that I burst into tears with him. Court and Ruby walk in, confused at the crying, sugary frenzy.

"What happened? Are you two okay?" Court asks.

"My candy," Rowen moans.

"My baby." I scoop Rowen into my arms and bury my face in his candy-coated chest. "That scared me." Phew. The perfect excuse for my momentary meltdown. Court cannot know I'm upset. Or he'll never leave me alone again.

So I start to laugh, to cover it up, then look at Rowen. "What did Aunt Tippy say on the farm? No crying over spilled milk."

"Or broken eggs," Ruby chimes in.

"Or smooshed cotton candy," Rowen says sadly.

I laugh even harder, then I set him down. "Right. Now, let's get you two cleaned up. I hope you had fun with Daddy."

Court is still standing at the edge of the room. His gaze narrows —like he's looking right through me. I just smile as I walk past him.

"Thanks again for taking them to the park."

"Hey, were you in my office while I was gone?" he asks.

Quick. Think. Why was I in his office? And how the fuck does he know I was in his office?

"I, uh, I was trying to print something, but I guess my printer is out of ink. I went into your office to see if I could connect to yours, but I couldn't figure it out." I shrug and do my best to look like a meek idiot that can't figure out a printer. Instead of a woman with a degree in marketing.

"Oh shoot. If I'd known you were out of ink, I could have picked some up. Next time, just call me." There's an edge to his voice, a warning. What he really means is, *Stay the fuck out of my office, Hannah.*

"No problem. I'll get the kids down for a nap, then I can go myself." There is an edge to my own voice. Because what I'm really saying is, *Fuck you, Court.*

Ten minutes later I stomp on the gas pedal and my car races down our street.

He knew I was in his office.

My heart pounds in my ears. How did he know? Does he have a camera in there? Or was he alerted when I logged on to his desktop? I need to go somewhere I can think—but I'm freaking out.

My phone rings. It's Court. I don't want to answer it, but he'll just keep calling.

"Hey, babe," I answer, trying to play it off, like I didn't just flee after turning *Bluey* on for the kids.

"You left in a big hurry. Where are you going?"

"Remember, ink for the printer?" I make a left turn, heading in the complete wrong direction for the office supply store.

"Where are you buying ink from?" he asks.

That's a weird question. "I don't know, that place next to the grocery store." Why does he care where I'm buying ink from—unless... Oh my god. Is he tracking me? I make a quick right turn and head for the interstate, just to see what he'll say.

"Where are you going, Hannah?" His voice is eerily calm. "Because I know you aren't going to buy ink."

"Jesus, Court. I'm—" I pause and look around. Bingo. "I'm going to the mall to get you an anniversary gift. Is that what you want me to say? And yes, there's a place there that sells ink. What is your problem?" I snap at him. Thank you, huge advertising billboard on the interstate, because I had no intention of going to the mall, I just needed a destination to tell my psychotic husband.

"Oh, Hannah, babe, I'm sorry. I, uh, I don't know what's gotten into me today," he backpedals. "Have fun at the mall." Then he hangs up.

My hands are trembling, I'm sweating, and my mouth is like sandpaper by the time I pull into the mall parking lot. I throw the car in park, chug the stale water from my Stanley cup, and turn up the A/C, hoping to cool down before I check my phone. I navigate my apps to settings, then scroll down to location sharing.

"You fucking asshole," I whisper. The little pin is glowing. My phone is sharing my location with him. And I know I did not turn that feature on myself.

I can't believe this is where we are at in our marriage.

Spying on one another.

He must have turned it on after I walked in on him and Sophia —so next time, they won't be interrupted. All I can think about is what else he's been doing, how long has this been going on.

"Grrrrr." I drop my phone in my lap and slam my hands on the steering wheel. "Court loves you, he adores you, he's the father of your children." I try to talk myself out of these mounting feelings of mistrust and betrayal.

Maybe I should just call Cassie back. She'll know what to do. Or even if she doesn't, at least I won't feel so alone. I pick up my phone and fumble because my hands are shaking—I accidentally open up the camera roll. The picture I took of Court's screen is staring me in the face.

The only evidence I managed to capture while snooping. I zoom in—trying to figure out what I'm looking at. As far as I can tell, it's a handwritten bill of sale for a painting. The date is faded, but it looks like it's from ten years ago.

"Wait... hold on..." I squint and look closer. No. That can't be... But right there, at the bottom of the scanned document, is a name I recognize.

Blake Carter.

Whoa, whoa, wait a second. Does this mean what I think it means? Court knows Blake? Or at least, met him ten years ago to buy a painting from the guy? I guess there's only one way to find out. Text the phone number next to his name and pray it's still him.

TWENTY-SEVEN

Is this Blake Carter's number?

Yes, may I ask who this is?

I'm really sorry to bother you. I'm your wife
Sophia's neighbor, Hannah McMillian.

Hannah, I've heard all about you. Is everything
okay? Is Sophia okay?

Shit. He knows *all about me*? I have to play this right...

I haven't seen her in a few days.

Oh, well, is there something I can help you with?

Fuck. I don't know. My palms are sweating. Why did I text him again? To ask him if he knows my husband? Damnit. I should have thought this through before I impulse dialed. I know Blake is a piece of shit human, and he put Sophia through a lot, but I literally have no one else I can talk to right now! I wonder what would happen if I told him his wife is having an affair with my husband? Or that she had plastic surgery to look like me.

I start, then pause.

...

Then I start again, but I'm freaking out. So I close my eyes and go for it.

> Sophia's not herself. She's behaving very strangely.

> Strange how?

> She's given herself a complete makeover. She's not the same woman I met when she first moved in next door. Maybe you should come to Florida... I think she needs help.

> Hannah, I hear you, but now is not a good time.

Wait? That's it? I tell him his wife is acting strange and needs fucking help and all he can say is it's not a good time? Of all the arrogant, self-important... "Raaaaawr!" I scream. I'm not about to let this go, but I can't just sit in my car all afternoon and badger a billionaire in a foreign time zone.

Not just any billionaire, I remind myself.

A billionaire my husband has done business with—that's how I've come to have Blake's phone number in the first place.

And that's when I start connecting all the dots. None of this is random. Sophia's infatuation with my life and my husband isn't because we're neighbors.

It must have started ten years ago.

When my husband, Court, bought a piece of art from Blake Carter.

And I can only imagine the art dealer who brokered the sale.

Sophia.

What a sneaky little bitch.

TWENTY-EIGHT

I stomp around the mall, fuming. I can't stop thinking about Sophia and her pathetic husband, Blake. How can he sit idly by while his wife makes a fool of herself and of me? She's been obsessed with my husband for years. While Blake's been living some bizarre double life, leaving Sophia to her own devices, she's decided to play the same game. Coming in to steal my life! Maybe that's what I should have said to Blake.

I buy the least sexy anniversary gift I can find—a black-and-white stone chess set. Then I buy my original alibi: an ink cartridge. As I'm leaving the mall, I spot the Apple store full of happy people learning how to use their new devices. I'm sure one of the first things they teach them is how to turn location sharing on and off. I feel like such an idiot—I cannot believe my husband.

My neck tingles and I rub it instinctively. It's like I'm wearing an electronic dog collar connected to a leash. One that Court can jerk and pull anytime he wants. I wish I could just throw my stupid phone in the trash.

But I have a better idea. I'll buy a burner phone. Then if I want to go somewhere without him tracking me—I'll have that option. I feel empowered for the first time all day and smile at the woman who sells me the new phone. She looks like she recognizes me.

"Is your name Hannah? Are you that influencer, with the twins?" she asks. "Sorry, you probably get asked that all the time. You look like her, but thinner."

I don't want to be rude, but I really don't want to do this right now. I nod once, "Yep, that's me, in the flesh." I laugh a little.

"I knew it. I just love your posts. All those nice things you do for your family—"

"Aw... thank you. I really appreciate it."

Then she leans in and whispers, "If you don't mind me asking, is everything okay? You don't have cancer or something, do ya? You know, my sister-in-law has lymphoma, and she lost a lot a weight too and—"

Jesus. People have no boundaries. "No, no cancer. It's just a lot of work chasing after twins all day and doing all my posts for social media."

She makes a surprised noise. "I figured someone like you got a team of nannies and housekeepers doing all that stuff for you."

"Nope. Just me." I chuckle nervously.

"Anyway, I won't waste any more of your time." She puts a hand on my shoulder. "I can tell you got a real beautiful heart."

My eyes fill with tears as I leave the mall and walk aimlessly through the parking lot to find my car. That thing she said about my beautiful heart has me all choked up. I've tried. I really have. And it's nice to hear that a complete stranger can see that in me through the online portrayal of my life, even if she thinks I look sickly. But I'm fucking tired. Tired of trying so hard to give Court the perfect life and be his perfect wife. I know, deep down, part of why I do it is to prove that Matt's death didn't break me. That even though my life with him was supposed to be the fairy tale, that I could still go on and have something enviable.

Look where it's gotten me.

I stepped on the scale this morning and I've lost fifteen pounds. My hair is starting to fall out. The only thing my husband wants from me anymore is sex. He doesn't care that I'm wasting away. He doesn't offer to take me out on dates, we don't travel to exotic places, he doesn't even let me hire the help I need to manage the house while I'm running a successful influencer business. Why the hell am I killing myself?

To what end?

So my husband and neighbor can gaslight me?

Fuck that.

Two can play this game.

It's about time I turn the tide and stand up for myself. Prove I am not some dog they can abuse for their pleasure. I might be Hannah McMillian, trad wife influencer, but in my heart I am still *Hannah Price*. Voted most likely to succeed, even though I came from nothing. A girl who survived. No matter what it took.

And what I want is my fucking life and my husband back.

Not this twisted version of ourselves we've become.

"Business must be running smoothly," I say, and give Court a kiss. He's sitting at the table drinking coffee and reading the news. I've just finished doing yoga in the backyard while the twins are still sleeping and the sun is rising.

He chuckles. "What makes you say that?"

"Well, it's been weeks and you haven't gone on any business trips."

He smiles—but it's strained. I can tell he's hiding something. "It's sweet you think work must be going well for me."

"Well, you never talk about it with me anymore." I pour myself a cup of coffee and join him at the table.

"Really, you want to talk about my work?" he asks.

"Well, I am supposed to be your best friend, right? The person you can tell anything to." I touch his arm. I'm baiting him... I want to see what he'll do.

He rubs his face. "What does that mean?" He's annoyed.

I sigh. "It means we've been out of sync lately. So I was thinking that if your work is under control, we could take the twins and go on a nice long holiday. Rent a house in Spain for a month.

You know, get away from here for a while." My eyes flick toward Sophia's house.

"You can't still be upset with her—you haven't seen her in weeks. Leave that woman alone." He stands up and glares at me. "I've already promised you a family trip to Disney." Then, through gritted teeth, he says, "And I've fucked you every day—isn't that enough for you?" He turns around and walks out of the kitchen.

God, he's so predictable.

I knew if I pushed him, it would go one of two ways. If he was innocent of doing anything with Sophia, he'd have jumped at the chance to get away with me and the kids for a month. But if he was guilty, he'd be defensive and walk out on me. I have no doubt that by tomorrow he'll be boarding a plane to anywhere—without me.

Sure, if he leaves, it gives my body a much-needed break from his ego-driven sex bombing. But it also proves the thing I was most afraid of...

Besides planning to tear my house apart for evidence of his indiscretions, I've also been waiting for him to leave so I can do my deep dive into Sophia. Because I swear to god, every time I open my laptop, he's suddenly right there. It's like he's got eyes in the back of his head.

Or...

I smack my forehead with my palm.

Of course. He's tracking my computer. He's a billionaire, in the crypto industry, which basically makes him a computer and tech genius. Through all his connections, he's probably got access to whatever kind of spy and security tech he could possibly want.

Looks like I have to go back and visit my biggest fan at the Apple store and buy a new laptop.

"You must have jinxed it," Court says a few hours later. He's standing at the door with his suitcase in hand. "Hopefully this won't take too long—but those guys in Québec, you have to stay on top of them, or the projects can spiral out of control pretty quickly."

I give him a quick kiss. "Safe travels."

"Where are the kids?" He looks around. This isn't the same send-off he's grown used to getting.

"Napping."

"I'll miss them." He says the words, but I'm not sure I can believe anything he says anymore. Not until I get to the bottom of this.

I give him one more kiss. Because despite him being kind of an aggressive asshole lately, and everything else that's been going on, I do love Court. Which is probably really stupid. But he's the father of my kids, he's the man I've built my life around, that's love right? The kind worth fighting for? I'm willing to do whatever it takes to find out what's really going on. I can't spend the rest of my life with a man who's keeping secrets from me.

TWENTY-NINE
SOPHIA

The garage door rumbles open. I put the car in reverse and just as I press my foot on the gas to back up, I see Blake in the rearview mirror. My heart leaps into my throat and I quickly throw the car in park. "I nearly ran you over—what the hell, Blake?" I chastise my husband when I get out. He just smiles like some psychopath and walks into the garage, casually wheeling his suitcase. "And how long are you staying this time?" I ask as I follow him into the house. My stomach growls. I guess going for a drive-thru burger is off the plate now. A little American indulgence I've allowed myself the last few weeks.

"I'm only here tonight. I have business." He leaves his suitcase in the hall and heads for the bar cart. I follow after him like a puppy, watching as he pours himself a Scotch.

"Where is it this time?"

"Does it really matter?" He gulps down his drink, then refills it before taking a seat in the leather chair in the study.

His work really isn't so demanding that it requires multiple cross-continental trips every month. I think he goes on business trips so he can have alone time away from his kids, or so he can fuck a flight attendant before eating at a Michelin-starred restaurant and reading a book by the pool of some luxury resort. When you're a billionaire, the money does most of the work for you, earning tens of millions in interest per year.

His whole I-work-so-hard image is such a facade.

I wasn't expecting him, so I don't have a lot in the kitchen, but I manage to whip up something—still grieving my burger. I boil pasta and sauté it with a little spinach and white wine sauce. We sit at the island, eating in relative silence—just soft classical music playing in the other room.

I'm on edge and I'm not sure why. I don't like it when Blake just shows up unannounced. I keep glancing towards Hannah's house, but the heavy blinds block out the view.

Blake pushes his plate away when he's finished eating and starts telling me about some building he bought in Paris. I'm only half listening, because I don't particularly care.

"Wait, you did what?" I almost drop my fork when my brain registers his words. Did he just say what I think he said?

"I bought you that apartment you've been wanting in Paris," he repeats himself. "I think the renovations are almost done, but I have a hard time understanding the French contractors on the phone. I'm going to send you their contact info. I'm sure you can handle it from here."

"I, uh, don't know what to say," I stammer. "Thank you." He bought me that flat in Paris? Jesus. I wasn't even serious when I said I wanted it.

Later that night, after hours of sex, Blake is showering and I'm sitting in the living room with the back windows wide open, having a cigarette. I'm thinking about his gift. The flat in Paris. It's supposed to be some grand romantic gesture—more than he's done for me in years. But I know Blake. He's not doing it because he loves me and he's sorry for everything he's been putting me through. He bought it to entertain me. He thinks I need a project. Something to keep me busy, like decorating a newly renovated 5,000-square-foot flat, instead of obsessing over the family next door. Hannah texting him about my behavior must have really freaked him out. He didn't tell me she messaged him, but I snooped on his phone and saw the conversation. How did she even get his phone number?

No matter.

If Blake wants me to go to Paris, I guess I'll go.

After he leaves the next morning, I spend a few days going back and forth with the contractors over the phone. They said the flat is move-in ready.

I peek out the windows, looking across the way at Hannah's house. I'm going to miss her and the twins, but since everything has gone sideways, moving to Paris is probably the best thing I can do. After that debacle when she returned from Iowa and caught me having a glass of wine at her house, when I'd told her I was moving to the UK, there is nothing I can do to fix it.

I did feel bad—it really was my intention to leave.

But fucking Blake. He forbade it. That was my first mistake, telling him my plans to leave. I should have just left and asked for forgiveness later. He was such a dick about it too—

why didn't he just tell me it was because he'd bought the flat in Paris and that's where he wanted me to go? He's always so secretive, it drives me crazy.

Buzz.

It's Blake.

"Good morning," I answer.

"When do you leave?"

"I don't know, a few weeks." I walk over to pour myself another cup of tea.

"No. Leave tomorrow. And, Sophia, get some new clothes— you're not doing that new look of yours justice. I mean, what are you, some American housewife? I was honestly a little disappointed in your appearance the other day." He hangs up.

My blood pressure rises. I look around nervously. Did he really just say that to me? I look down at myself. I'm in a pair of sweats and a baggy off-the-shoulder sweatshirt. It's comfy—I'd planned on snuggling up on the couch with a new novel all day. But apparently not. Apparently I need to turn up the volume on my looks and get on a plane to Paris tomorrow.

Why do I do this to myself?

Let him dictate the kind of woman I'm allowed to be?

I glance at my Joan Miró painting and think about my sister, Lauren... She never would have let a man treat her the way Blake treats me. She demanded respect. Maybe that's why she was better than me.

Or maybe that's why she's dead.

Tears stream down my face. My limbs feel heavy, the weight of all the bad decisions I've made over the years bearing down on me. I collapse in a heap on the floor, allowing myself a few minutes to let the darkness in.

I wish I could call Hannah.

She always knows how to pull me up when I start spiraling into a depressive state. But since calling her is out of the question, I decide to call her friend Sinclair. The only person I know who can help me right now.

THIRTY

HANNAH

"Oh, the drama." Sinclair says. His forehead is Botox frozen, so I can't tell if there should be worry lines cut into his features. His text was vague, wanting to know if I was home alone and if so, whether he and Jamie could come over for dinner. He even said they'd bring the food. Who was I to refuse a visit from my best gays and a delicious meal?

"Well, hello to you too." I lean in and give him a kiss on each cheek, then I open the front door all the way for him and Jamie to waltz inside. They've come bearing Italian food, a bouquet of flowers, wine, and what I assume is—*gossip*.

"Girl, you are gonna freak out when I tell you what happened today." Sinclair heads right for the kitchen and begins puttering around, getting out plates, wine glasses, and a vase.

"Babe." Jamie smacks him on the arm. "You said we'd feed her first, before you fill her pretty head up with all this nonsense."

"What do you think I'm doing?" He's scavenging around, opening drawers and closing them.

"Looking for this?" I hand him the corkscrew.

He winks at me, then quickly tackles the cork and fills our glasses. The twins are passed out in my bed upstairs. I let them run around the mall all afternoon, then I fed them Happy Meals.

Jamie's finished with the flowers and moved on to plating the food. It smells amazing. "Should we eat in the dining room?" he asks.

"Nah, let's just hang out here." I sit on one of the barstools at the kitchen island. I don't want to stare out the dining room windows at Sophia's house. Even if I can't see her, I know she's in there and it makes my blood boil.

"Okay, take a bite so I can say I let you eat first." Sinclair hands me a fork.

I roll my eyes but oblige, taking a big bite of eggplant parmesan. It melts in my mouth. I hope whatever story he has isn't the kind that ruins an appetite. Because man, this is delicious. I sip my wine, then quickly take two more bites to satisfy my friends and my stomach.

"I'm dying—just tell me the news."

I've lifted up the fork to take another bite when Sinclair exclaims, "You will never guess who came into the store today and wanted me to dress them."

My hand trembles and I set the fork back on the plate without eating. There could only be two people Sinclair would be this amped up about coming into the store. Either it was his celebrity crush, Ryan Reynolds—or it was *Sophia Carter*.

After the immediate shock of learning Sophia went to Sinclair for fashion advice wears off and my head clears, I'm able to speak again. "Tell me everything. Start at the beginning."

"Okay, well, I was busy with a client and Jamie took the call," Sinclair says.

"She said she was referred to Sinclair by her husband. Which I didn't question; Sinclair dresses a lot of men in town." Jamie is animated when he talks, waving his hands around. "First, I offered her an appointment in a few weeks. But she said no, it was an emergency, it had to be today because she's getting on a plane tomorrow morning."

"But you've never dressed Blake Carter, have you?" I interrupt.

"No. But we didn't know who she was yet, so the husband was irrelevant," Sinclair says.

"Anyway, she said she needed couture and her budget was limitless. So I told her to come in and we'd make it work," Jamie says.

"Oh, Hannah, you should have seen her when she arrived. Frazzled. She looked like she hadn't washed her hair in days. Big dark sunglasses, baggy clothes. I was worried she was a vagrant!"

"Which is why I asked for her card before we started." Jamie smiles. "Amex Black. And that's when I saw her name—Sophia Carter."

"With the hair up and sunglasses, I didn't recognize her, but once I got a good look at her face—I knew it was the same Sophia that's been stalking you. It was the woman I met at the bar. Her face, it's uncanny." Sinclair shakes his head and tops up each of our glasses of wine.

I'm thankful Jamie made me eat something before this conversation started.

Because I have in fact lost my appetite.

There's no way this is a coincidence. Sophia using my personal shopper. The same man she met at the bar when she was debuting her new look, *as me.*

"She had to recognize you, Sinclair."

"She didn't let on if she had," he says and clucks. "And in the name of professional clothiers, I did not reveal that I knew her identity."

"He was so professional—you should have seen him," Jamie nods in agreement.

"God, she is such a sneaky bitch. I hate that she ambushed you like that."

"Yes, but this is good news, babes. Maybe now she'll leave once and for all—she'll fly off and meet up with her man, in her new wardrobe, and have no reason to return."

I've been texting with Sinclair and Jamie to keep them up to speed on the drama. But I didn't tell them my latest revelation, that

I found Blake's phone number on a scanned receipt on my husband's computer. I also might not have told them about walking in on Sophia and Court the day we returned from Iowa. Until I know for sure if something is going on between them, I don't want to go accusing my husband of having an affair all over town. Telling Cassie is one thing. Telling my two catty gay friends is something else entirely...

So maybe I haven't kept them up to speed on all the drama.

I do appreciate the info, even if I can't tell them I'm probably the reason why Sophia is about to see her husband. My text with Blake must have left an impression. Why else would he be in such a huge rush to see her?

"Well, I hope you didn't dress her in anything that I own," I say. It's about the only thing I can say.

"Lord, no!" Sinclair exclaims. "But... I, uh, well..." He pauses.

"You don't have to say it. I know you were being professional. I'm sure she looked—" I stop myself from saying *fabulous*. Even though that's probably exactly what Sophia looked like when she left. "I'm sure she looked lovely when you were done with her." I reach my hand across the island, and he takes it and squeezes and nods once with a grateful smile. "And if I know you, you called Kenlie to give her a blowout."

"Well, I couldn't let her walk out looking like a hot mess. I fucking burned those baggy clothes," he exclaims.

Jamie leans toward me and whispers, "Not really, but I did put them in the trash."

"So, did she say where she was going on this spur-of-the-moment, need-a-new-wardrobe vacation? Or how long she'd be gone? Did she make any phone calls? Or texts?"

"Honey, I can't tell you that. It would break client-clothier confidentiality," Sinclair says with a straight face.

I look at him, then at Jamie, then back at Sinclair, and all three of us burst out laughing until tears are streaming down our cheeks. I get up and go pick out another bottle of wine from Court's collection—choosing one I know costs a small fortune and will give him a coronary when he sees it's gone.

According to Sinclair, Sophia was on her phone, mostly texting, sometimes speaking in hushed tones while he was putting looks together... "But I did hear her arguing with someone in Paris. Sounds like she's buying an apartment there—but it's not ready, so she has to stay at a hotel. She was pretty aggravated," he says.

"Hmmm... Paris, huh?" As long as it's far away from Florida, I don't care where she goes. It's just too bad it's one of my favorite cities.

After another few hours of wine, laughter, and gossip with Sinclair and Jamie, my friends depart for the night in an Uber—leaving their car in the driveway to pick up tomorrow. I'm glad they came over and we could spend some time together. I seriously contemplated telling them about finding Court and Sophia together in their swimsuits and everything else that's happened, but I thought it might ruin the evening. I'd just end up crying and they'd try and console me or try and pack my suitcases for me—telling me I'm too good for Court. It would turn into a whole thing.

Instead, I chose to just have fun.

I honestly can't believe we didn't wake up the twins, who are still asleep in my room when I creep upstairs to go to bed. Thankfully there's plenty of room in the bed, and I crawl in and snuggle up next to my babies.

"No matter what happens, at least I have you," I whisper before closing my eyes and falling into a heavy, wine-soaked sleep.

THIRTY-ONE

I have a strange text message from Court when I wake up.

Did you have fun last night?

As far as he knows, I was home alone with the kids, like I always am. He doesn't know Sinclair and Jamie were here and that we drank a bottle of his expensive wine and gossiped like schoolgirls. And maybe I'll keep it that way. Maybe I won't respond to him at all.

I look out the window while I'm making coffee. I wonder if Sophia has already left for the airport. Sinclair thought she said her flight was early. So I hop on my computer to see what time the international flights to Paris are leaving from the airport—a flight that long, she wouldn't be taking private. But as soon as I log on, I panic. Wrong computer. I need to set up my new one—and use a secure internet connection. One my husband isn't secretly monitoring.

The burner phone I bought is going to come in handy—I'll set it up and use it as a personal hotspot to connect my new computer to the internet. It takes me thirty minutes to get them both up and running. There's a sense of freedom and relief at being able to search for things online with privacy. Something I'd taken for granted before.

Armed with my trusty notebook, I start making a checklist of things to search about Sophia, with tidy little squares I can check off as I go.

- Flight
- Website
- Social accounts

Looking back at the previous pages of my notebook, I feel guilty that I haven't been keeping up with my regular routine. Checking analytics. Responding to comments. Checking my influencer contracts. If it wasn't for my pre-scheduled posts, my social page would have gone dark weeks ago. Not to mention, I can't remember the last time I checked my bank account.

But I don't have time for all that right now. I have to uncover the truth about Sophia and my husband. First things first. Did Sophia get on a flight to Paris this morning?

Hmmm… No direct flights from the small international Fort Meyers airport to Paris. So maybe she took a private plane to Miami and caught the Paris flight from there. There's one way to find out.

"Hello, Sunshine Charter," the man on the other line answers.

"Good morning, sir." I turn on the charm. "I was hoping you could help me out with something."

"I'll try. How can I be of service?"

"Well, aren't you a doll? I was just talking to my best friend Sophia, before she got on her plane to Paris in Miami. And see, she realized her Louis sunglasses were missing, must have left them on her charter flight this morning. I told her not to worry, I'd call and see if y'all found them."

"Sure, I can check. You said this morning?"

I can hear him clicking on computer keys.

"Yes, sir."

"Okay, yes, we flew Sophia McMillian to Miami. If you hold on for a second, I can radio the pilot and see if he found her sunglasses."

My jaw is on the floor.

Did he say *Sophia McMillian?*

"Thank you," I squeak. As soon as he puts me on hold, I hang up. I cannot believe that bitch used my last name to check into her flight. What a complete cunt.

I take a few deep breaths. Reminding myself this was what I wanted. To uncover what's really going on. I check the flight box off on my list, then I move on to the next item. Website. If Sophia really is an art broker to the ultra-wealthy, and if that's how she met my husband ten years ago while brokering a deal between her husband and mine—I should be able to find something about her online. Even if she doesn't have her own website, maybe she's connected to a big firm. Like Sotheby's.

I search as many keywords as I can using her first and last name, but I keep coming up empty handed. So I check Sotheby's website and scroll through their listing of employees. I don't find Sophia, but it doesn't mean she doesn't have mutuals there. I decide to call and poke around, choosing a broker that's been with them for twelve years. I give myself a minute to think up a cover story before dialing the international number.

"Hello, this is Kate," the woman answers.

"Hi, Kate. I have a strange question about a piece of art I'd like to sell—and I was hoping you might be able to help me."

"My client list is rather full at the moment, but if you want to ask, I'll let you know if I can be of any assistance," she says. "First, may I have your name and contact information?"

"I'd prefer to keep this anonymous for now. I'm going through a divorce. And, well, the painting was a gift from my husband. I don't have a receipt, but I know the name of the broker at Sotheby's who sold it to him ten years ago. I assume you keep records of those kinds of things?"

"We do. And this is actually a very common question. Typically in divorce cases, you'll receive paperwork indicating you were awarded the painting. We will accept that as proof of ownership if you're looking to put the piece up for auction with our firm," she explains.

"Okay, wonderful. So knowing Sophia Carter sold it to my husband makes no difference to you?" I throw out her name, just to see if I can get a reaction.

"Hmmm... Sophia Carter. Now there's a name I haven't heard in a while."

I have to keep myself from squealing.

"Do you mind me asking what painting she sold your husband?" she asks.

Shit. I scramble. I have to play this right. *Think*, dammit—then I recall something Sophia said the day she moved in about a priceless piece of art.

"It's a Joan Miró. Not my taste, but worth quite a lot," I say.

Kate gasps on the other end. "Oh. Um. Yes, well..."

Now I've caught her off guard. I have so many questions I want to ask this woman, but I'm afraid I'll ask the wrong one and tip her off that I'm not just some greedy divorcée trying to sell off my share of the settlement for cash.

Better to end the call now. "Thanks for your time. I'll be sure to call you back once I get the divorce papers. You can sell this ugly piece of shit for me."

"Yes, yes, I'd be happy to. I wonder if... No..." She pauses.

"You wonder if what? It's in perfect condition," I assure her, even though I have no idea. I feel caught in defense of my own lie.

"Oh, I'm sure. I was just wondering if I should reach out to Sophia to see if she has any interest in buying the piece back herself. She must have sold it to your husband after her husband died. Although, I don't know why, it was always her favorite..." Kate's voice trails off.

Shit.

I hang up.

My hand is shaking.

Sophia's husband is dead? But how can that be? Not only is he alive, because I've texted with him, but Sophia's on a flight to Paris to meet up with him. What the fuck is going on? I get back on Google and start searching—trying every combination of names and places I can, to figure out what's happening.

But it's like the internet has been wiped clean of any records of Sophia Carter, art broker, wife of Blake Carter, billionaire financial real estate mogul who may or may not be dead. Then I search for Blake Carter. Nothing. Next I try Court McMillian to see if I can find anything about my husband online. Nadda. Hmmm... I search for myself. A million results pull up on the screen. My social pages, affiliate links, brands I represent, articles and interviews I've done. Stuff going back to college. I even find a picture of me and Cassie at some "Save the Whales" rally we went to during our sophomore year.

I'm starting to feel like I'm going crazy.

Do I need to hire a private investigator to uncover the truth about Sophia and Blake? Who are they really? Why do they have this connection to my husband? Is Blake dead or alive?

Maybe Sophia had another husband who really did die, and she married Blake right afterwards.

Sophia McMillian.

The man at Sunshine Charter said Sophia McMillian traveled with them this morning. Not Sophia Carter. What if...

So I Google "Sophia McMillian" and scroll through pages of random people, hoping and praying to find something. But by page six of the feed, I'm still coming up empty handed and feeling like this is useless. Until I spot a backlink on an art gallery's website, to a social profile for a woman named Sophia McMillian.

Click.

The page opens up to an old profile that looks like it hasn't been used in at least five or six years. I scroll down. It's mostly images of art, statues, and a few food shots. Just like Sophia's current social page. But I keep scrolling, hoping to find something to identify this page as my neighbor... That's when I come across a picture of Sophia, the way she used to look before she colored her hair and had a nose job. Standing next to her in the picture is her husband. He's got his arm around her waist and he's holding up a drink with a little umbrella in the other hand. The caption says:

Happy wife, happy life—Blake took me to Fiji!

I gag.

The man in the picture with her is not the mysterious Blake Carter.

The handsome, fit, older man is the same man I've shared my life and bed with for the last five years. I'm staring at a picture of my husband.

Court McMillian.

Sophia's voice echoes in my head. *Blake has a second wife and a family.*

Oh my god, oh my god. I'm going to be sick. I leap up from the table and barely make it to the kitchen sink before all my coffee comes rushing up in a burning, acidic mess.

"Mommy!" Rowen screams and rushes to my side.

My stomach roils when I hear his little voice and I puke again.

How could Court do this to me?

How could Sophia?

What kind of sick, twisted game are they playing? I splash some cold water on my face, and Rowen hands me a dish towel.

"Here, Mommy," he says. "Please don't be sick again."

I dry my face, force a smile, and ruffle his hair. "I'm okay, RoRo, sorry to scare you."

Ruby wanders in carrying a blankie and stuffie, her hair in a big matted tuft on one side. "What's the matter?" she asks.

What's the matter is their dad is a lying piece of shit.

"How would you kids like to go back to Aunt Tippy's farm?" I ask. There's no way in hell I'm staying in this house for one second longer than I have to. Court or Blake or whatever the fuck his name is might come back at any moment—and I really don't want my kids to witness what will happen when he does.

"YAY!" they both shout at the same time.

"Good. Why don't you go watch *Bluey* and I'll fix you some pancakes. Then I'll start packing."

THIRTY-TWO

My brain is moving at a thousand miles per minute trying to piece the Sophia-Court puzzle together as I throw clothes in my suitcase. But like solving any difficult puzzle, sometimes it's best to start at the beginning... And the truth is, in the beginning, while I was busy sizing up Court and seducing him to be part of my perfect life fantasy—he was the one luring me into his own dark and twisted web.

And if he was willing to do that, build our marriage on lies, have children and raise them on lies... What else is he capable of? Clearly nothing is off limits with this man.

I can hardly see straight as I head for the twins' room. I start throwing clothes in their bag, but I'm overwhelmed, my heart's beating irregularly, and I fall to my knees. I bury my face in my hands.

"What am I going to do?" I sob. If Court and I have to share custody, then what? Am I supposed to sit back and watch as he takes my kids to Sophia's house? Is that where he'd live if I kicked him out? And what about when he has business trips? What about custody then?

"No!" I gasp, realizing something. What if all of his business trips aren't really business trips? What if he's going home to other families? Maybe Sophia isn't the only other wife he has. Court could be using a dozen aliases, all of which he's been able to hide from me, by wiping his digital footprint clean.

Suddenly everything makes sense. The reason why he won't let me post pictures of him online. The reason I can't share his name on my social page. The reason we don't have a nanny or a housekeeper. It's not because he doesn't want those things. It's because he's afraid someone might find him. Not a business rival—*one of his other wives*.

I'll be damned if I'm going to let him have joint custody of my kids. He'll have zero custody. And instead of Court hiding his identity and whereabouts, it will be me.

As of today, right now, my trad wife influencer brand is officially dead. I'm going to take my kids and go off-grid.

It seems like a perfect plan, until I do some research.

Taking children away from a biological parent, even during a divorce, is considered kidnapping. Now, if Court had been abusing me or the twins, I could file for a temporary restraining order as part of the divorce. Giving me custody during the proceedings. But —he's never laid a finger on any of us, and emotional abuse seems much harder to prove. Especially because all of the evidence I have right now is extremely shaky.

Not to mention, my husband has billions of dollars.

He can and will hire the best attorney money can buy. Plus, he could pay off anyone willing to speak on my behalf and make any digital evidence disappear. It will be his word against mine in front of a judge. And what if Court or his attorney decide to go digging into my past? It would only make sense, if I'm accusing him of these heinous acts, that he would try and find something to lord over me.

And if he uncovers the secret I've been carrying around for the last twelve years, not only will I lose custody of Rowen and Ruby, but I could go to prison for the rest of my life for what I did.

Hannah Price, how come you look so sad? Matt's voice rings out in my head.

Tears streak hot down my cheeks and I grit my teeth and put my hands over my ears to block out the voice in my head. He always shows up at the most inopportune times. I need to focus on figuring out a way out of this mess with my husband, not relive the worst day of my life with Matt.

"Go away, Matt," I hiss at his ghost.

But, Hannah, I love you, please don't shut me out, Matt says.

"If you loved me so much, you wouldn't have made us go to that party. You wouldn't have put me in this position."

Aw, come on, you're not still mad about that, are you? His voice slurs, just like it did that night.

"Well... look what happened."

You killed me.

THIRTY-THREE
HANNAH

Seventeen years old

"What'd your Aunt Tippy say? Can you go to the party tonight?" Matt asks as we get in line. The auditorium is so loud on the other side of the heavy red stage curtain, I can barely hear him.

"Yeah, she said I can go," I tell Matt, even though I don't really want to go to another drunken bonfire. I want to go home and finish packing, which is what I told him earlier. But look at him, he's so excited—how can I say no? I give him a kiss. "You better go find your spot in line or you won't get your diploma."

"Maybe I want to get mine with you." He puts his arm around my blue commencement-gown-clad shoulder. Then he reaches up and grabs my yellow tassel. "So I can move your tassel for you."

I smack his hand away before he can move it.

"Matt, go!" I yell at him and point toward the front of the line.

"Fine." He gives me big puppy dog eyes before he finds his spot. I watch as he high-fives and fist-bumps everyone around him.

"I can't believe you're gonna leave him here," Vanessa Princeton leans in and whispers. She's standing behind me, since we are lined up alphabetically.

"What's that supposed to mean?" I turn around to ask.

"You're going off to college, and four years is a long time. Aren't you scared someone's gonna steal him from you?" She wags her eyebrows at me.

"God, Vanessa. No. I mean, sure I've thought about it once or twice. But Matt would never cheat on me."

She scoffs at that. "He's a man. That's just what they do."

I roll my eyes. Like Vanessa knows anything. Matt would never do anything to hurt me. He knows I'm gonna come back to see him as often as I can. And once I graduate, we are getting married and building the kind of life we both always wanted growing up. I can picture it in my mind: our perfect house, our perfect kids. No deadbeat moms, drunken dads, grinding day in, day out for peanuts.

Thankfully the graduation music starts, saving me from having to explain myself any further to Vanessa.

After the ceremony is over, and Aunt Tippy and Uncle Fran give me flowers and a hug and take more pictures of me than they have the entire time I've lived with them, I take off my gown and smooth out my yellow dress. June nights in Iowa are balmy.

"You ready to party?" Matt asks as he strolls up behind me. He jingles the keys to a car. "Dad let me borrow the Firebird tonight. Yeeee-haw!" he shouts.

"Really, why?"

"Why'd he let me borrow the bird? Probably because I just graduated," Matt replies.

"Noooo." I laugh. "Why the *yee-haw*? Please don't turn into a hillbilly after I'm gone. Just because we grew up in the country, doesn't mean we have to—"

"Oh, Hannah." He kisses me mid-sentence. "Have some fun, babe. You know I was joking." Matt unlocks the car door for me and opens it, bowing with a sweeping gesture. "Ladies first."

He drives like a maniac, singing along with Rascal Flatts, all the way to Grady Donelly's bonfire party. The field is packed with cars when we arrive. Looks like the entire school is here.

"Matt, lay off the booze! You promised we'd go shopping tomorrow morning for the room organizers I need," I chastise, watching him tilt a silver flask up to his lips while he's driving around, trying to find a spot to park in the field.

"I know you're a big-time college woman now, but this is our last night to be wild and free. After tonight, we aren't kids anymore."

We get out of his dad's car and start walking in the tall grass toward the bonfire in the distance. I lace my fingers through his. Vanessa's warning rings in my head—about someone trying to steal him from me. If I'm too hard on Matt tonight, I might push him into the arms of someone else. I take a deep breath.

"You're right. Tonight we should just have fun. We can grow up tomorrow."

"Atta girl." He throws his arms around me, spins me. "Yee-haw!"

I laugh and give him a kiss when he sets me down. "I love you, you big goof."

"I love you more, Hannah Price!" he shouts into the air. Then he gallops like a wild horse toward the group of guys standing around a beer keg and shouts, "KEG STAND!"

Oh boy, this is gonna be a long night.

But I'll try my best to have fun.

"Matt!" I scream at the top of my lungs, standing up on wobbly legs. I look around the field where I've been ejected from the car. I spot Matt slumped in the driver's seat and limp forward, leaning on the open door, trying to make sense of what happened. Blood gushes from a huge gash on the side of his head. "What are you doing? Get out."

He was so drunk, there was no way I'd let him drive us home.

So why is he in the driver's seat?

It was me. I *know* I was driving.

"Matt, stop fucking around, there's smoke." I grab his arm and tug. He's not responding. He's probably got a concussion and he reeks like booze.

"Fuck, fuck, fuck!" I don't know what to do. I look around for my cell phone to call for help, but I don't see it anywhere.

I should have been paying more attention to the road—instead, I was kissing Matt. I'm such an idiot. Who kisses like that while they're driving? But I was trying to be "Fun Hannah" and prove to Matt that I'm the only girl for him. I never even saw the deer. The front of the Firebird clipped it and spun the car in a full 360, and we ended up smashing into a tree and careening into a ditch—that's when I flew out of the car. I can't believe I'm not hurt.

Matt groans and blood bubbles out of his mouth. "Say it was me," he chokes out.

"What? No!" I shake him. But his eyes roll into the back of his head. "Stay with me, Matt, I love you, stay with me."

I try and pull him from the car. But his body is dead weight. I'm used to hauling bales of hay in the barn with Uncle Fran—this should be easy. Noxious black smoke pours out of the car's front end. I tug and jerk, trying to get him away from the car in case it catches on fire, but my arms feel like Jell-O and I can't get him more than a few feet from the driver's seat.

"I love you, Matt, I'm so sorry..." I stroke his face and wipe the blood from his hair. His breathing is labored at best. I don't know what else to do but hold him and tell him I love him. Tears stream down my cheeks and puddle on his face, mixing with the blood and bits of glass. I rock back and forth in a panic.

I sob, calling out his name, over and over, begging him not to leave me.

They said I was in shock when they found us an hour later. My voice gone from screaming. Matt lying dead in my lap. But I didn't understand. He was breathing—*he's breathing, stop, what are you doing? He's alive!*

They said I was so brave for trying to pull him out of the wreckage. They said I was stupid for getting into a car with a drunk driver—I could be dead.

Just like Matt.

Every time I opened my mouth to say I was the one driving, the words came out as mumbles no one could hear. They weren't listening! They kept talking over me. The EMT, the police, the doctors, Aunt Tippy... and then Matt's dad, Tom. He hugged me and told me how sorry he was that Matt almost killed me too. And how grateful he was I pulled Matt from the car so they could have a funeral with a body.

What was I supposed to do?

His funeral was a week later. I wanted to stand in the back and hide. In case someone stood up and pointed at me and yelled, "It was Hannah! Hannah was the one driving. She killed Matt." Instead, I marched to the front of the room and sat next to Matt's cousins and aunts, and I cried for the pain I'd caused all these people. I cried because I was a liar.

But most of all I cried because Matt offered to take the fall.

I don't know what was going through his mind.

Aunt Tippy loaded me and my boxes in the farm truck the next morning before sunrise and drove me to Iowa State. All I wanted to do was crawl into my bed and rot—but then what would the lie about Matt be for? If I was going to carry this terrible secret around with me for the rest of my life, I had to make it a secret worth keeping. I had to make sure my life was worth something. A way to honor Matt.

What was a life worth, anyhow?

A million dollars?

A billion?

THIRTY-FOUR

Present day

I'm sitting on the edge of my bed with half-filled suitcases around me. Since I've come to the realization that I can't take my kids and go off-grid, I need to come up with a new plan and fast.

"Come on, there's got to be something," I say to my phone screen as I scroll through online message boards of women going through divorces in Florida. "Anything! Someone's got to know how to get rid of a lying, cheating prick like Court."

That's when I see a message thread called "Moral Fitness". I click on it and start reading. Page after page of helpful tips from women who were able to prove to the judge that their ex-husbands did not have the moral fitness needed to raise children. Gambling. Drugs. Police records. The list of items goes on. I know Court isn't exactly some drug-dealing criminal, but he has lied about who he is! He has another wife. And if he was willing to do that, to me, what else has he been willing to do? Maybe he really is a criminal mastermind. Maybe all his business trips are to drug factories. I just don't know!

But I do know that if I can get some solid evidence to show a judge that my husband isn't really who he says he is. Proof of his lies. It should be enough to show his moral fitness has been compromised. That's the only chance in hell I've got to get full custody of the twins.

It's not going to be easy.

I've spent the last five years living with Court and I had no idea he wasn't who he said he was. I feel sick again. I have no idea how I can get my hands on hard evidence. I get up and pace around—pausing to look at the pictures of me and Court hanging on our bedroom wall.

"Why did you do this to me?" I ask one of the photographs. It's breaking my heart to see the way Court is looking at me there—with what I thought was complete adoration. It was our first trip together, a little weekend jaunt to Mexico.

But the truth is, that look isn't love.

It's something sick and sinister. Because while he was looking at me like that, there was still another woman in his life—Sophia. *Because they never split up...* She told me the truth when we had our day of beauty, lying on my bed. Sophia said she couldn't have children, so she basically gave him permission to go off and start a new family. What does that make me—their fucking broodmare?

I rip the frame off the wall. "You're a greedy, selfish asshole," I say to his image. I'm ready to smash the frame and burn the picture. Destroy any evidence that Court and I were ever together, purge him from my life. But wait—that gives me an idea. What if I take pictures of Court with Sophia? That could be the evidence against them I need!

Then I groan when I really start thinking about it. The likelihood of catching them together again is one in never million. The only reason I caught them this time was because they didn't know I was coming home. I snuck up on them.

However... if I could orchestrate a time and place for Court and Sophia to be together, then I could follow them, like a private eye. I just wish I could find out if Sophia was really in Paris. That would be the perfect place for a stakeout—far away from the twins, who I'll leave with Aunt Tippy on the farm. And I know Paris better than any other big city in the world. I was so enamored by the famed "City of Light" after Court proposed to me under the glittering Eiffel Tower, that I spent months obsessing over it.

That's when I realize.

I *do* have a way to find out if Sophia's in Paris.

> Hey, can you do me a huge favor?

Who is this?

> It's Hannah. New number.

How do I know this is you and not your lookalike?

The phone rings once, twice, three times before he finally answers. "I promise, it's really me," I say when he picks up the line.

"Girl, you had me scared for a minute." He laughs nervously.

"So, about that favor... Can you get ahold of Sophia and say you have a new dress she'll love and you'd like to send it to her? I need to know where she's staying in Paris."

"What are you up to?" He clucks.

"Nothing. I just need to know..." Then I think of something. If I want to sneak around Paris and go unseen, I'm going to have to change my look. And who better to help me out than my personal stylist? "Sin*clair*..." I exaggerate his name. "Have I told you how amazing you are?"

He scoffs. "Why are you buttering me up? What else do you need?"

"Well, since you asked, it would be a huge help if you could send some clothes to Paris for me."

"Honey, you aren't going to confront Sophia on foreign soil, are you? Look, the girl has problems, but please don't do anything you'll regret. You're not cut out for international jail."

If he only knew what I've discovered about Sophia and Court, he'd be singing a different tune. But I can't tell him anything. Or Cassie, for that matter. I cannot involve my friends in what I'm about to do—in case things go sideways. Plausible deniability.

"Will you help me or not?"

"I just worry—"

"I'm not asking for anything crazy. Just basic French clothes. I have to look like a local, not a tourist. I'm traveling light and won't have time to shop."

He lets out a long sigh.

I know he wants to tell me I'm being stupid and reckless—and maybe I am. But what else am I supposed to do? Post about Court's behavior on my social page for the entire world to see? He'd sue me for defamation and probably still get joint custody. Or do nothing, and just keep living my life with my head in the sand as his happy little trad wife? I'm already sick from the stress... If I let my husband keep playing this twisted game, *it will kill me.*

"Please, Sinclair, I need your help."

"Fine. Text me the address. I'll make sure you look très boring," he concedes to my request. "And as soon as I hear from Sophia, I'll let you know."

"Thank you."

"And girl, be careful."

After bathing the children and putting them to bed early, I finish packing. It's hard, walking around the house, trying to decide if anything is worth saving. Because as far as I'm concerned, once we leave for Iowa, I'm never coming back to this house again. It's a house built on lies. The children's things are the hardest to reconcile abandoning. Thankfully they seem to love the farm—and I'm hoping after some time and shopping to fix up their room, they'll be okay with the fact that they are never coming home again. I know it won't be easy for them to understand their daddy is gone. But someday, when they're grown, I'll tell them what really happened, if they want to know.

I still haven't heard back from Sinclair about the hotel Sophia is staying at in Paris and I'm beginning to wonder if maybe that's not where she went after all. The only thing I really know is that she took a private jet to Miami. She could have gone anywhere in the world.

There's a pit in my stomach.

My entire plan rests on Sophia being in Paris. I can lure Court there, if he isn't already, but I have to know that Sophia is there too.

To keep myself occupied I get online and find a hotel, but I realize that if I book it with my credit card, there will be proof I was in Paris—and I can't tip off Court. Even if I use my influencer bank account, he might have access to it. He was able to turn track location on my phone. I can't put anything past him.

Shit.

How the fuck am I going to manage this?

Maybe I'm just being paranoid. But all it will take is one loose end and he'll know I'm up to something. I really didn't want to do this, but the only person I know with the kind of money I need right now is Cassie.

It's me. Court is stalking my phone. I had to get a burner. Call me.

She calls within seconds.

"Tell me everything now," she demands.

An hour, a bottle of wine, and a box of tissues later, I've told Cassie every single tiny detail of what's been going on since the last time I spoke to her when I was tearing the bathroom apart looking for Viagra.

"Oh, Hannah, honey. Look, I know it's hard right now, but you can get through this," she says in her most comforting voice. "I have people. If you want me to make Court or Blake or whatever the fuck his name is disappear, I can do that."

"No, no, didn't you hear a word I said. Plausible deniability," I sob.

"Babes. You and that bottle of wine just spelled out your entire harebrained plan... and as far as I can tell, the only thing you're guilty of is wanting to take pictures of your lying piece-of-shit husband so you have a chance at getting full custody of my godbabies."

"Uh-huh," I moan.

"You know, you'd make a really bad Bond villain."

I start laugh-crying because she's right. And I don't want to be the villain, I want to be the hero of this story. I want to save my sweet Ruby and Rowen from growing up with a father they will never be able to trust. A man they can never truly know.

"Buuut... female Bond villains are always sexy as hell, so at least you've got that going for you," Cassie says.

"Not sexy enough," I complain.

"Oh please. Your husband is a billionaire narcissist. Even if your pussy was made out of pure gold, he was always going to stray. That's what they do, Hannah."

I whimper and sniffle again.

"Stop crying. I'm going to text you my black card. Whatever you need, it's yours. Use my name everywhere you go, except for customs."

"How do you know this stuff?" I wipe my nose and straighten up.

"Oh, honey, you don't want to know what I've done for the sake of anonymity."

"Someday I do, Cassie. I want to know all the things."

"Well—then someday we'll trade war stories. In the meantime, I hope you know how much I love you and I'm here for you and the twins... Would it make you feel better if I stayed with them in Iowa when you're away?"

It would make me feel better knowing she was there at the farm. But—I can't ask her for her credit card *and* to take care of my kids. Plus, Aunt Tippy might lose her mind if she walked in on Cassie working.

"You're the best. I don't deserve a friend like you. I'll call you when I'm done collecting evidence and you can meet me at the farm. We'll celebrate." I offer up an alternative instead of turning her down outright.

"You've got yourself a date. Now, be a good little trad wife and go post on your social page—it's been dark for thirty-six hours."

"Shit." I was so set earlier on my plan to abandon my influencer life for a life under the radar and off the grid, I've forgotten to keep up appearances. I'm about to log on to my new laptop, when I remember—I should use my other phone and laptop soon or Court might get suspicious, if he's monitoring them.

"I'll wait for your call, love you," Cassie says her goodbye and hangs up.

It's already so late, but in the influencer world that means nothing. Keeping a high-quality algorithm means posting throughout the day and night. I scramble—all the premade content I worked on is used up. I literally have nothing prepared—not to mention the way I'm looking these days is anything but glamorous.

So I run to the kitchen, film a few shots of my hands setting out ingredients, and hack those together with a couple videos I never posted when I was baking cupcakes. I layer it with a voice over— teasing some new cooking concepts I've been working on. Which obviously I haven't, but it will make it look like I've been a busy, little housewife.

Just as I'm about to go to bed, I get a text from Sinclair.

> She's in Paris, staying at the Ritz.

> You're an angel. I'll text you my hotel info tomorrow. I'll be staying under the name Cassie Bronovich.

> Be safe.

When I finally crawl into bed in a worn-off wine daze, I feel like I could sleep for days, but I know I have a million things to do if this is gonna work. What is it they say? No rest for the weary. Or is it the wicked? Either way, I vow to myself a week of bedrest when all of this is over.

My alarm is chirping before my mind has even quieted for the night.

Using Cassie's card and name, I book myself a hotel in Paris across the street from the Ritz. I want to be close to Sophia and Court, but not under-the-same-roof close. Then I text Sinclair the address.

Now, the only thing left to do is guarantee my husband will be there.

"Mommy, you're so pretty," Ruby says. She's come into my bathroom after I've showered, fixed my hair and makeup, and put on a pink sundress.

"Thanks, sweetheart." I smile and boop her on the nose. She giggles and runs off. I gaze at my reflection. It's been a long time since I put this much time and effort into my appearance.

I'm nearly ready to set my trap. I contemplated filming a video to send to Court, but I was worried if the twins heard me speaking, they wouldn't understand the lie.

The lie I intend to tell my husband is cruel.

Not as cruel as the lies he's told me.

But it's the only thing I can think of that will catch Court off guard and force him right into the arms of Sophia in Paris. If he isn't already there.

I attach my phone to the ring-light stand in the kitchen. The room is sunny and bright. Which is what I'm going for. It takes twelve attempts to get the right smile—flirtatious, with a glimmer of tears in my eyes. In my hand, I'm holding up a pregnancy test I've doctored with a pink marker to indicate positive. I came across an old box of them when I was tearing apart the bathroom on the hunt for bottles of Viagra to explain away my husband's sudden sex obsession.

Before I can change my mind, I text Court the picture.

> I was going to wait until you got home, but I'm too excited!

The phone rings. My heart is pounding. It's time to see if I can lie to my husband as well as he's been lying to me.

"You're gonna be a daddy again!" I exclaim as soon as I answer the phone.

"Hannah, I'm in shock. I don't know what to say." His voice sounds both strained and excited.

"Are you happy? Tell me you're happy."

"Yes, of course I'm happy, I just..." He pauses. "I didn't think we were planning on having more children, so this comes as a surprise, is all... How are you feeling? Have you been to the doctor yet? You look incredible—glowing already."

"Thank you, babe." I smile. He bought the lie. Hook, line, and sinker. "No, I haven't gone to the doctor yet. I just found out last night."

"I'll cut the rest of my business trip short to be there with you," he says.

"You would do that for me?"

"Of course, you're my wife. Nothing is more important than being there to support you and our new baby."

If only that was true.

My fist clenches at my side.

"Actually, I have an idea. I want to do a babymoon."

"A baby what?" he asks.

I laugh. "Everyone does it now. It's like a honeymoon. For the soon-to-be mommy and daddy, before the bundle of joy arrives."

"Can't that wait?"

"No, I mean yes, but the twins won't stop begging to go back to the farm, and I'm feeling great right now. You remember the morning sickness I had last time—through most of the pregnancy?"

"I suppose we could go somewhere next month," he hesitantly agrees.

"No. I want to go now. I miss you and I need you. Just me and you. I've got it all worked out—I'll take the kids to the farm, get them settled in for a few days, then we can meet up in Paris. Just like when you proposed. It will be so romantic. Pleeaaase!" I beg.

"Really? Paris?" He sounds surprised.

"Well, we did just have our anniversary... So being in Paris to celebrate this new baby, well, it seems... *perfect*."

"Yes... new baby... Paris... perfect," he mumbles. He doesn't know that I know Sophia is in Paris. Which makes his hesitation all that much sweeter.

"Yay!" I exclaim. "Book us a suite, oooh... or better yet, a château, and send me the reservation. I'll take the twins to Aunt Tippy's house and meet you there."

He exhales before asking, "How long will you need to get them settled before you can meet me here?"

Here.

He said meet me *here*. So that bastard *is* in Paris. I can't let on that I know.

"Hmmm..." I pretend to consider it. "Well, today is Tuesday, so how about I meet you in Paris on Saturday? Does that give you enough time to finish your work and fly out?"

"Oh, um, yes. Well, that sounds doable."

"Twins need me, babe, I'd better run. I love you." I muster all the fake excitement I can.

"I love you too, Hannah." He says it the same way he always does. Until this very moment, I'd never noticed the sadness, verging on contempt, in the way he says it. I always took that tone for sincerity from a man who'd not spent much time with a woman. But now that I know the truth, everything is unraveling.

THIRTY-FIVE

The farm is much the same. It honestly feels like we never left, except for the narrowed look in Aunt Tippy's gaze. She's too smart for her own good and she knows I'm up to something. The twins are out in the barnyard with Frannie, helping him feed the spring calves their bottles, giving me and my aunt some alone time.

I'm sitting on the window seat, clutching a pillow to my chest, staring out over the yard. The daffodils are in full bloom and a mama cat is walking along the edge of the garden with a kitten dangling from her mouth. She's heading for the little garden shed, no doubt moving her brood after our arrival, hoping to keep Ruby from over-loving them.

Aunt Tippy sits on the edge of my bed and faces me. "Are you gonna tell me why you're back so soon?"

"Court's having an affair."

"With that neighbor woman?" she asks.

"No. Not with Sophia—he's been having the affair with me." My voice is flat and emotionless. Aunt Tippy's face contorts as she tries to reconcile my last statement. "Apparently he's been married to Sophia for over ten years... I don't even think Court's his real name."

She doesn't respond and I turn my head to gaze back out the

window, watching as the mama cat exits the garden shed and runs back toward the barn. I wonder how many trips she'll have to take to move all of the kittens.

"Well, what are you gonna do?" Aunt Tippy finally asks.

Tears bubble up and cascade over my lashes. I've really been trying to keep it together, but it's hard.

"Tears ain't gonna help. What's your plan, Hannah?"

I sniffle once, then straighten up. Aunt Tippy is right. Tears won't help this situation. "I'm going to Paris to get hard evidence—that is, if you don't mind me leaving the twins here with you for a while? Otherwise, it's his word against mine when I file for divorce. His lawyers will paint me as a crazy woman."

"Of course they can stay. Do you need money?" she asks.

I look at my old, farm-worn great-aunt. I know she doesn't have money to give me. I'm the one who sends her money to take care of this place.

I shake my head. "Cassie's helping me out for now. I do have my own money, I just can't use it right now—Court's tracking my computer and probably my bank accounts."

She shakes her head. "That man is a snake. And you know what we do with snakes?"

"Cut off their heads?"

"Or stomp the shit out of 'em." She laughs. "Remember that nasty black bullsnake in the bathroom, when you was about twelve or thirteen?"

"Yeah, about gave me a heart attack," I exclaim, remembering the way I jumped. "Slithered up the shower drain when I was brushing my teeth. I went to turn on the shower and there it was, hissing at me."

"And what'd you do?" Her eyes crinkle around the edges.

"I beat it to death with the wire toilet bowl brush," I reply, before I start laughing.

"You've always been tougher than I imagined a pretty thing like you should be. But I suppose with the upbringing you got before you came to Happy Farm, you had to be tough."

Then Aunt Tippy stands up and opens her arms.

I pull my body from the window ledge and wrap my arms around her.

She promises not to tell Uncle Fran. It would only worry him. As far as he knows, the twins are staying for a few weeks because they missed the place. Which is true.

Before I can leave town, I have to set up an alibi. Court thinks I'm staying here the rest of the week to get the twins settled in. The best way to prove that is by posting pictures on my socials to look like I'm here at the farm. With Aunt Tippy's help, I take plenty of pictures. Thankfully, Ruby and Rowen love playing dress-up, so they don't mind changing their clothes five times to capture all the shots I need. Some with dirt on their faces in the garden, planting tomatoes and watering with matching green cans. Next, a few of them laughing while they bottle-feed the calves in the barn. Some with them screaming and running when the chickens chase them from collecting the eggs. Aunt Tippy even gives them a few cooking lessons—rolling biscuits and putting lattice tops on cherry pies.

Once I edit and upload the pictures to auto-post each day, it will look as though I've been here the whole time and not like I'm catching a secret flight to Paris.

The next morning, before anyone else has risen, including the sun, I load into the rental car and hit the road. I left the cell phone and laptop Court is tracking plugged in at Aunt Tippy's house. I'm sure he'll try to text and call me, but I can't worry about that. He has the phone number to the farm. He can call and speak with Aunt Tippy. She's under strict orders to make up every excuse in the book.

Hannah's out in the pasture with Fran.

Hannah and the kids are feeding the chickens.

Hannah's in the shower.

As long as he thinks I'm at the farm, that's all that matters. I'm hoping I can get to Paris and back before the Saturday deadline for our "babymoon" even arrives.

Armed with only the clothes on my back and a few personal items in a backpack, I grip the steering wheel as I merge onto the interstate, hyper-focused for any deer that might try and jump the fences and run out in front of me. I have to fly to Chicago to catch the flight to Paris. But as I approach the tiny single terminal at Sioux City Airport, I begin to panic and almost turn the car around. Sure, I can use Cassie's credit card to book my flight, but I still have to use my own name for the ticket. With Court's money and connections, how long will it take before he figures out I was on one of those small planes?

I put my turn signal on and merge back onto the interstate, opting to drive the hundred miles south to Omaha, where there's a much bigger airport, with hundreds of flights coming and going each day, providing me with a bigger shield. I slide into a deep trance as I drive the long, nearly empty interstate, the sun just starting to peek up over the horizon. Nothing but miles and miles of wide-open fields on either side of the pavement. It's beautiful, but rather than enjoy the morning solitude, all I can do is wonder why the hell Court has done this to me...

THIRTY-SIX
SOPHIA

The shower pressure is perfect in Paris, not like that shit in Florida, like piss dribbling out of the faucet. Here the water is hot, rich, velvety, and the steam envelops me in a misty cocoon. I could literally live in this shower. Eventually, after I've enjoyed the water pressure long enough, I drag the razor blade over my legs, making sure not to miss a single hair. *That's one of his biggest pet peeves.*

Sometimes I imagine scraping the blade over my flesh, peeling it away from the muscle and bone, letting the water run red with my blood, ending this whole preposterous charade. But then I think—what would be the point? I'm sure the devil will be waiting when I die, and since I'm already living in hell, does it really matter? It's all the same when my day of judgment comes... At least here, there's fine art and dry martinis. So I'm careful with the blade. Setting it on the ledge when I finish shaving.

My phone buzzes. Blake.

I'm on my way back to the hotel.

Sometimes I wonder what her text would sound like, if she was the one responding. Bubbly? Cheery? Childlike? It feels fake when I try to imitate her. So I stick with my own voice.

I'm getting dressed.

Don't put clothes on yet. I have some exciting
news on the status of our new apartment. I think
you'll be pleased.

When he's excited, so is his libido. Instead of clothes, I stand naked at the bathroom mirror, apply my makeup, and brush my fake blonde hair. I can't wait for Blake to go back to America so I can color it dark again. Then I open up the closet and choose an outfit for later—something short and tight. I'm sure Blake will want to go out for dinner and drinks after we fuck.

I was so disappointed the flat wasn't ready when I arrived in Paris that I've been in a foul mood for days. Which hasn't gone unnoticed. Blake's been quick to point out that my bedroom performance has been lackluster.

Besides the renovations not being complete, I attribute at least half of my bad mood to nerves. I'm not nervous to be around Blake. I'm just nervous to live with him again. It's been ages since we spent more than four or five days together under the same roof.

I let out a long sigh.

Then I go pour myself a drink and spread my naked body across the bed, waiting for Blake and grumbling over what a mess I've caused. Things were going great for me on my own. My career was flourishing. I had a gorgeous penthouse flat in Beijing, where I could come and go as I pleased. Blake only came to visit a few times a year. It was perfect.

Then my curiosity had to go and get the better of me.

I wish I had never looked her up online.

Hannah Price McMillian. Trad wife superstar. With her gorgeous long blonde hair, and flawless natural American beauty. She looked just like a movie star—an Amanda Seyfried or Jennifer Lawrence type, that beautiful girl next door.

I really had no intention of ever meeting her in real life. But once I started following her, she made me smile with her wholesome approach to being married. She was cute and real and tried so hard. She obviously had no idea she was married to one of the richest men in the world. If she did, there's no way she would have made that entire series on making rainbow ice for mocktails.

Or maybe she did know, and she didn't care. I became obsessed with finding out more and more about Hannah. Reading between each line in the descriptions of her pictures and posts. Scouring the internet for information about her. How did she not know her husband was harboring dark secrets—that he was a monster? The question of whether Hannah knew about Blake gnawed at me, like a splinter under my skin, impossible to ignore. Until I couldn't stand it any longer. I bought the house next door to Blake and Hannah just so I could find out.

Blake wasn't angry when he found out.

He was fucking furious.

He put his fist through the bedroom wall. Then he shoved me on the bed and ripped my clothes off. I screamed at him to stop. I told him he should have thought about my feelings before he put me in this situation. If he didn't want me in his life, all he had to do was say so.

The sound of his belt coming off his waist made me recoil and cry out.

But he didn't care.

He's always been a vile creature. A pervert.

I should have just stayed away, like we agreed six years ago when he came up with this stupid idea of having another wife. One he said he could trust. One that would bear his children.

I look at my phone. It's been twenty minutes since his last text. I wonder what's taking him so long? I get off the bed and go pour myself another drink, wrapping a bathrobe around my body. Then I turn on the TV and snuggle up in the lounge.

Before long, my head is bobbing with sleep, and I lie down to close my eyes. I dream about Blake, what it was like before he left to be with Hannah. We were in the middle of another argument, about having children.

You don't even like children, I argued.

That's not fair, he protested. *Lauren would have wanted me to have more children.*

Don't you dare talk about what Lauren would have wanted. You're such a prick, Blake.

Oh, I'm the prick?

Yeah, you are. Even though I knew I was the reason Lauren was dead. If I hadn't been so jealous of her... She had the perfect husband, the perfect children, the perfect life. She'd always been so fucking perfect. From the day we were born, three minutes apart, to the day we graduated uni. She was always number one, and I was nothing more than the genetic extras in her shadow. Our parents said so. Our classmates and teachers too.

But not Blake.

He was always kind to me.

Leaning on me for comfort whenever he and Lauren were in a fight.

Well, I want more kids. So what do you suggest I do?

I don't know, Blake... Hire a fucking surrogate who will raise the little rat for you. Or better yet, why don't you just fucking leave me and get a new wife? Or are you worried I know too much?

You're belligerent.

I wished he would kill me and be done with it. If I told him I'd had a hysterectomy to guarantee I would never carry his children, I bet he would. Instead, I narrowed my gaze, lowered my voice and said, *Why don't you leave? Move back to America and take a new wife. Become someone else entirely and have a family. I'm releasing you from whatever the fuck this is between us.* I stood up and walked slowly to the wet bar to pour myself a stiff drink.

When you're a billionaire, you can be anything you want. You can be anyone you want. So in a moment of deranged desperation to spread his seed, my husband, Blake Carter, became Court McMillian. And within a few months, after arrangements were made—building up his new persona, creating documents, deeds, IDs, and such—he moved to the States and started his hunt for the future mother of his children. The piece, he claimed, that had been missing from his life—since Lauren died.

I jolt awake when I hear the door to the hotel open. I fling off the robe and run to the bedroom. Doing my best sexy pose on the bed, willing my breasts to look perky and my skin taut and inviting. Trying not to cry. I deserve this. It's my fault Lauren is dead.

"Sophia, where are you?"

I couldn't stand that my sister had the life I wanted.

"In here."

So I seduced her husband.

"I have wonderful news."

I made him fall in love with me.

"I can't wait to hear."

I made him love me so hard that he killed her and their children to be with me.

How could I ever leave him now? Even when he decided to have another family with another woman? What I'd never expected was for Blake to actually love Hannah. For him to find joy in her perfect American embrace. For their whirlwind romance to turn so quickly into marriage and children. Twins, no less.

As if the devil himself was standing next to me with a red-hot poker, jabbing it between my ribs, burning my already black heart.

"Sophia, you'll never guess. First, the apartment is ready. You can move in tomorrow. And the best news of all—Hannah's pregnant again!" he exclaims as he enters the bedroom. He sees my naked body and his eyes light up with feral passion. He unbuckles his belt and slides it off his pants. I tremble. I know he's not going to hit me, not tonight, not when he's this elated. But it's muscle memory and I can't help it.

"It's too bad you freaked Hannah out so much. It would have been nice to have you next door when the new baby arrives. It will be hard for me to get away after it's born." He quickly removes his shirt and comes closer to the bed.

I swallow the lump in my throat.

"Yes, I remember. You only came to see me once the year the twins were born."

He crawls onto the bed, and moves toward me, like a lion, slowly, with hunger in his eyes. My flesh ripples—with fear, with desire, with pain and self-loathing. I wonder if he ever looks at Hannah the way he's looking at me now. He comes at me with his mouth and I turn my head so his lips and teeth can drag across my neck.

I wish more than anything he'd take a bite and rip out my jugular.

So I could lie on the bed, covered in my own blood, while he fucks my lifeless body.

I regret not slitting my wrists in the shower.

THIRTY-SEVEN

HANNAH

"Ahhhh, Ms. Bronovich. Welcome to Paris." The concierge at the hotel greets me. "Your personal belongings arrived last night and are waiting in your room."

"Merci," I reply and accept the plastic key card to get into my room, heading straight for the elevator.

All I want to do is take a shower and grab a nap before I start trying to pinpoint where Court and Sophia might be. I know which hotel—but if I'm going to get pictures of them together, holding hands, kissing, acting like a married couple in love—I'm going to have to find them out there in the city. I can only hope that's what they'll do, because without any evidence of them still being together, Court will somehow spin this entire thing in his favor, he's smart like that. So I have got to nail his ass for being an immoral human.

I swipe the key across the pad and step into my room. It's gorgeous. There's a huge bouquet of fresh flowers on the table, with a card from Cassie that reads:

You're the strongest woman I know. Take this fucker down. I love you XO.

And in the bathroom, there's a giant basket full of personal items—makeup, shampoo, deodorant, everything I might possibly need—with a note from Jamie that reads:

Who says you still can't look fabulous even in your darkest hour?
We love you.

I fall to my knees.

Clutching the two cards to my chest.

I'm not sure I deserve to have friends so amazing. Someday, I will pay them all back for everything they've done for me. But first, I have to get up off this hotel bathroom floor, stop crying, and go on the hunt to find Court and Sophia.

I decide to take a shower and wash the grime of travel off my body. Then I order room service before I crawl into bed and nap for a few hours on a full stomach. I was too amped up on the plane to sleep.

Unfortunately my dreams are fevered. I hear my mom screaming at one of her boyfriends. The screams turn into the sound of metal ripping apart in a car crash. Matt's dead body is in my lap and his beautiful, handsome face decomposes like I'm watching a video sped up. I open my mouth to call for help, but my voice is gone.

I wake up in a cold sweat and have to take another shower to clear my head.

Then I open up the suitcase Sinclair sent. It's everything I might need to look the part of a local woman hitting the town for dinner. There's shoes, undergarments, and simple, elegant clothing.

While I get dressed, I trawl Sophia's social page, hoping to find a clue where she and Court might be. The last time I checked, she hadn't posted anything in a week. But in Paris, there are so many picture-perfect landmarks. How can an art junkie like her walk around the city and not be inspired to take and post a photograph?

But there's nothing new on her social page.

I pace around the hotel room as long as I can, refreshing her page over and over, before I decide to wing it and start walking around the city. I grab the purse Sinclair included in the suitcase, along with a scarf and sunglasses.

Court will want to avoid the places tourists hang out, but Sophia, on the other hand—

she'll want to see the art. So I Google some of the lesser-known museums and look for the ones with Michelin-starred restaurants within walking distance.

I know my husband.

He'll agree to do her art thing, for a quality meal.

Near the first museum, I step into a French bookshop and buy a romance novel. Something a local might be reading at a café. And that's what I do—order a cappuccino and croissant at a small café and sit at one of the outdoor tables. I pretend to read the book, while really gazing at the museum entrance across the street. I'm watching for couples, but it seems to be a lot of tour groups. So maybe this museum isn't far enough off the beaten path.

I look up another museum, one closer to the hotel, then I hail a taxi, rather than walking across the city. As we drive, I watch out the window, looking for people holding hands.

That's when I spot a couple that, from my vantage point, look an awful lot like Court and Sophia.

"Please stop—arrêtez-vous ici, s'il vous plaît," I tell the driver and jump out of the taxi, tossing some paper money at him. Duolingo French lessons for the win.

I look around, right, then left, trying to find the couple I just saw walking by. I spend the next hour walking up and down the same two blocks. Going in and out of the various restaurants and cafés. But no matter where I look, I can't find them. I feel foolish, my head hangs low, and I decide to go back to my hotel room.

As I turn the corner, I hear a familiar laugh, coming from a narrow alley.

It's Sophia.

My heart rate spikes and my eyes dart around in a panic for

someplace to hide. I narrowly duck into a door frame, hidden by the shadows, just as Sophia and Court breeze by.

"See, I told you that little wine and cheese shop was divine. Why don't you ever listen to me?" she says, and laughs. I'm not sure, but something in her tone sounds different, like she's trying too hard to be happy and cute.

I stay in my hiding spot for a few minutes before stepping out and heading back to the main street. I stay close to the edge of the buildings, peering around the side, hoping I haven't lost them. But I can't risk them seeing me. That was too close. I look up and down the street—and spot them getting into a taxi at the end of the block.

Before I can talk myself out of it, I hail a taxi and jump in.

"Follow that taxi!" I yell and point at their vehicle, which is turning right.

"Madame?" The driver questions me.

"Shit. Sorry... Suivez ce taxi," I say. The driver shrugs and drives forward, turning right. I cheer him on for making the correct turn. Then I point again at what I think is Court and Sophia's taxi. When it changes lanes, so does my driver. "Oui! Oui!"

"Ah, tu veux que je les suive," the driver says, understanding my request. For several miles, we follow them. Thankfully, the traffic in Paris is ridiculous, so they never get too far ahead of us, and we blend in with the hundreds of other cabs and cars all seemingly going in the same direction.

When their taxi pulls to the side of the road to drop them off, my driver slows and pulls over a few cars back. He turns his body around and looks at me with a grin. "Like Bond girl," he says in broken English.

"Oui." I laugh, nodding. I stay in the cab for a few minutes and watch out the front window as Court and Sophia run across traffic to the other side of the street. There's a small restaurant with a green awning. The place is packed—the outside tables are filled with couples and friends out having dinner. Sophia and Court go through the main entrance to be seated inside. Now's my chance to get out without being seen.

I thank the driver for his help and give him a large tip.

"Bye, bye, Bond girl," he says and gives me a wink.

I don't immediately run across the street toward the restaurant. Instead, I stand next to a group of locals who are chatting and smoking cigarettes, hoping to blend in with them. I take out my phone to see how far I can zoom from here. But it's not close enough to see what's happening inside the restaurant. Not to mention all the cars driving by—they keep blocking the view.

Several more people have joined up with the smokers and they start moving en masse to cross the street. I stay with their group, using them as a human shield until I'm on the other side. They're heading into the restaurant. But I'm scared if I go in, even with a group of locals, Sophia or Court might see me. So instead, I sneak down the side of the building, pressing my back against the cold stones. There's a window to my right.

Oh my god, I can't believe I'm this close.

I just have to figure out how to see inside the restaurant without looking like some peeping Tom, staring into the windows. I try to loosen up my stance, putting a foot up on the wall and casually leaning, like I'm waiting for friends to arrive. I take out my phone, and hold it up. Maybe if I flip the camera angle I'll be able to see inside the window.

As soon as the screen flips, I squeak and fumble, nearly dropping it.

Sophia and Court are sitting at the table next to the window.

My breathing is labored as I return to the front of the building to make sure they can't see me.

Goddammit. Why is this suddenly so much harder to do in person than it was in my mind? How am I going to get pictures of them? Sweat forms on my brow and palms. People are starting to look at me funny.

"Est-ce que ça va, madame?" A man puts his hand on my shoulder, checking if I'm okay.

I nod and move further down the street, away from the restaurant. If I stay here any longer, I'm bound to get caught. This would be so much easier if I had an accomplice. Someone who could go in and take the pictures for me, because Court and Sophia will recognize me if I walk in there.

I think about that for a few minutes.

They will recognize me... But what if I wasn't the me they are used to seeing?

Sophia's changed her looks to carry on this charade. So why can't I? It's a gamble to leave this restaurant without any evidence at all, considering I might not find them again. But it's a gamble I'm willing to take.

THIRTY-EIGHT

Looking at my reflection in the mirror the next morning is like looking at a different woman. The remnants of last night's extreme makeover are littered all around the bathroom. Scissors. Piles of hair. Empty bottles of temporary hair dye. Plastic gloves. Stained towels. Tubes of lipstick. Open eyeshadow palettes.

The hair is the most drastic change.

From long and blonde, to shoulder length and brown, with heavy bangs. The smoky-eye makeup and red lips help add to my new look. With a pair of fake reading glasses, I've gone from Malibu Barbie to some kind of sassy French librarian. I take a quick selfie, so I can share it with my friends later.

There's something very liberating about changing your entire look.

I'll have the freedom to go into any location and not worry that Sophia or Court will recognize me. As long as I don't get too close.

Before leaving the hotel, I do a quick scan of Sophia's social page, to see if there are any clues about their whereabouts today. Much to my surprise, there's a picture of a historic building some-where in Paris. I don't know the location by the name alone, but a Google search says it's five kilometers away, on the banks of the River Seine near the Eiffel Tower. The caption says:

My new flat. Is this even real life?

That bitch!

She stole my line—from the very first picture I posted to launch my lifestyle brand—I said, *Is this even real life?* Because being with Court felt like such a fairy tale. If I had only known what a nightmare it would turn into...

Heat rises in my face.

Cassie warned me Sophia might try and crawl into my skin.

She's stolen my look, she tried to steal my kids, and apparently my social media is next. I storm out of the hotel and take a taxi to the address of her new apartment. The rage I'm feeling right now has me contemplating something dramatic. Like screaming her name at the top of my lungs until she opens up a window so I know what floor she's on. Then calling Interpol to tell them she's building a bomb or something equally as terrifying. See how she likes tangling with me then.

Instead, I walk over to the tree-lined path along the River Seine, and gaze out over the sparkling water. Taking slow, deep breaths, trying to calm myself...

"You came here to get evidence. Not cause a scene," I remind myself. So I find a nice bench with a view, sit down, and get on my phone, looking for property information, while keeping an eye on who's coming and going, to find out who exactly owns Sophia's new apartment. After paying one hundred euros on a property website, I pull up the sales report. It looks like the entire fourth floor of the building was recently purchased by one Monsieur Court McMillian. He paid a whopping thirty-six million euros for the place. And from the pictures, it was previously split into several smaller apartments. I'm sure he paid the enormous bill for the renovations to transform the multi-flat into Sophia's luxury dream home. I know he didn't spend that much on our family home. Not even a quarter of it. I just can't wrap my head around his thinking.

Well, they can both go fuck themselves. I've done my research. In the state of Florida, marital assets, like property purchased during a marriage, are split equally during a divorce—even with a prenup. So in reality, this apartment isn't Sophia's at all.

It's half mine.

That is, if our marriage is even legal. Ugh! All of this is so frustrating. One minute I feel empowered, and the next I feel completely overwhelmed and stupid. My bottom lip quivers. What the hell am I even doing? Sitting on a bench across the street from Sophia's new apartment. Am I just going to sit here all day, when I should be home, with the twins. Tears well up in my eyes when I think about my kids, the reason I'm here, going through all this hoopla in the first place. I would do anything for them, absolutely anything.

"Alright, pull yourself together, do what you came to do, then you can go home." I wipe the tears, straighten up, and look at my laptop.

I check my social page, so I can see my babies' faces—it looks like the kids and I are having a grand old time at the farm baking pies with Aunt Tippy. Then I check Sophia's page again. She posted another picture—only moments ago. A fresh piece of quiche Lorraine, with two forks taking a scoop from it at the same time. She's tagged the café, and with a quick click on their business page, I discover it's walking distance from here. Just across the bridge heading toward the Champ de Mars park.

I put my laptop in my bag, adjust my fake glasses, and start speed walking, hoping I can catch up with them before they finish eating at the café. Years of chasing Ruby and Rowen has prepared me for this. I'll have to remember to thank Sinclair for sending me sensible ballet flats for daytime wear.

The streets are bustling with tourists, but I still make it to the café in under fifteen minutes. Barely breaking a sweat.

Please, let them still be inside, I beg the universe when I see the blue facade of the café. Small circular tables filled with brunch guests dot the sidewalk out front. I can tell the inside of the café is going to be cramped—there's no way I won't be seen.

"But I'm not me. I'm someone else," I remind myself, my

fingers instinctively reaching up to touch my short dark hair. Why would they pay any attention to some random French woman going in to buy a coffee and croissant?

The bells jingle when I enter, and I get in line with a group of young girls, hoping to blend in. My eyes survey the busy restaurant floor and I spot the happy couple at a table near the back. I don't want to look too obvious, but the savory café air is choking me. I'm certain Paris isn't having an earthquake, but I swear the floor wobbles under my feet.

Get some evidence, my brain screams at me.

"Oh!" I gasp, remembering my mission. I quickly pull my phone from my pocket and start taking as many pictures of Court and Sophia as I can, using the row of girls placing their order in broken French as a barrier. One looks at me and smiles, following my gaze and giggling when she sees I'm staring at and taking pictures of Court.

His hand gently brushing crumbs from Sophia's lips.

Her big, adoring eyes.

Him holding her hand as he helps her from her seat and guides her to the door.

Shit. They're leaving. I turn to chase after them—but the woman at the counter yells something at me in French, which my brain is too scrambled to recognize. I throw some money at her, even though I didn't order anything, then run out of the café.

"Where did you go?" I mumble and scan the street until I catch a glimpse of Court walking around the corner toward the park.

For the next two hours, I follow them. Capturing dozens of incriminating pictures. Kissing, touching, laughing. If I didn't know better, I'd swear Sophia was putting on a performance for a romantic comedy—she's practically *Emily in Paris*, with all of her over-animated expressions and poses.

The Sophia I know is a much more serious woman. But that was the old Sophia. This is the new Sophia—wearing clothes like I might wear, her hair styled just like mine used to be, her facial features eerily like mine. While I, with this new dark hair and smoky makeup, look a lot more like Sophia used to. Oh, the irony.

Is she pretending to be me right now? Is that what this is all about? She thinks I am overly cheery and dramatic, like a character in a top-ten Netflix show? Court seems oblivious. He's only half paying attention to her antics. He keeps getting on his phone, making calls and probably checking emails. He's never been great at being present in the moment...

Regardless, she's doing enough fawning and kissing on him for me to capture more than enough evidence. There's no judge in the world who would call me crazy when they see these pictures. I'm feeling quite smug as I follow the pair back across the bridge and take a final picture of them going into the apartment building together.

That shot is the icing on the cake.

I collapse on the same bench I sat on earlier to look at all the pictures I just took, transferring them from my phone to my computer so I can see them better. My nose crinkles. Ugh. I hope the judge doesn't think that's me with Court, and not Sophia. I zoom in and out. I'm so focused on my screen, I scream when a young woman sits down next to me.

"Excusez-moi!" she exclaims with a panicked look on her face. I laugh and shake my head and try to apologize, putting my computer away. I'd better get back to my hotel—I've got more than enough evidence. I throw a final glance at Sophia's new apartment, when I see someone standing in the window on the fourth floor. I squint—is that Sophia? Yes, I think so. Her face is somber and she's looking right at me.

Then she holds up a sheet of paper and presses it against the glass.

There's a single word written on it.

RUN

I shouldn't let Sophia keep controlling my life. But when someone says "run", you run. My muscles fire as I leap from the bench and start pounding the pavement. I was thankful for the ballet flats earlier, but after spending hours walking and now running, my feet are screaming in pain. Once I'm a few blocks from the apartment, I slow down and flag a taxi.

The driver asks where I'm going. "Où allez?"

I squeak out the hotel address between heavy breaths and a pounding heart. That was probably the weirdest thing—no, no, what am I saying? That's probably the least weird thing to happen to me when it comes to Sophia.

After a terrifying taxi ride, with me craning my neck in circles like an owl, I'm standing in front of my hotel room door. I set my bag down so I can lift my shirt a little to retrieve my key card from the money belt, where I've stashed it alongside my passport. But before I swipe the key, I spot something stuck on the side of my bag. I squat down to look at a small flat white disk.

That's odd. I don't recall my bag having a tag like that.

I use my nail to pick at the side of it and it comes off rather easily—the sticky substance holding it to my bag gets on my fingers as I turn the object over and over in my hands. I'm not one hundred percent certain, but I think this is an AirTag. A kind of tracking beacon.

That girl on the bench must have stuck it to me—and now I've led someone to my exact location. Was that why Sophia was warning me? When did she figure out I was following them? And who exactly am I running from? The only logical conclusion is my husband.

Well, the joke's on you, Court. Track me all you want. I'm still filing for a divorce when I get back to Florida. I have all the evidence I need to prove to a judge I'm not crazy, you are still with Sophia, and you can't be trusted to have custody of our kids.

I hear a noise and glance up. There are two large men in suits walking down the hallway. I stand and look around for other hotel guests. But I'm all alone. The hair on the back of my neck stands up.

Sophia's warning.

RUN

Shit, shit, shit. I fumble with the key card and just as the men reach my location, I swipe it and duck into my room, slamming the door shut behind me and flipping the safety lock. Oh my fucking god. Did Court send these men after me? He's not just tracking me online?

My heart pounds in my ears and I look through the peephole.

"Oh my god, oh my god," I'm chanting. But wait—what's this? They aren't facing my door—they are going into the room across the hallway. I turn around and press my back against the door.

"Pull yourself together," I pant.

But how can I? I slide to the ground, sobbing, and pull my knees up to my chest. I thought Court and I had built something special. I thought I was the one woman he'd met traveling the world, who was finally worthy of the ring on my finger... I look at the diamond and hold my hand up, turning it this way and that. It used to mean everything to me—a symbol of our love. But in my heart I know, the dynasty we were building is over.

Now the only thing that matters is getting home to Rowen and

Ruby. I tug at the ring and it slips off easily, with the weight I've lost from this trauma, and I drop it on the floor. It clangs against the tile as it rolls away.

I've been in Paris for less than forty-eight hours—my favorite city in the world—and after today, I never want to come back. I stand up and take a deep breath. I need to pack and get the fuck out of here.

Knock, knock, knock.

I jump. "Jesus Christ!" I've had about all I can take for one day. I go to the door again and look out the peephole. There is a familiar face on the other side of the door.

"Hannah, please let me in."

FORTY

I open the door. "What the fuck do you—"

"Shut up, Hannah, I'm here to help you." She barges in and shuts the door and locks it. "You're in danger. Not just you, but you and the twins."

"Did you put the AirTag on me?"

"I needed to see you in person." She smooths her hair out of her face and takes a deep breath.

"Oh please. You're a whack job. Telling me to run. Putting an AirTag on me. Following me to my hotel. What kind of pathetic shit are you up to?" I'm shaking. I'm so mad at her. I don't want to be this close to the woman who's wearing my face and hair. The woman who's been sleeping with my husband and lying to me for months. Then I remember—he was her husband first—and my stomach lurches.

"You don't look well, Hannah, I think you should sit. Let me get you a glass of water," Sophia offers.

"As if I'd drink anything you gave me. I'm not a complete country idiot."

"Do you really think I'd poison you? You're pregnant, for Christ's sake, what kind of monster do you think I am?" She shakes her head and laughs under her breath, then takes a sealed bottle of water from the mini fridge and hands it to me.

"Riiiight, and why should I believe a word that's coming out of your mouth? You are the biggest fucking liar." The irony isn't lost on me that I'm calling her a liar, when she thinks I'm pregnant. I crack the bottle and chug the water. Trying to regain some kind of composure.

"We used to be friends."

"Really? We used to be friends? Let me tell you something, Sophia. Where I come from, friends don't do this kind of shit. Husband swapping. Face swapping. Or whatever twisted game you and Court are playing with me. This obsession—it ends now, Sophia. I'm filing for a divorce, and you can have him. But you cannot have my kids, do you understand me? They are mine." I point at her.

"He's never going to let you have them. And he's never going to let you leave," she whispers.

"Ha, we'll see about that. Now that I have proof he's been lying to me for all these years, I don't think there's any judge in the world that wouldn't grant me a divorce and full custody," I argue.

"Hannah, it's not that simple... But it can be. I'm going to tell you something, but you have to promise to do a favor for me in return."

"Why would I ever do you a favor?"

She lets out a rattled groan. "In my house, there's a safe behind the Joan Miró. I'll text you the combination. Inside of it is a sealed manila envelope with the name 'Lauren' on the front, and next to it is a small box with some audio tapes in it. I want you to look at what's in the envelope. But it's mine; I need it back. The tapes though—those are yours. Destroy them and then you're free."

"What do you mean, then I'm free?"

"I don't have time to explain everything. Just go to my house, get the envelope and tapes, and get far away from there." Sophia's clearly frazzled and starts shaking. Her eyes go wide and she looks around the room. "If you don't, you'll be trapped like me." Her eyes glitter with tears.

"What did he do to you?" I ask and she starts crying.

I oughta kill this woman.

But something about seeing her in such a fragile state reminds me that I would have once done anything to protect her. I was willing to give her any amount of money and help to get her away from her husband. It just turns out he's the same man I want to get away from. Before I can tell her I'll go home and look at the envelope and tapes, her phone buzzes. She looks at it and goes white as a ghost.

"Fuck. I have to go."

"But—"

"Go home, Hannah, before it's too late."

I have so many questions. But the only thing I can do is nod.

"Sophia?" I call out to her as she's leaving my hotel room.

"Yes?" She looks back at me.

"You're a terrible fucking person." If this is the last time I see her, she needs to know how I really feel.

"I know."

It took me less than thirty minutes to pack up my bag and hail a taxi to the airport. The sooner I can get home, the better. I'm not sure I really care about what Sophia's got in her safe. The only thing I need to do is go to the bank and wire all of my influencer money to a new account. One that Court definitely doesn't know about. I have this horrible feeling in my gut he's going to try and steal everything I've earned in order to manipulate me. I should have moved the money before I took the kids to Iowa, but I was scared. If I moved it too early and he found out, he would know I was on to him.

I exhale slowly and rub my temples. I'm not tired, thankfully I was able to sleep on the flight, but I am mentally exhausted. Trying to figure out what's going on with Sophia and Court has consumed me. And I'm not sure I'm any closer to really uncovering the truth. But now I have to layer the stress of Sophia's visit to my hotel room. She was clearly shaken, scared, and worried about me. But she's a damn good actress. It might have all been another act.

By the time I reach our neighborhood, I'm shaking with anxiety.

I don't even want to look at my house.

After this, I'm never going to see it again. The place I've spent the last four years living with Rowen and Ruby... Every milestone in their lives, first smile, first words, first steps. All of our knickknacks and mementos. When I leave, I'm starting my entire life over from scratch. It's scary and overwhelming.

I pull the rental car into Sophia's driveway, trying my hardest not to look at my house. Then I text Sophia to let her know I'm here.

> I'm at your house. What's the code to get in?

The sound of the windshield wipers is calming while I wait for her to text me back. I close my eyes, so I'm not tempted to stare at my house. No, not my house, I remind myself. It's a place of lies. Thankfully, Sophia responds after a few minutes, texting me the combination to the safe along with the code to her back door.

"You better not be lying to me again, Sophia," I mumble at the screen. The back door lock clicks when I enter the code. Even though this entire thing feels like one big setup, and I'm probably making a terrible mistake by going into her house, she's piqued my curiosity. What could she possibly have in a manila envelope with the name Lauren on it that has anything to do with me and Court?

I take a few steps into her house. Out of habit, I slip off my muddy shoes, feeling a little foolish—because who cares if I get Sophia's floors dirty? But it does feel nice to let my feet breathe. My feet might be comfortable, but my heart sure isn't. It doesn't know how fast it should beat—if this was a scary movie, any second now is when Sophia would jump out of a closet, wielding a butcher's knife and yelling, *Gotcha, bitch!*

But this isn't a scary movie, I remind myself. There's one way to prove it. "Ooops!" I exclaim as I tip over the replacement vase I purchased after Ruby cracked the original one the first time we came over to Sophia's house. I watch with satisfaction as it shatters on the stone tiles. Except I'm barefoot, and now there's little shards of glass between me and the safe hidden behind the wall on the other side of the room.

At least I know I'm alone in the house.

That much noise, even the scariest of hidden psychos would have come out to investigate what the hell I'm doing.

Since I can't walk across the glass, I decide to go upstairs to Sophia's room, since the staircase is right in front of me. I'm sure she has plenty of shoes I can borrow, plus I'm kind of a snoop, and surprisingly I've never actually been in her bedroom before.

Sophia's bedroom looks like a page from a Crate & Barrel catalogue. There is nothing personal about it. Plain grey and white furniture and bedding. Her closet has an assortment of things with more color, most of which I've never seen her wear. Things she must have worn in Beijing. I spy a lemon yellow sundress, next to the dress she wore to the club that night. I can't stand being in her closet any longer, so I grab a pair of sandals. They are a little small, but they'll do for now. I make my way back downstairs, across all the broken shards of glass, and over to the priceless painting. What an odd thing to use to cover a safe—priceless art should never be touched or moved without a great deal of care. As an art dealer, Sophia should know better.

That's when a lightbulb goes off in my head. Putting her safe behind the painting is actually the perfect place to hide it. Because Court would never look there.

Until this moment, I wasn't sure I believed her, but she really is keeping secrets from him.

"Here goes nothing." I feel guilty taking the painting off the wall. For about two seconds. Then I toss it haphazardly to the side of the room, feeling alive.

FORTY-ONE
SOPHIA

When Hannah opens the manila envelope with my sister's name on it, she's going to be confused at first. The pictures, awards, letters, and other personal effects are stacked in chronological order. Starting with pictures of us as babies. She might not realize right away that she's looking at a set of twins. Although, as a mother of twins herself, she might recognize the similarities. She might even notice how our mother clearly favored Lauren, dressing her in far finer things than I, and *never* in matching outfits.

By the time we were in primary school, there was a strong family resemblance to one another, especially in our school uniforms—the only matching clothes we'd ever owned. Maybe, if she hasn't already, that's when Hannah will start putting the pieces together.

When she finds the letters Lauren wrote to me, lamenting being at boarding school without me there to really make her shine, she'll begin to see the picture. Our parents thought it best that we attend separate boarding schools, seeing as being together might confuse our teachers and peers. I was never really sure what that meant. Both schools were prestigious, and both Lauren and I were successful academically, as Hannah will see when she reads our final marks on our graduation certificates.

Of course, Lauren wasn't just top in marks, she was beautiful and popular. While I, on the other hand, frequently went to the headmistress's office. Something about being mean, spiteful, and having a chip on my shoulder. It was only because I was top of my class that I kept my spot in school, seeing as I was not well-liked.

I really didn't want to go to uni with Lauren. We'd never been close, but she insisted. She said it would be the only time we'd have with one another, before finding husbands and having families of our own someday. So, much to our parents' chagrin, who said we were bound for disaster, we moved into a shared room at our Oxford college.

Our first term together was incredible. Lauren was the sister I'd always dreamed she might be—we did everything together and she proudly told everyone I was her twin. Thankfully my body had caught up to hers, and I'd learned how to do my hair and makeup in a much more stylish fashion. Before long, guys were asking me on *almost* as many dates as Lauren. I knew it confused my sister, and she tried her best to conceal it, but I could see the jealousy building inside of her. She'd held herself above me for so long, how could someone like me be getting almost as much attention as someone like her?

Of course, Hannah won't learn any of that from the contents of the envelope, but she will know Lauren and I were together at Oxford.

It was there that we met the dashing, handsome, unknown American financier, Blake Carter. He was friends with our economics professor and searching for a student to help him with some advanced research in cryptocurrency. I was obsessed. From the moment we met, I fawned over him with every breath I took. I would do anything for that man, and I mean anything. But no matter how hard I tried, Blake only had eyes for Lauren. And Lauren took the opportunity to put me in my place.

This is the point where Hannah's jaw might fall slack.

She will see Lauren and Blake's beautiful wedding photo... and me standing in the background, with a longing gaze at my sister's new husband. Followed by the pictures of the birth of their twins, and me pretending to be happy, while secretly plotting how I might steal Blake away from my sister. He should have been mine in the first place, if Lauren had just stayed out of it.

Then things will turn dark, when Hannah reads the small article I clipped from an Italian newspaper. If she's smart enough to put it through Google Translate, she'll discover Lauren and the children died in what Blake described to the police as "a tragic boating accident."

But we both know he left them in the middle of Lake Como to die.

Otherwise why would he spend tens of millions of dollars scrubbing the internet clean of any trace of the accident, or his marriage to Lauren? Why would he forbid me from having pictures of the children, or letting me honor their memory in any way?

Conveniently my parents died in an automobile accident six months later, leaving me sole heir to their estate. I've always assumed it was Blake's doing, so he could finish scrubbing my family's existence from memory. I'm sure Hannah will assume the same thing, especially when she reads my handwritten notes saying as much.

She might wonder why I'm still alive.

Or how I came to marry Blake after my sister's death, if I thought he was their killer.

While Blake and Lauren were building their life together, I was making powerful friends in the art world. Friends who Blake longed to do business with—the kinds of men money alone could not buy introductions to. Well, for a price, I provided Blake with those highly coveted introductions. And that's why I know he killed my sister. She found out he was sleeping with me as payment for the introductions.

I imagine she threatened him, just like she'd threatened me, when I told her about the affair. I didn't mean to tell her, but I was being petty. It was another day at their summer home on Lake

Como, and she was lording her picture-perfect life over me, telling me it was a disappointment I'd turned down several decent marriage proposals to gallivant around the world, sleeping with my clients. And that's when I snapped and told her the only client I slept with was her husband. I regretted it the moment I said it, when I saw the look of pure disappointment on her face, and I promised not to do it again.

But she vowed to divorce him, take the children away, and tell the world we were horrible people. I really didn't care. I'd already lost everything the moment I told Lauren. She was the one person in the world who really loved me and I broke her. I snuffed out the light in her because I was a jealous bitch. Something I'd have to live with. Blake, on the other hand, refused to accept that his burgeoning reputation might become tarnished if Lauren told the world the truth. So he decided to kill her. With Lauren out of the picture, and me as his replacement wife, he'd be free to make himself both the victim and hero of his own story.

Maybe that's why Blake is drawn to Hannah—she's a lot like Lauren. Beautiful, smart, gentle—but with more agency than my sister ever had. Unlike Lauren, Hannah has a dark side. One she's going to come face-to-face with when she listens to the tapes in the box.

FORTY-TWO
HANNAH

A huge clap of thunder booms outside. I nearly jump a foot in the air. "Jesus, that scared me." I fan my face. Now that I have what I came for, I really should get out of here and go to the bank. Who knows how long it will take to set up a new account?

But there's one last thing I want to do before I leave.

When I was in Sophia's room, I noticed one of those expensive soy wax candles on the dresser, which means there's got to be a box of matches or a lighter nearby. So I run upstairs, and rifle through the drawer until...

"Bingo!"

I click the button on the long stick utility lighter, and a yellow flame appears. I walk into Sophia's closet and set the kelly green dress on fire. I don't have time to wait and see if the entire wardrobe goes up in flames, I just know I feel a hell of a lot better sending her a message this way. You want to fuck around with me? I don't think so.

I trot back down the stairs, grab the thick manila envelope and box of tapes, then as I am leaving, I decide to light the blackout curtains on fire.

I know how spiteful and petty it is to want to destroy Sophia's house.

But from the moment she moved in next door, she's done nothing but try to destroy my life. This is the least I can do to pay her back. Plus, there's a storm still brewing outside and storms mean rain. I can't imagine anything burning in the middle of a Florida rainstorm, where the water pours from the sky like a high-pressure shower head.

I crawl into the driver's seat of my SUV rental and check the mirror. My dark hair is windblown and I look wild. Thunder rumbles in the distance. It won't take long for the storm to pass right overhead. I speed down the road and out of the neighborhood, without looking over my shoulder for a final farewell. What's the point?

I check into a vintage surfside motel on Sanibel Island. The kind that still accepts cash and uses a book to write down the guests' names instead of a computer. The kind of place Court would never find me. Even so, I use a fake name to check in.

After bringing in my things, I lock the chain and go sit in a chair looking out the sliding glass doors at the ocean. The rain has stopped, and the moon is shining on the water.

Transferring my money at the bank to a more secure account was much easier than I'd expected—thanks to the manager being another one of my "biggest fans." She was blown away by my new hair color... which I promised there would be a big reveal post about next week, so it was our little secret for now.

Lie.

I'm shuttering my socials.

I know the truth now. I'm not Hannah McMillian, the perfect trad wife influencer. My marriage is a sham and my life is anything but perfect. Even before Sophia, everything I did was carefully curated to create a version of myself and my children that wasn't real.

It's always been a big fat lie.

I let out a long sigh before getting up to pour myself a glass of wine and put the batteries in the small tape player I purchased after going to the bank. I was in a bit of a daze as I walked around Target, loading up the cart with snacks, drinks, and other necessities. As hard as I tried not to think about Sophia, I couldn't help but remember when the twins and I took her on a shopping spree and we had our three-day pajama party.

Wine in hand, I stare at the manila envelope and box of small cassette tapes.

I'm not sure which one to dig into first.

As I sip my drink and contemplate, my phone buzzes.

"Hey, Sinclair," I answer.

"Girl, your house is on fire!" he shrieks.

"What?"

"It's all over the news. Sounds like lightning struck Sophia's house and the wind blew the flames to your house. I'm sooooo sorry!" He's practically sobbing.

I quickly turn on the small TV, flicking the channels until I find the local news.

There's a news anchor in a red jacket, holding a microphone, standing across the street from the smoldering rubble that was once my home. Firemen and fire trucks are behind her, blocking most of the view, but from what I can see—both of our houses are completely destroyed. All that remains is the steel framework.

"Fire Chief Alex Branzino has stated that a lightning strike and high winds were the culprit. Thankfully the homeowners of both properties were not present at the time of this devastating blaze. Heavy rains prevented the fire from spreading further in this luxury neighborhood. Tom, back to you."

"Girl, are you still there?" Sinclair asks.

"Oh, um, yes, sorry—I just turned on the local news. I'm honestly in shock." And I am—I mean, seeing my house destroyed is stirring up so many emotions. It was the only home Ruby and Rowen ever lived in, and I took that from them.

No. I shake my head. Court took that from them. He forced this mess on us all.

"Wait, the local news? But aren't you in Paris?"

"About that—"

"Hannah. Where are you?" Sinclair's voice drops into his serious octave.

"I, um, can't talk right now. I'll call you later—I'm safe and I have the evidence I need. Love you." I hang up before he starts asking too many questions.

That's right. I have the evidence... and that's what I need to do, look at all of it. Because as soon as Court hears our house has burned down and he realizes I didn't come to Paris for our baby-moon, he's going to put all the pieces together.

The clock is ticking.

I carefully unseal the thick envelope labeled *Lauren*. I slide the contents out and set them on my lap. The first item is a baby picture—actually, two babies. I flip it over. The names *Lauren & Sophia* are carefully penned on the back.

It takes me a few minutes of looking through pictures and school records to understand.

Sophia and Lauren were sisters. Twins, no less.

"Oh god," I mutter to myself.

But why did she want me to look through a bunch of things about her mysterious twin sister? And why didn't she ever tell me she had a twin, unless—something must have happened to her. To Lauren. But how does this have anything to do with me and Court?

As I go through each item, I can't help but wonder—how could Sophia and Lauren's parents be so cruel to them as children? Clearly, their parents favored Lauren. It's evident in the clothing choices, the birthday gifts, and cemented by little notes written by both Sophia and Lauren. I feel guilty looking through everything, as if I'm invading their private sibling relationship. Something I never had growing up, but something I've nurtured and encour-aged between Ruby and Rowen. As the mother of twins, I couldn't imagine favoring one over the other, creating a lifelong divide.

Then I come across something I'm not at all prepared for.

My stomach churns, and I think I'm going to be sick. I'm

staring at a picture of Sophia in a bridesmaid dress. She looks miserable. The bride—her sister, Lauren. The groom. None other than my bastard husband, Court.

"What the fuck? He was married to your sister?" I say to the photograph. As if Sophia might uncross her arms and start talking back to me.

I can hear her voice. *Well, I loved him first.*

I quickly shuffle through the next few pictures and documents, trying to understand how Sophia ended up with Blake if her sister was married to him.

I gasp, "Oh Jesus Christ," and drop everything on the bed when I find a picture of Court—it's so eerily similar to one I have at home. He's smiling, proud, and holding something in his arms. Not just one something, but two. Twins. He's in a hospital, standing next to a very tired-looking Lauren. My uterus contracts, remembering myself in that exact same position four years ago, with Court holding Ruby and Rowen.

He wasn't just married to Sophia's sister. He had children with her. Twins.

My vision blurs, my heart pounds. I can't breathe. Ruby and Rowen have half-siblings out there, somewhere in the world. So many questions are running through my mind. What happened to Lauren and her children? Why did Court marry Sophia?

"Pull yourself together," I say and will my hands to stop shaking. I slam down the rest of my wine, then get up and pour myself another glass. I take a few bites of a chocolate bar and run to the bathroom to splash my face with cold water.

I'm scared to look at the rest of the pictures and documents, now strewn all over the hotel bed, because in my heart —I think I know. Lauren and her twins aren't out there in the world, living their best lives. They are dead. That's why Sophia said my life was in danger. Not just mine, but the twins' too.

I find a small newspaper clipping, written in Italian. It takes me a few minutes on Google Translate to decipher it. It tells of a boating accident and the drowning of Lauren Carter and her two small children. The only survivor, one Blake Carter.

"How fucking convenient," I mutter.

I pace around the hotel room in shock.

I can't wrap my head around this revelation. I have to know more. What kind of boating accident? Was another boat involved? Was Court hurt? Did they find their bodies? I get on the internet and search for the accident. But I come up with nothing... I can't find a single thing about what happened that day on the lake. I can't even find a single thing about Lauren. It's as if she never existed.

I rifle through the other documents on the bed and come across a couple of torn-out journal entries from Sophia.

July 8

I keep thinking that any second I'm going to wake up from this nightmare. But I haven't slept in days, so I know this isn't sleep induced, this is really happening. Lauren is dead. The girl everyone adored, with her picture-perfect life, is gone... and so are her precious, darling babies. I can hardly bear to think about their cherub faces without wanting to climb up to the roof and throw myself off. I know their deaths are my fault, even if I can't prove it... yet. I've always been insanely jealous of my sister, but at least she understood me. She's the only person who could. I'm so fucking angry that she's gone. I didn't want this. I didn't want her to die! Why couldn't I just leave well enough alone? Why did I have to seduce her husband? If I'd just had some fucking self-control, Lauren and the children would still be alive. But, like Mother used to say, "You'll destroy this family someday, Sophia. You think you're cleverer than the rest of us, but you're not. And until you learn that, we're all doomed." She was right...

July 15

Blake and I were arguing again during dinner last night. I've never seen him get so drunk. It honestly scared me. Then, for some idiotic reason, or one too many martinis, I called him a murderer, and he started laughing. He stuck to the same story he told the police: He said Lauren and the children fell off the boat when he swerved to miss a log floating in the lake, and when he returned, they'd already drowned. But I know Lauren would never take the children on the boat without life jackets. She's a fanatic about their safety. So I called Blake a liar and punched him in the face. He overpowered me and pinned me to the ground, and said, "So what if I'm a liar? I did it to be with you. I married the wrong sister." The truth is, it doesn't matter that I know he killed them. I can never tell anyone what he's done, or I risk him exposing my secrets. Our lives and careers are too intertwined, for now. So in order to protect myself, I agreed to marry him. I'd rather kill myself, but if I die, who will be left to remember Lauren? To pray for her and the children? Someday I'll take my revenge on him. Until then, being his wife is my punishment.

I drop the pages, my hands shaking. He killed them? He left them in the fucking lake to drown? How many times have I let him take Ruby and Rowen to the beach alone... Holy shit, he could have killed them too.

I scream at the top of my lungs.

"Shut up!" Someone next door pounds on the wall.

I pace around the small space. "I don't feel sorry for you, Sophia, because what you've done is unforgivable. But it doesn't make Lauren's death your fault." I say the words out loud, as if somehow she can hear me across the ocean. My entire body trembles, thinking about what she's endured. Years of living with a man she knows could kill her. A man who killed her sister.

It takes me thirty minutes to calm down. I'm sure I'll never fully understand the depth of Sophia and Blake's codependency issues. I keep calling him Blake in my head, when I think of Court in Sophia's life. I guess it's easier to think about him as two separate people. Which is what he's done, created two lives. Both of which he's royally fucked up. And all the money in the world can't save him now. He's not just a liar and an adulterer. If Sophia's journal entry is to be believed, he's a murderer too.

"You're the devil. If you really killed your wife and kids..." I shake my head. I'm so disgusted by everything I've uncovered. It's late, and I'm physically and mentally exhausted, but I'm so close to knowing everything. All I have to do is listen to the small tapes in the box. They're the kind used during interviews, or sessions with a psychiatrist. Once I do that, I'll be free. That's what Sophia said.

Each one is labeled with a month and set of initials.

I have no idea what to expect when I listen.

I exhale deeply, then roll my head from side to side to work out the tension in my neck and shoulders. Okay, here goes nothing. "Well, let's find out what was so important that you had to record it." I pop the little tape into the tape recorder and hit play.

"Barry Whitemore, private investigator. Date, June 6th. Investigation of candidate number three, April Jones. After spending two weeks following Ms. Jones, interviewing former partners, employers, and deploying other background techniques, my recommendation is to terminate further surveillance. The candidate does not have the required life experience..."

I click to stop the tape. I'm so confused.

"What the fuck is this?"

I pull out the tape and pop another one in.

And another.

They are all the same. Private investigator, Barry Whitemore, providing information on female candidates. Giving detailed, and sometimes extremely personal information, about the women, to whoever the recipient of these tapes is.

Why does Sophia have these? Was she interviewing housekeepers or personal assistants? What does any of this have to do with me? Or Court? Or his possible murder of her sister? I'd thought maybe she recorded him confessing, and I'd be able to go to the police and have him arrested, freeing myself and the twins from his influence once and for all.

That's when I see a tape with the initials *H.P.*

My throat tightens.

"Barry Whitemore, private investigator. Date, August 10th. Investigation of candidate number six, Hannah Price. After spending a week following Ms. Price, interviewing her current employer, and deploying other background techniques, my recommendation is to continue surveillance... I've scheduled a flight to Sioux City to interview childhood contacts..."

Barry's voice keeps going, talking about his interviews with various people in my life. What a bastard! Posing as a doctor, a journalist, a former professor, giving people I knew reason to trust him and to tell him information about me.

Then he says something that unlocks everything.

"After interviewing a young auto mechanic, Nathaniel Taylor, about Ms. Price's involvement in the death of Matthew Aarons, it is my recommendation to place Ms. Price as your top candidate..."

I stop the tape.

I can't breathe. My chest heaves up and down as I try to suck in air, but it's not working. I slide open the glass doors, hoping some fresh air will help, but it's thick and humid and only makes the sense of suffocation worse.

Nate Taylor—he was in the grade below me and Matt in school. I always thought he had a crush on me, which was cute, but I was with Matt and that wasn't going to change. Nate's dad owned the auto body shop where the Thunderbird was taken after the accident. I don't know why Matt's dad didn't just have it smashed in a compactor. It was half-burned, and a horrible reminder of Matt's death.

The death I caused.

And covered up.

I think I know what Barry's going to say next, but until I hear it for myself, I can't know for certain. I hit play on the recorder.

"Mr. Taylor indicates he and his recently deceased father worked on the car after the accident. After secretly dosing Mr. Taylor's beer with Rohypnol, I was able to conclude Ms. Price was

most likely the driver, based on the blood spatter and damage to the vehicle. Mr. Taylor has indicated a deep fondness for Ms. Price and has not made his theory public. I believe you can use this information to your benefit at a future date..."

I turn off the tape, run to the bathroom, and throw up the cheap Target wine and bag of Cheetos I ate for dinner. I can't fucking believe Court. He had me followed by a private investigator when we started dating. Not just me, but every woman he dated over the course of a year. And I thought when we met he hadn't been out with a woman in years. God, I'm so stupid. And worse yet, he had some kind of rating system. He was looking for a woman with a tragedy he could exploit.

"Wait, wait, wait..." I run back and look at the case with my initials. *September, H.P.* Which was when we met. But we didn't have our first date until October. It took Court a month of visits to the bar before he finally worked up the courage to ask me out.

I rewind the tape to the beginning and hit play.

"Barry Whitemore, private investigator. Date, August 10th. Investigation of candidate number six, Hannah Price."

August 10th. Barry said August. Not September when we met, not October when Court finally asked me on a date. But August. Nausea consumes me again. And while I heave and cry into the toilet, my broken heart finally shatters into a million tiny pieces. None of it was ever real. Not our first meeting. Not our whirlwind romance. Nothing about my husband is or was ever mine. Somehow, he found me first. He knew all about me, where I grew up, where I went to school, who I hung out with, and about Matt.

I feel more violated by this revelation than I do by uncovering the truth about Sophia and Lauren.

My limbs are weak, and I collapse on the bathroom floor. I curl up and wrap my arms around myself, praying to find the strength not to die. But my heart and mind have suffered too much... My breathing slows and I whisper, *"I love you, Ruby. I love you, RoRo."* Then everything goes black.

FORTY-THREE

I wake up on the bathroom floor. Confused, I pull myself up and rub my eyes. After my first round of vomiting last night, I recall getting up, and getting sick all over again when I stopped to really think about Lauren and her children. She was so young when she met him, a college student, and she trusted him. She must have loved him, and what did he do? He had an affair with her sister and then he killed her and their kids. If he got away with it once, he could do it again.

After showering and drinking some coffee, I walk down to the beach, the waves lapping at my feet. I find a quiet spot to sit and run my hands through the sand, using it as a sort of meditation to help me think. I can only assume my husband has been lining pockets to cover up what he's done, but money alone can't protect a bastard like that forever. Crypto billionaires might use stealth wealth to fly under the radar, but they are not immune to the law.

I imagine taking the envelope of pictures and documents about Lauren along with the interview tapes to the FBI. I'll tell them everything I know and let them deal with Court. But a nagging feeling in my gut says that's a futile exercise. Based on my internet searches, it's clear Court's been able to use his power to scrub his name off almost everything. It could take a forensic analysis team months, maybe years, to uncover anything. And that doesn't mean they'll even find enough to prosecute him. The Italian article said Lauren's death was ruled an accident. So why would the American FBI even open it up as a case?

Not to mention, what would happen to me and the kids during an investigation?

Would we have to go into witness protection? Abandoning Aunt Tippy, Uncle Fran, Cassie, Sinclair, and Jamie? I know they'd all understand I have to do whatever it takes to protect me and the twins, but still—I'd hate to be all alone.

"Shit," I grumble and rest my head on my knees. I can't go to the authorities. If I give them the tapes about Court using a private investigator, they *will* dig into my past. They'll find out that I caused Matt's death. Which means, instead of Court going to prison, it could be me.

Okay, so maybe going to the authorities is not my best option. So how do I save me and the twins? What would Cassie do?

Easy. She'd kill him.

I scoop up some sand and let it pour from my hand, like grains spilling slowly from an hourglass, giving myself time to reconcile what I'm considering—killing Court.

Because if we run, he will find us. If I go to the authorities, I will end up behind bars, leaving the twins in his care. If I tell him I'm leaving him, he will kill me and the twins. He's done it once before, with Lauren—there's nothing that will stop him from doing it again.

So what other option do I have? Even if I go to jail for killing him, the twins will be safe. Aunt Tippy would raise them on the farm and Cassie could help. They would be safe and alive.

When the sand is gone, I've made up my mind to kill my husband and come up with a semblance of a plan. It's not foolproof. But it's something. I stand up, brush myself off, and go back to my hotel room. First, I call Aunt Tippy to check in on her and the kids. If anything bad had happened, she would have called me.

Thankfully, all is well, as I expected. Ruby and Rowen have

missed me something fierce, but as she says, there's no time for tears on a farm when there's plenty of work to be done. Today's adventure—one of the chickens managed to hide a nest in the back corner of the yard, and there are fifteen baby chicks for the twins to run around mother-henning. I remind Aunt Tippy to stay vigilant and keep my babies close before we hang up.

Knowing my babies are safe at the farm gives me the strength I need to make the next call.

"Hello?" Court answers on the first ring.

"We need to talk, in person."

"Hannah, honey, oh my god—where are you? I've been trying your phone for days."

"Cut the crap, Court."

"Excuse me?" His tone shifts dramatically.

"I want you to come home to Florida and meet me in person so we can discuss the terms of our divorce like civilized people."

He laughs. "Divorce? I'm not giving you a divorce. On what grounds?"

"On the grounds that you're having an affair with our neighbor. I know you've been in Paris with her. I know you bought her an apartment." I'm not going to tell him I discovered they've been together for over ten years.

"Hannah, sweetheart, you've completely misunderstood everything. Baby, please. I'm not having an affair with Sophia. I only bought her the apartment to move her away from you, just like you wanted. That's all. It was a trade. I bought her the apartment and she signed over her house to me. A simple business transaction."

God, he's good. If I didn't know what I know, there's a strong chance I would have believed him.

"I don't trust you. And I know you don't trust me, because you put tracking on my phone and computer. So we need to end things before it gets ugly."

"As ugly as burning our house down?" he says snidely.

I let out a loud laugh.

"I didn't burn our house down. Sophia's house was struck by

lightning and the wind blew it to our house, or do you not check the local news on your phone?"

"Whatever you say, Hannah. I'm sure we can just let the judge figure it all out," he says. "And maybe, when we're talking to the judge, I'll ask him what the penalty is for vehicular manslaughter."

And there it is.

The threat.

I was prepared, but it still feels like a punch to the gut. I want to scream and rage at Court. To tell him to fuck off. But this is the part of my plan where I have to cry and beg for forgiveness. I sniffle once, then twice, and let my bottom lip quiver. "Court, why?" I whisper. Then I choke cry, until finally real tears and real emotion comes from my body. "Please, I'm sorry, I didn't mean it, I don't really want a divorce..."

"Oh really, Hannah? You didn't mean it?"

"You know this whole thing with Sophia just had me scared and fucked-up in the head. What was I supposed to think?" I sob. "I just want to know you're mine. I love you, Court."

He lets out a long sigh. "I love you too, Hannah."

"I'm having your baby, for Christ's sake, and you bring up Matt's accident? Why are you trying to hurt me?"

"I don't know. Because it hurts me that you said you want a divorce." He's angry now.

I sob uncontrollably until he tells me to calm down. "Breathe, baby, breathe, it's not good to get so worked up when you're pregnant. Please, calm down. It's gonna be okay, we can work through this."

I gulp and stop crying almost instantly.

"Come home, please. Get on the first plane you can and come home. We need you," I beg. I'm completely disgusted with myself and I'm going to need another shower after this.

"Do you want to meet me in Iowa? I can surprise the kids—how does that sound?"

I rub my temples, I'm ready for this call to be over. "Shouldn't we look for a new house first? We can't bring the kids home to a hotel."

"Ah, you're right. Okay, well, I'll catch a flight tomorrow morning. Why don't you meet me in Miami? Let's start over fresh, in a new city."

"You want to move to Miami?" That's a curveball.

"It makes sense. The crypto market is hot in Brazil. Flying direct from Miami will be faster for me."

"Sure, okay, whatever you want. I'll head to Miami and get a hotel. I'll text you the address—we can go house hunting right away." I'm saying what I think he wants to hear.

"Wonderful. See, isn't it better when we just communicate?" he says.

Oh, the arrogance.

My face burns and I clench my teeth. I want to hang up and throw my phone across the room. But I have to remain calm.

"I love you, I'll see you tomorrow," I do my best not to grumble and then I hang up. My hands are trembling. What the fuck am I doing? Luring my evil husband back to the States might be the biggest mistake I've ever made. I reach a hand up and push the hair out of my eyes. Dark hair. Crap. If Court sees it, he's gonna freak out and suspect I'm up to something.

I stand up. I guess I'm going to Miami. But first, I need to see my hair stylist.

FORTY-FOUR

I've always hated hair extensions. They are uncomfortable and make my hair too full—like I'm some Texan beauty pageant contestant. All I need is a sparkly crystal tiara and a sash that says, *Miss Husband Killer* stitched across the front.

But at least I'm mostly blonde again. The stylist had a hell of a time trying to get out that temporary brown hair dye. I promised her I'd never, ever, color my hair again. The dark color washed out my complexion, not to mention if the twins saw me like that, it might scare the bejesus out of them. They've only known me with one look.

It's after midnight, but Miami is one of those cities that never really sleeps. After checking into the hotel, I walked across the street to a little Cuban restaurant. It's packed with an eclectic mix of people eating, drinking, and dancing. I was lucky to snag a spot at a high top in the back. The meal is spicy and flavorful and my drink is strong. There's music playing and a liveliness that helps keep me present and calm my nerves.

I don't feel like I'm plotting to kill my husband—instead it feels like I'm exploring the new city I just promised him I'd move to.

All day long I've tried to come up with the easiest way to kill

Court and deal with the body. Shooting him? No. Too messy, and how would I get a gun?

Hire a hitman? No. I wouldn't even know where to begin. Plus, that would leave a paper trail.

It has to be something simple.

Something I am capable of doing.

Then, on my drive here, while listening to the P.I. Barry Whitemore tapes again, something he said triggered the perfect plan. Rohpnyl. Also known as Roofies. Whitemore used it to drug Nate and get him to spill his secrets. So what if I used it to drug Court enough so I could overpower him? Then there's a million different ways I could kill him. I could convince him to go swimming with me and drown him—a little nod to Lauren. Or I could make him drink an entire bottle of Scotch and he could die of alcohol poisoning. Or I could shove him down the stairs in the hotel and watch him break his neck.

So maybe my plan isn't rock-solid yet.

But it starts with getting some Rohypnol. Which is why I'm out so late. I overheard the bartender at my hotel saying to another guest they could score some cocaine from the waitress here. The one with the red flower in her hair.

I sure hope it's not an undercover sting—because I really don't want to go to jail tonight for trying to buy drugs.

"You want another drink?" my waiter asks.

No, what I want is the waitress with the red flower in her hair to come help me.

"Ummm... do you have anything stronger?" I whisper and slide him a hundred-dollar bill. He cocks his head, takes me in, and winks once. I watch in horror, ready to run out of the busy restaurant, if he goes to anyone other than the waitress.

I'm holding my breath.

He moves smoothly, grabbing empty plates and drinks, before casually saying something to the woman. She looks in my direction, catches my eye, and nods once. A few minutes later, she comes to my table and sits down in the empty seat across from me.

"You're familiar." She narrows her gaze. She's younger and even prettier than I could tell from across the busy, dark restaurant. There's an edge about her—she's tough. I bet she doesn't put up with anyone's crap.

"Oh, ummm, yeah, I have an influencer account," I say softly.

"Why you asking for stronger shit?"

I let out a long sigh. I think the only way she'll give me what I want is if I'm honest. "My husband, he's been hurting me. I just want something to make him pass out so I can escape."

She leans back and crosses her arms. I'm not sure she believes me.

"I'm sorry, this was stupid." I get up to leave and she grabs my wrist.

"No. Sit."

I sit back down and tears well up in my eyes. My lower lip trembles. If she doesn't help me, I'm not sure what I'm going to do.

"Crush up two and put it in his drink. He'll sleep for twelve hours and won't remember shit the next day." She slides a small bag with four pills to me.

"Thank you." I clasp her hand and squeeze.

She stands up to leave, then smiles, as if she's just remembered something. "Are you the one that put veggies in cupcakes?"

I nod.

"That was smart. I make the zucchini ones all the time. I hope you get away from him."

I could hug her for her kindness, but instead I tuck five hundred dollars in cash under my plate, walk out of the restaurant and cross the street to the hotel. I'm not sure how long I have until Court arrives, and I need to be prepared.

I've put some of the crushed-up pills in the decanter of Scotch, which should be Court's preferred drink after a long flight. To be sure, I also put some in the orange juice.

Buzz.

My phone rings.

Unknown Number.

I quickly decline the call, but my heart is racing. Then I receive a text, also from an unknown number.

It's Sophia, are you awake?

Did you just try and call me

Yes.

Call again.

Buzz.

"Hello?" I answer, wondering if this is a trap.

"We're on a private jet. He's sleeping and I'm hiding in the bathroom. We should be there in a few hours," Sophia whispers, barely loud enough for me to hear. Court arriving in Miami at two a.m. really throws a wrench in my plans. I can't very well convince my roofied husband to go swimming in the middle of the night, which is the method of killing I've chosen. Drowning.

"Did you get into the safe?" she asks.

"Yes, I have the envelope," I assure her.

"And?"

"I burned your house down."

She sighs. "Just leave the envelope at the front desk under the name Mary O'Leary."

"Okay..." I pause. "I'm going to kill him."

There's a pause on the other end. "About time." Then Sophia hangs up.

FORTY-FIVE

I pace around the hotel room nervously. I look at the clock—again. 3:15 a.m. He's got to be close. My heart pounds when I crawl into the bed and pretend to be asleep. If this doesn't work, I'm putting myself in serious danger.

Click.

The door.

He's here.

He quietly moves about the other room. Probably putting down his suitcase and taking off his shoes. Then I hear him open the bedroom door and let out a sigh. My body stiffens, preparing for him to come crawl into the bed... But then nothing. He must have turned around. My lungs release the breath I was holding. That was close. Phew.

I strain my ears for the sound of liquid pouring and a crystal glass tumbler setting down on the table. A few moments later, a grin spreads over my face when I hear the TV click on softly and the sound of glass clinking on the end table. Oh thank god, my note worked.

Court,

I'm so glad we agreed to start over. I love you. If your plane lands early while I'm still sleeping, why don't you slip into bed with me, instead of sitting around drinking Scotch and watching the news until the sun rises. Ha ha.

Love,
Hannah

I might not know the real Blake Carter or Court McMillian or whoever he is, but I do know a few things about the man I've been married to for the last five years. Like the fact that he loves to turn on the news and have a Scotch when he comes home after a long flight—no matter the time of day. Using a little reverse psychology on such a clever man—well, that's the icing on this shit cake.

I'm going to bed. My husband is checking in later tonight— please give him this key and note. His name is Court McMillian.

Yes, ma'am.

It was a gamble, leaving the note at the front desk. I wasn't sure what name Court would try to check in under. But what other option did I have? It would be too suspicious to text him—he'd know I was tipped off about his early arrival.

I wonder if the concierge thought it was odd that my husband arrived with another woman? Nah... They probably see all kinds of freakish stuff late at night. This is Miami, after all.

Then I hear the glass clink against the table again.

That's a good husband. Drink up all your roofied Scotch.

But then—I have a moment of panic. What if he's not really drinking the Scotch? Maybe he poured water in the glass—maybe he's not going to fall into a stupor. Against my better judgement, I get up to peek out, but I can't see his glass from this angle. Plus it's dark—the glow from the TV is the only real light.

A bead of sweat forms at my brow and my hands tremble when I push open the door all the way. I fake a yawn as I walk out, hoping it will hide how nervous I am. "Babe, you're here. I thought you'd come crawl into bed with me." I cross the open space to where he's sitting on the tan leather couch. I can tell by the glaze in his eyes and lines on his face he hasn't slept in days. There's something else too, I've never noticed before—but he looks so old.

"Sorry, honey, I, uh, you caught me. I know you said come to bed if I got here early, but you looked so peaceful, and just the mention of a Scotch and the news, well, how could I resist?" He chuckles and pats his lap. "Come sit with me. I've missed you."

As I get closer, he narrows his gaze.

"Something's different."

I reach up and touch my bangs. "My stylist went a little crazy."

He doesn't wait for me to reach his lap. He stands—a little wobbly on his feet. "I like it, very sexy." He wraps his arms around me and leans in for a kiss. I turn my head so his lips touch my neck. I have to be careful not to kiss him on the mouth. I don't want to drug myself.

"Mmmm... that feels nice," I say, trying not to gag. Just being in his presence, knowing what he's done, makes me feel like I'm touching someone with the plague.

"I spent a lot of time on the flight picturing our new life," he slurs.

"New life?"

"You know, a new house, a new baby." He drops to his knees and starts kissing my belly.

Ugh. Gross.

"Why don't you come to bed? Let's get some sleep, we have a big day tomorrow—house hunting." I help him to his feet and lead him by the hands to the bedroom.

"Wait, I want you to get naked," he growls as I'm about to crawl into bed. "I want to worship your body and fuck you."

I turn around. He's got that hungry look in his eyes. He is the predator and I am his prey. Oh great—this is what I was afraid of. I really, truly, do not want to have sex with him right now—or ever again.

"But honey, I'm tired... Let's just get some rest," I coax.

Court frowns and takes off his belt, gripping it tightly in his fist.

"I said, get naked." His voice goes from light-hearted to deep and dark.

"Or what?" I laugh nervously. "You'll hit me with your belt?" My pulse is rising quickly. How long is it supposed to take for the roofies to knock him out?

"I might... You know, Sophia likes it when I spank her with my belt," he says and slowly smiles. "I bet you'd like it too. Let's find out. I love that I can tell you about her now. I hated hiding it from you, baby."

Oh my god. This intoxicated idiot just admitted the affair he's worked so hard to convince me was something I made up in my head. So maybe the roofies are working. I should pretend to be more shocked, but I'm so sick and tired of this game.

"Court, what the fuck is wrong with you?" I want to leave, but he's blocking the door. "Get out of my way."

"Turn around and bend over. Let me show you how Sophia likes it."

"Fuck you."

He smirks. "You know, that's what Lauren said when I told her her sister liked a good spanking."

"You're out of your mind. Just go to bed and leave me alone." If I can get out of the room, I'll wedge a chair under the knob and lock him in here until I can figure out what to do. I wasn't expecting him to behave like this.

"Leave you alone? I don't think so, Hannah. Get your ass on the bed," he demands and lunges at me.

I scream and duck, but I'm not fast enough, and he wraps his arms around my shoulders and wrestles me to the bed. "Court, stop it, you're hurting me!" I kick and thrash and punch, but he's got his full weight bearing down on me.

"Stop moving!" he yells, then he takes the belt and lashes me once across my chest. The sting of leather on my breasts makes me scream out in pain. I throw my hands up to protect myself from the belt, and its sharp metal buckle. I ball my fists and start swinging wildly. Somehow, I make contact with the side of his head. His eyes and nostrils flare. He drops the belt and his hands slip around my neck and I stop moving.

"All I have to do is squeeze," he threatens. "Is that what you want? You want me to squeeze the fucking life out of you, Hannah?"

I've seen Aunt Tippy wring the life out of a chicken more times than I can count. I hear her voice in my head. *Just hold it right there and squeeze.* Tears stream out of the corners of my eyes. I don't want to die. I have to defuse this situation as fast as I can. "Court, please, it's been a long day." My voice is strained from the pressure he's putting on my throat. "You're tired and I've been antagonizing you. I'm sorry..." I whisper, reaching a hand up to cup his cheek. "I love you."

His features soften and his hands loosen from around my neck. He sits back slowly and waits a few seconds before he climbs off of me.

"Yes, it's been a long day." He rubs his palms over his face. "I'm sorry, I shouldn't have done that."

My head is spinning. I have to get out of here—there's no way I can overpower him. Even drugged, Court is strong. I've completely miscalculated this. But my body is frozen. My breasts sting and I can still feel his weight sitting on my stomach and his hands around my neck. He takes his shirt off and flings it over the chair before walking out of the bedroom. Hopefully to pour himself another glass of roofied Scotch.

A lamp flicks on in the other room, and the soft glow illuminates the doorway.

"What are you doing here?" Court demands.

"Oh you know, I was just listening to you play with your food before you eat it," Sophia says. I wasn't sure if she'd find the extra room key I put in the manila envelope. I'm not even sure why I put it in there—I'm still not sure if I can trust her.

There's only one way to find out. I convince my body to get off the bed and walk into the other room. I'm shaking, and blood is dripping from the laceration across my chest.

"Are you okay, Hannah?" Sophia asks me.

"I, umm..." I really don't know what I'm supposed to say. I'm damaged, broken, beaten, physically and mentally.

"Don't talk to her, she's fucking fine. She's a prude, but she's fine." Court's words should sting, but I don't even recognize this man—he's not the man I fell in love with. Because that man wasn't real. God, I'm such an idiot.

Then he goes for the Scotch and clumsily fills up another glass.

"Blake, darling, why don't you set that drink down and come show Hannah what really turns you on," Sophia coos.

Court slams back his drink and drops the glass on the carpet. Jesus. There's no way he'll still be standing in ten minutes—not with that much Rohypnol-infused alcohol in his system. He approaches Sophia slowly.

He looks at her, then over at me. "You two really do look alike."

She starts to smile and opens her mouth to say something, but then Court slaps her across the face. Her head flings to the side, her blonde hair whooshing in an arc. Blood gushes from her nose.

My hands fly up, covering a scream at my lips. I gasp for air.

Sophia raises her head slowly, laughing, then wipes the blood on the back of her hand and arm. "You must be very tired, Blake. Is that all you've got?"

"Sophia, no," I cry out. Why is she egging him on?

Court pulls his hand back and hits her again.

"What are you doing? Stop it, Court, you're hurting her!" I run over and start hitting the back of him. I'm not going to stand by and watch him beat the shit out of her. I don't care if she thinks she deserves it for luring her sister's husband into bed with her. She didn't kill Lauren. She doesn't have to endure Court's abuse.

Court spins in a rage and punches me.

I tumble backwards and fall hard on my ass.

"Ooof!" The air escapes from my lungs, and pain explodes in my face and radiates up my spine. I moan, trying to get up. I can't believe that asshole just punched me. I'm about to say as much, when a noise silences me.

Click.

I quickly scramble to the side, to get out of the path of the weapon. Court turns around slowly, knowing what he's about to come face-to-face with. Sophia is pointing a gun at his head.

He swallows hard, then puffs up his bare chest. "Put the fucking gun down."

"No." Sophia doesn't flinch.

"You're nothing without me." He raises his voice, but the words are slurred and slow to leave his lips. "I'm all you have, Sophia." He steps toward her and his legs wobble under his weight. Then he rubs his hands over his face and neck and takes a deep breath.

Sophia cocks her head and smirks, looking at him with intrigue in her eyes. "I think your other wife has drugged you." She lowers the gun, stopping when the black barrel is inches from Court's heart.

Court tries to laugh, but he starts coughing.

Then he looks at me and growls. "Did you fucking drug me?" He coughs and gasps a few times.

"No. Eyes on me. Don't look at her. Don't talk to her," Sophia says calmly.

"Or what? You're gonna kill me?" He puts his arms out to balance himself.

"Uh, Sophia, it wasn't real poison, just roofies," I squeak. I don't want her to get a false sense of security—he might start trying to hit her again.

"Well, in that case." Sophia pulls the trigger.

I don't have time to scream or cover my ears. The gunshot is deafening. Court immediately drops to his knees and his body slumps forward, landing face down on the floor, barely missing Sophia's feet.

"Whoa, that felt good," Sophia says. Her bloodied face looks more alive than I've ever seen it before.

I'm gasping for air, trying to reconcile what just happened.

"Are you okay? That fall didn't hurt the baby, did it?" She offers me a hand and helps me to my feet.

"There is no baby."

Sophia throws her head back and laughs. "Brilliant. You really had him with that one." Then she walks over to his dead body and kicks him. "You hear that, you dead fucking prick? How does it feel to be lied to?"

I brush myself off and feel my jaw. I'm in a daze and my ears are still ringing from the gunshot. The entire hotel probably heard it, which means the police will be swarming this place any minute.

Sophia stands over Court, spewing all kinds of pent-up rage at him. I hate to interrupt what looks very therapeutic for her, but we have to get our stories straight. "What are we going to say when the police come?"

"The truth. I shot him in self-defense. Just get rid of any roofies. I'll tell them he ate my anti-anxiety meds on the plane and went crazy. My room is just across the hall. I'll say I heard him screaming at you and came to investigate."

"Are you sure?" I ask.

"I've got this covered, Hannah. Just ask for a lawyer and don't say a thing."

It's the first and probably only time I've wanted to trust Sophia —because the rest of my life depends on it.

FORTY-SIX

"Are you sure you don't want me to go to the funeral?" Cassie asks, shielding her eyes from the sun. "I don't mind. I brought a *killer* black dress." She laughs and takes a sip of her wine. She's sitting on the back patio of the house I rented for a few days in Fort Myers while I've been taking care of the final arrangements.

"No, it's fine... and I see what you did there." I roll my eyes and she smirks. "I just want to get it over with and get the fuck out of Florida as fast as we can." I suck in a breath of the salty sea air and look out over the water. This might be the last time I see this view of the ocean for a long time. I can't say I won't miss it...

After finishing my glass of wine, I leave Cassie on the patio and slip into the house to get dressed. I wiggle into the black dress Sinclair and Jamie sent over for the occasion and walk outside so Cassie can zip me up.

"You do make a smoking hot widow," she teases.

The dress is rather short, but I suppose that's no accident. Sinclair is brilliant when it comes to styling me. There's sure to be photographers slinking around the edge of the cemetery, trying to capture pictures of the disgraced trad wife social media influencer. He obviously wants me to play up the scandal.

The newspapers have run multiple articles about what they

think happened that night. *Deadly Neighborhood Sex Triangle* seems to be the favorite headline. My picture-perfect online image shattered overnight. If they only knew the truth—well, my carefully curated image would still be tarnished, but maybe I'd be more sympathetic.

It doesn't really matter.

For the first time in a very long time, I don't care what anyone thinks of me. All that matters is that I'm free. And apparently, so is Sophia. I have no idea how she did it. Got the cops to rule it self-defense.

But she's good... Very, very good.

I imagine money exchanged hands somewhere along the hierarchy of the Miami police department. Or maybe Sophia gave up information to one of the lettered federal agencies on Court's real identity, or Lauren's murder, or his questionable international business dealings. Something I was too scared to do because of what happened the night Matt died.

Whatever she did, it worked.

The police hardly questioned me at all, mostly talking to my very expensive attorney, while I spent two days recovering at the hospital from a bruised jaw and tailbone.

After I disposed of the roofies that night, Sophia became a stage director. As if she'd been preparing for it her entire life. She told me to lie on the floor and sob and cry when the police arrived, and not to stop until they took me to the hospital.

I promise you'll be with Ruby and Rowen by the end of the week. She looked me in the eyes as she said it—and then I really did start wailing. In the chaos and drama, I hadn't allowed myself the pleasure of thinking about my children. Not until that very moment, and then I completely lost it. I didn't have to pretend... I was inconsolable when the police arrived.

"Well, you look fabulous." Cassie stands now and gives me a kiss on each cheek. "I'll have everything ready to head to the airport when you get back. Are you sure you don't want to stay one more day to see Sinclair and Jamie?"

"No, they're planning to come visit me and the twins in Iowa once things have settled down."

She nods.

My phone pings. The limo is here. I take my friend by the hands. "I can't thank you enough, for everything." Without her credit card and my little *What Would Cassie Do?* game, I'm not sure I would have survived.

"You don't have to thank me..." She squeezes my hands, then walks me to the door. "Oh, now that you're single, I want to set you up on a date with my personal trainer, Archie—he's a total babe and not a douchey billionaire." She grins from ear to ear.

"Oh Jesus, Cassie, you're trouble. I'll be back in a few hours to pick you up." Armed with my phone, and a smile on my face thinking about the possibility of dating someone normal again someday, I load into the limo and head for my husband's funeral.

FORTY-SEVEN

I gaze out the window on the way to the cemetery, knowing this is a foolish endeavor. There was no one to call and inform of Court's death. He was an only child, and his parents are both dead. He had no other relatives I was aware of. Honestly, I'm not even sure he had any real friends.

Court was a loner.

And since our house burned down, I couldn't even dig around his office for business contacts. His phone mysteriously disappeared the night he died, although I have a sneaking suspicion Sophia took it. Which is probably for the best—I'm sure it was filled with things I don't want to see.

Pulling up to the small cemetery, I'm thankful to see the funeral director was true to his word. There's a dozen or so people, dressed in black suits and formal attire, standing around the casket. I was embarrassed to think about standing at Court's graveside alone, so I did the only thing I could think of. I paid the funeral director to hire people to attend the service.

Yes of course, Mrs. McMillian, don't worry—this is a common occurrence. I'm not sure if it made me feel better or worse to know I'm not the only wife who has had to hire people to attend her husband's funeral.

The driver opens the door for me to step out just as thunder rolls somewhere in the distance. Great. I didn't bring an umbrella. The weather in South Florida is so unpredictable, I should have known better. But I'm sure the service won't take long. The for-hire minister has instructions to perform a short, somber sermon followed by a small recount of some of Court's finer accomplishments.

On my urging, Court donated money to several local charities such as the library and wildlife refuge. He used to say that without me, his life would be meaningless; he'd have no one to spend his money on, or no one to tell him where to spend it. I thought that was charming. But in reality it was just more proof of his narcissism. He spent his money on fine wines, expensive clothes and art, lavish foreign apartments, and plastic surgery for the woman standing twenty feet away from the grave.

Sophia.

Court's voice echoes in my head. *"Sophia likes it when I spank her with my belt."*

"Apparently not, you fucking asshole," I mutter to myself as I cross the well-manicured green lawn toward the grave site. As soon as the funeral director sees me take my place, he signals for the service to begin.

I can't help but stare at Sophia. I'm honestly surprised she came, even if she was his wife longer than I was. She killed him, for Christ's sake. There was so much drama between them I'll never know about, but I refuse to let it eat me alive for the rest of my life. The only part of Court I choose to remember is the part of him he left behind, Rowen and Ruby. With their cute button noses and sandy blonde hair.

Suddenly my heart aches—not for Court. Not for Sophia or her sister Lauren. But the other children. There were only a few pictures of them in the manila envelope. Toddlers, maybe two years old. A boy and a girl. No names. Just small faces, with button noses and sandy blonde hair.

I feel sick… How could Court kill his own children? No matter what kind of fight he had with Lauren about his affair with Sophia, how could he do that to his own flesh and blood? If Sophia had never moved in next door, unraveling all the lies, I would have continued raising the twins with a killer. A man capable of murdering them.

It makes my skin crawl thinking about it.

The sermon is over just as the sky opens up. I look over at Sophia. She's gripping her umbrella handle and being led away by her driver. As she gets into a limo, I pray this is the last time I ever see her. But something in my gut tells me it won't be. The rain pelts me and I feel foolish still standing at the grave. All the fake mourners have run off, and grave diggers in muddy coveralls are approaching to lower the casket.

I feel empty.

This funeral charade was pointless. I guess if I'm being completely honest with myself, I thought that someone who knew Court might show up out of the woodwork to offer me their condolences and tell me what a wonderful man Court was. Offering me a glimmer of hope so I can stop feeling so guilty that I let Court charm his way into my life. But even if a thousand mourners arrived to sing his praises, none of it would change the fact that he was a liar, an abuser, and a murderer.

Buzz.

My phone rings, and I fumble with it in the rain.

"Hello?"

"Get out of the rain."

"What do you want?" I sigh. There's no telling what words might pass over Sophia's lips. I think the only thing I've really learned about her is that she's as unpredictable as the Florida weather.

"Do you know what they say about neighbors?"

"Fences make good ones?"

She laughs. "Don't be daft, Hannah. No. They say, love thy

neighbor as thyself... You taught me to love myself again. You made me want to be free." Then she hangs up, and I fall to my knees and cry.

"Mommy, why are you crying?" Ruby asks.

"I'm just so happy," I reply. The old farmhouse smells like fresh paint. I still have little flecks stuck to my skin and in my hair. I was here until well past midnight with a brush and roller to make sure the walls have time to dry. Sinclair and Jamie arrive tomorrow to help me start decorating. I can't wait for my friends to see everything I've done to the house. I know they'll be proud of me, maybe even a little jealous. But I have a plan for that. I'm going to show the guys a little boutique for sale downtown—it could be the perfect place to start their own clothing store, if they want to leave Florida too.

"You did a fine job fixing this place up." Aunt Tippy walks in, carrying a casserole dish. Uncle Frannie's right behind her with a basket of eggs. They head for the sunny kitchen where I've got the paper plates and plastic silverware ready for brunch. I help them get settled, then grab the fruit salad out of the fridge and set it next to the steamy breakfast casserole.

"We're real proud of you, Hannah." Frannie rests a hand on my shoulder. "I'll still be sorry to see you and the twins leave Happy Farm, but I know you want your own space."

"Don't worry, we're just down the road, *neighbor*. I'm sure the twins will be at your place all the time." Buying the old rundown Thompson farm next door to Aunt Tippy and Frannie was the first thing I did when I landed in Iowa four months ago. Instead of running from Matt's ghost, I've tried to honor his memory. This place was supposed to be our dream, and now me and the twins are starting a new life here. It feels right.

The screen door slams and Rowen comes running in like a bat out of hell.

"ROWEN!" Aunt Tippy yells.

He stops dead in his tracks.

"You turn around right now and—"

"Aunt Tippy, it's fine! Really, thank you, but this house is meant for the kids to live in and be loud and dirty and just to enjoy. Rowen, honey, why are you in such a hurry?" I walk over to my son to see what he's got in his hands.

"An egg, Mommy! Our chickens laid their first egg!" He holds out his hands to reveal a lovely brown egg.

"Let me see," Ruby says and wedges her body between me and Rowen.

"Ooooh, pretty. I want one," Ruby says. Rowen grabs her by the hand and they go rushing off together, back outside.

"Those two are like a tornado. You should set some rules," Aunt Tippy says, giving me a look.

"Honestly, Aunt Tippy, I'm tired of having to make sure everything is picture-perfect. A little mess, a sunburn, a bad hair day, it doesn't matter anymore." I grab the coffee pot and add another splash to my cup. Then I pour a cup for Uncle Fran and take it to him at the kitchen table, where he's taken a seat by the window, overlooking the garden and chicken coop. The twins are racing around, playing tag, with the egg.

"You're probably right. I suppose I was a little hard on you as a girl. You're doing just fine with them twins. I hope you know I'm real proud of how hard you worked to turn this place into a fine home."

My heart swells.

I have worked hard. I could have hired someone to do all the physical labor for me—that's what I've spent the last five years doing. Hiring people. Pretending. But not anymore. I rolled up my sleeves and put in the long days and nights to build something truly meaningful. To be a woman, mom, niece, and friend the people I love can be proud of. I'm even learning how to cook. No more gourmet delivery meal service for me and the twins. From now on, I'm going to try and be as real as I can be.

Huge thanks for reading *The First Wives*. I hope you were as obsessed with Hannah and Sophia's friendship as I was writing it. If you'd like to keep in touch with all my new releases with Storm Publishing, you can sign up below.

www.stormpublishing.co/se-reed

And if you want to join other readers in hearing all about my new releases and bonus content, you can sign up for my newsletter.

www.writingwithreed.com/subscribe

If you enjoyed this book and could spare a few moments to leave a review, that would be hugely appreciated. Even a short review can make all the difference in encouraging a reader to discover my books for the first time. Seriously, thank you so much.

I've always felt that adult friendships can be messy and complicated. Especially if you work full-time, have children, a spouse, and family obligations. I wanted to explore those feelings with this book. How cultivating a new friendship can easily turn into obsessing over details in another person's life, potentially fueling envy and jealousy. And how our performative behavior on social media can mask who and what we really are. Although this book is a work of fiction, whenever I write I like to draw inspiration from people, places, and events I've come across in my own life.

Thanks again for being part of this amazing journey with me, and I hope you'll stay in touch – I have so many more stories and ideas to entertain you with!

xo

S.E. Reed

ACKNOWLEDGMENTS

First, I have to thank my loving husband and children for always supporting me. I know I spend a lot of time on my computer writing, or leaving scattered papers with notes all over the kitchen table, but you never judge my addiction. You know it's just who I am and I'm so lucky to have a family like you. I am incredibly grateful.

To my daddy: I love you more than all the stars, because they go on forever and ever.

To Emily Gowers, my kind-hearted, and brilliant acquiring editor and mentor at Storm Publishing. Thank you for seeing something in my writing and giving me your blessing to write this story. You've been such a joy to work with. You're always available, encouraging, and willing to spend time brainstorming. Also, you don't judge me for my overuse of exclamation points!

To Dana Hawkins: I'm obsessed with you. Seriously though, I'd like to say that I think about how different things might be right now if we'd never met. But that would be a lie. I never think about my life without you in it.

To Theresa Green, E.L. Johnson, Emily St. Marie, Abigail Wild, Bruce Buchanan, Diane Billas, and Mariah Stillbrook... I love you guys. Thank you for your hearts, your wisdom, and your friendships.

To my Sunday writing group, Ginny Myers Sain, Casie Bazay, Jenni Howell, Alyssa Villaire, Tracy Truels, and Vanessa Montalban. Our calls and emails over the last few years are something I cherish and look forward to. Cue the song "You've Got a Friend in Me" from *Toy Story*.

Hugs and love to my BRPSC peeps. You girls are the best!

And finally, to all my other friends and family around the globe, thank you! I'm always grateful for the conversations, encouragement, and laughter whenever we connect or see each other in person.